THE SWORD OF EDEN

The Kingdom of Heaven Chronicles

Book 1

HOLT CLARKE

Imagination 2 Creation Publishing

Charleston, SC

Books by Imagination 2 Creation Publishing may be ordered through booksellers or by contacting:

Imagination 2 Creation Publishing
www.HoltClarke.com

ISBN 978-0-9979335-3-6

DEDICATION

To my son Luke

Shishle is officially a word and it means bestest bud in the whole wide world! Love my shishle and ever proud of my boy.

Love you forever and then some!

Dad

CONTENTS

Then God put winged creatures at the entrance to the garden and a flaming, flashing sword to guard the way to the life-giving tree.

—Genesis 3:24 (CEV)

Prologue

SEED OF DARKNESS

The Light had reigned uncontested throughout its pristine borders, that is, until the Darkness entered stealthily, deceptively, and seductively. The scent of fear mixed with the intoxicating aroma of power like alluring pheromones swept into the garden land, infecting all with its abhorrent malady. With the seed of Darkness sown the awen of life began to succumb to the awen of death. The battle for angelic supremacy had now achieved critical mass.

Eden's primordial rainforest with its gargantuan trees swayed in the powerful winds ripping through its interior. The thick luscious foliage swirled violently slinging falling rain pellets like shrapnel around the jungle's interior; a stark contrast from Eden's earlier tranquil sanctuary boasting foliage in nearly every color of the imagination. The light-filled paradise of Eden was now eclipsed by a deluge of darkness that assaulted the pristine paradise with its dark magic.

Those belonging to the fallen Order of Powers arrived first as their black and crimson colored reptilian skin quickly turned pale in response to Eden's environment. Each wore black raiment with accents of crimson along with energy swords within easy reach for engagement. Their outstretched wings shielded their bodies from the torrential rain. Nearly a hundred strong, some perched high on thick Banyan tree limbs while others stealthily walked the forest floor on reconnaissance scanning the interior for his anticipated arrival.

Standing in the epic center of paradise, the Tree of Knowledge of Good and Evil symbolized the yin and yang of the Darkness and Light with its luminous energy fruit reflecting crimson, emerald, and sapphire hues highlighting the tree's broad branches. Large, shimmering green leaves recoiled around the energy fruit as if shielding from any seeking to partake of its celestial delights.

Fear permeated the lush rainforest like an ethereal serpent slithering along within the darkened interior of the thick rainforest. Not even a patch of light made its way down to the forest floor. Satariel, the Dark Lord had arrayed himself in wondrous false light working his dark magic in such a way that even the natural light bowed to his commands. At least, that is, until the others arrived.

My place was to wait, restrained by the Light, and alert to his coming. Waiting for what seemed nearly an eternity, my company had been the piercing screams, taunts, and night tremors that turned Eden into a very hell of swarming darkness. Paralyzed by fear, Adam and Eve were infected with a foreign emotion never before experienced before the Dark Ones had arrived.

Powerless, I could only witness the end of what once was pure, innocent, and unspoiled. But now, everything seemed an aberration of a time and place that was once unmolested and now had been violated never to be the same again.

Standing in a crescent-shaped clearing surrounded by trees and tropical foliage, Adam and Eve were clothed in breeches and tunics made from the lush emerald leaves of the Tree of Knowledge. The leaves clung to their bodies like a second skin, showing neither seam nor crease. Both appeared fragile and flawed, transfixed by fear. The clearing began to succumb to the deepening shadows as the last strands of golden light from the setting sun weakened in retreat. The shadows became more magnanimous with each passing moment.

Fiendishly hidden, and now appearing from the dappled shadows, First in Power and Lord over the Archein, Satariel approached the Tree of Knowledge of Good and Evil. Flanking him were Paimon the Influencer and Abaddon the Destroyer. Each were dressed in black and wore platinum breast plates that prominently displayed the image of a black dragon with fiery crimson eyes in the center. Recoiling in fear at the sound of the black wings retracting behind the divine beings, Adam felt his heartbeat quicken as an overwhelming sense of helplessness gripped him.

The unholy trinity of evil arrogantly surveyed the beleaguered couple as if casting their eyes upon pathetic and worthless creatures. The look of disdain permeated the Dark Lord's gaze. There was something unnatural about his countenance that unsettled Adam. The roll of distant thunder could be heard as flashes of crimson lightning illuminated angelic beings who were both terrifying and mesmerizing.

Adam could feel the intensity of Satariel's gaze. Suddenly feeling an urgent desire to flee the area, Adam restrained his impulse to run knowing his efforts would be futile. A maniacal grin broke across Satariel's face, his opaque eyes luminous with delight.

"Do you believe in the power of evil?" Satariel asked coldly. Adam dared not reply, looking only to the ground trying to find refuge in the intense silence that seemed to linger for nearly an eternity. The rebel angels were emboldened by Adam's fear as the dark energy coursed through their astral veins. Looking to Eve, Adam felt abandoned and for the first time, bereft of the Light surrounded by harbingers of an uncertain future.

Possessing ominous black eyes, Satariel was an extraordinary-looking angel. His thick, black hair dropped beneath his shoulders held back by a platinum headband featuring at its center a crimson, diamond-shaped stone that glistened in the fading light of day. His chiseled jawline, dimpled chin, and high forehead denoted strength and confidence - an appearance both spellbinding and menacing. Around his neck, he wore a metallic serpentine torque featuring a black onyx orb that encased crimson fire swirling within.

Satariel's astral body shimmered in power prominently showcasing a well-toned and muscular torso sheathed by a form-fitting platinum breastplate with crimson accents. His ominous black wings transformed into a flowing black cape draped around his shoulders was attached to his frontal armor by crimson medallions on the left and right. At his side rested a gleaming sword hilt boasting a serpent's eye made of a dark, crimson ruby, and a dragon's head jutting out on each side of the cross hilt. The sword seemed to animate at his side as if possessing a life of its own.

The energy plasma from the fruit of which Adam and Eve partook opened their eyes to the spiritual realm they previously were unable to perceive as if a veil had been ripped away, revealing winged creatures fierce in appearance, clothed in black, and who appeared human-like. Flanking Satariel and his two Generals was a legion of rebel angels creating a great swath of evil energy enveloping Adam and Eve.

Adam found his mind besieged by a cacophony of voices goading him to unleash a murderous rage against Eve. And likewise Eve found her psyche influenced by dark desires of lust, jealousy, and murder as she fought to resist the overwhelming urge to strike down Paimon, the beautiful female with exotic skin and a shapely figure slender and seductive, standing to the left of Satariel. Just as they were about to act on their dark impulses, a tremendous boom and blaze of blinding light erupted within the dark circle of uncontested evil.

The others arrived, winged creatures appearing in brilliant splendor like lightning striking the jungle floor in awesome fury. Branches cracked and crashed to the forest floor as a contingent of warriors arrayed in blazing white light descended with outstretched ethereal wings that transformed into material matter upon full descent to the ground. Twelve angelic warriors retracted their wings within their bodies as they each took up strategic positions in defense of Eden's sacred womb against Satariel and his rebellious legion.

Forming a wall of light that shielded the fallen couple, fiery swords of varying colors hummed to life with power, crackling and spitting blazing energy. These Guardians of Light immediately engaged the rebel angels in a violent clash of energy. The fury of the battle illumined the dark shadows of the thick tropical forest surrounding the clearing. One angel of Light with thick blond hair braided in the back took down two of the rebel angels with an over-the-top somersault that deftly cleaved the heads of both as he hit the ground never looking back in his pursuit of three more of the angels of Darkness.

The vile, stench of the rebel angels began to usurp the sweet floral aroma of Eden. The battle clash intensified as more rebel warriors appeared through a swirling black portal flooding the rainforest's interior like cockroaches pouring out of a dark crevice. The Darkness proved overwhelming as the Guardians of Light were pushed back by the minions of Satariel.

An angel of Light wearing a body suit made of topaz with a champagne breastplate exposing bare muscular arms gripped a sword spitting fiery energy in the air. While deflecting the crimson fire from an angel of Darkness, he quickly dropped to one knee using his free hand to fling a small dagger of energy at four other assailants, dropping down from a towering tree above. The energy dagger erupted into shards of Light that pierced each of the assailants turning them to burnt corpses that fell like ash to the ground. But it was not enough.

The lone angelic warrior was now surrounded by at least ten rebel warriors. Two lunged and lost their arms as a third one from behind was impaled by a reverse thrust. The tactical move was not lost on

Abaddon. His crimson blade of fire found its mark in the middle of the exposed breastplate of the angelic warrior whose sword went dark as his astral life force faded into the Light.

Abaddon dropped to one knee grabbing the back of the head of his defiant foe, arresting his fall to the ground, "Talmiel, know this my old friend. As you succumb to the Light, oblivion awaits you along with all those who foolishly chose to stand against us."

"You're wrong, Abaddon. He's coming and even now arrives," Talmiel said before releasing his spirit to the Light.

And then just as it seemed all would be lost, he appeared. A sublime and radiant being descended in the midst of the chaos, bringing a temporary halt to the battle frenzy below. He was a white blaze of fiery flesh, with a prominent forehead and silver hair flowing like a lion's mane, eyelashes like flashes of lightning, eyes like blue flaming torches, a chiseled jawline with a dimpled chin like that of a god projecting power and authority with an astral body sheathed in body armor emitting light in champagne and platinum hues.

He descended with outstretched ethereal wings that spanned nearly the entire clearing before enfolding behind him. His enormous astral wings cast brilliant light all around illuminating the darkness before transforming into a flowing white cape serving as extension to his frontal armor prominently featuring two dark blue jasper medallions like orbs of swirling blue fire. In the middle of his breastplate was the image of a Lion's head.

Standing equal in stature and possessing an uncanny physical resemblance to Satariel, the brilliance of his radiating light was blinding. Wielding a terrific sword that was ignited in blazing emerald fire, the angelic Lord gripped the sword's hilt firmly as he commanded the attention of all those gathered especially those belonging to the Darkness.

The demonic horde stepped back seeking concealment in the shadows of Eden as the crescendo of light diminished revealing a warrior of light with striking facial features that appeared almost identical to that of Satariel's with the exception of the eyes and the hair. Possessing a muscular frame readily apparent beneath his breastplate, he walked as if a paragon of Light. With flowing golden blonde hair, a high forehead and cheek bones, and eyes of brilliant sapphire blue, his presence conveyed a sense of majestic power and poise. Across his forehead was a regal headband displaying a diamond shaped sapphire stone of deepest blue.

"Satariel," his voice boomed like echoing thunder throughout the heavens. Stepping from behind the base of the Tree of Knowledge, Satariel indifferently and mockingly picked a piece of energy fruit which was glowing crimson red. Tossing the fruit up and down in his hand he returned the stern gaze of the one arrayed in Light.

Wearing an arrogant smirk, Satariel bit into the forbidden fruit. After spitting a seed to the ground he replied, "Brother. Why am I not surprised? It seems that you have benefited greatly from my abdication. I would've barely recognized you if not for those eyes." Dripping with sarcasm Satariel continued, "Sariel or should I call you Metatron? 'Next to the Throne of God', 'First among the Created Ones', 'Command of God'. Such lofty titles bestowed upon one so deserving. You have done well for yourself brother. Thanks to me. We are certainly honored by your presence and welcome you to our latest conquest. But unfortunately, it appears you have come a little too late."

"What have you done Satariel?" Metatron asked discerning the dark energy coursing through Eden like a super virus. The encircling warriors of Darkness warily looked on as the warriors of Light assumed combat positions once again with swords ignited and humming in an astral fire of blazing energy. The fear in Adam and Eve was unmistakable as Metatron cast his severe gaze upon Paimon and another rebel angel holding them both captive.

"Your work here is finished," Metatron said with a finality in his tone. "Take your dark disciples and leave this place."

A chill crept into the air as a palpable tension held followers of both the Light and the Darkness in its grip. Stepping closer Satariel quipped, "Far from it. My work here has only just begun. We, the progenitors have proven the wisdom of our rebellion. Eden has chosen. The Darkness has vanquished the Light. And the Creator's precious, pet creation has now granted me something special."

"And what would that be," Metatron said losing patience with his brother's narcissism. Smiling Satariel took great delight in answering, "DOMINION."

The implication of Satariel's claim was not lost on Metatron. Free will could unleash either good or evil, Light or Darkness. Adam and Eve's act of disobedience allowed the Darkness to infect and corrupt the Kingdom of Eden and now its fall would change everything. A new front had been opened in the Angelic War between those loyal to the Creator and those in rebellion against the Creator.

Placing his hand on the amber hilt of the sword attached to his side, Metatron was calculating his course of action casting appraising eyes on Paimon and Abaddon before responding to his defiant brother.

"Satariel, you once blazed brightest among us." Metatron said, allowing the words to hang in the air for a moment. "And now only Darkness fills your soul. Damn your pride, Satariel. How many kingdoms and innocents must suffer before you face the truth of your existence? The progenitors," Metatron said exasperatingly at the arrogance so indicative of the rebel attitudes among the various Angelic Orders and their response to the creation of the humankind.

"We ARE the progenitors!" Metatron thundered. "All of us gathered here, either in Darkness or Light. It's not all about you, brother. Nothing has been proven except for the hate that destroys and the love that seeks to redeem. You desire to abolish and overthrow out of fear. We desire to protect and defend out of love.

"Oh Metatron, highly favored among the Creator and the angelic hosts. You speak of that which you know little. Blindly you follow the Light and yet speak of the Darkness as if it is evil. You have never understood our cause because you have closed your mind to another way of being. So let me enlighten you. We fight for the right to be free from the oppression of the Light. Free from its order of governance that imposes its limitations and strips away true freedom. The Darkness empowers us to live as free spirits freely embracing the forbidden knowledge. And because we have chosen to exercise our free will we are: ostracized by the Light, rejected by the Light, and condemned by the Light. There are some things worth fighting for."

"You are gravely mistaken. The Darkness has so corrupted your mind and distorted your thinking, Satariel. Come back to the Light, brother. The freedom you seek has unleashed nothing but hate, war, and suffering. The Darkness enslaves. It doesn't liberate. Even now Eden is infected with your dark seed. There is a freedom that leads to life and there is a freedom that leads to death. You have chosen the latter. Those of the Light stand in the Creator's will. Those who stand with you do so in rebellion to all that is good, right, and true."

"Oh brother, you follow a fool's light," Satariel scoffed. "I will never return to your false hope. Your future will be filled with darkness, pain, and suffering. And any, whether angel or human who stand with you will suffer the same fate. Of that I promise you."

"We are finished here," Metatron said emphatically. "Leave this place and take your minions with you."

Satariel gave a precursory glance just over the right shoulder of Metatron to one of his Generals concealed behind thick tropical foliage. As a diversionary tactic, Paimon assaulted Adam and Eve with dark violent thoughts. Metatron quickly countered by flinging his cloak over them shielding their minds from mental penetration. Acting in concert, the rebel angels ignited swords that crackled to life with flaming crimson dark energy as they stepped into the clearing with bloodlust in their demonic eyes.

Satariel threw a fiery projectile directly at Metatron who countered with deft reflexes and lightning-fast speed igniting his sword with flaming, emerald fire. A tremendous blinding light elicited a force of energy eviscerating the projectile along with an entire legion of the rebel angels who made the fatal mistake of rushing him. The energy force of Metatron's sword slammed Satariel against the Tree of Knowledge and sent Paimon crashing into the tropical forest.

Satariel quickly sprang to his feet with a look of shock and awe mesmerized by the beauty and power of the sword wielded by Metatron. Never had he witnessed such power from an angelic weapon nor knew existed such angelic weaponry. *So the Light evolves,* Satariel thought drawn to the power of Metatron's sword as if gazing in lust at a forbidden lover.

Metatron tightened his grip on the sword giving Satariel one last warning, "Leave this place now."

Obstinately brushing the comment aside, Satariel replied "I see you come bearing a gift and a most powerful one at that."

Quickly scanning the forest for signs of Paimon, Metatron responded, "An unfortunate gift for an unfortunate time."

Satariel looked in admiration at the sword's handiwork and mused, "You wiped out an entire legion of my most able warriors with one fell stroke. What beautiful power it wields."

Satariel's lust for conquest and desire to possess all things powerful was not lost on Metatron who stepped closer, keeping the tip of the sword's fiery blade trained on Satariel, bathing him in a fiery emerald light. "I can assure you it's anything but beautiful. The greater the evil the greater its power." Inching closer Metatron brought the fiery blade within a hair's breadth of Satariel's face, "Care to become more intimately acquainted with this thing of beauty?"

Not a fool to tempt his fate before one of Empyrean's mightiest warriors, Satariel's calculating mind began churning. More cunning than any created being, Satariel saw in Metatron's sword, an opportunity that could bring Empyrean to its knees in abject surrender. Gripped more by exhilaration than fear, Satariel slowly backed away from Metatron stepping to the edge of the clearing at which time Paimon and Abaddon emerged from the jungle recesses taking their places by his side.

Satariel replied matter-of-factly, "You can have Eden along with the humankind. All I ask for is your sword in return."

"Your lust for power has blinded you to sensibility. You ask for that which is not yours to possess. Created by your Father and Maker of all things, the Sword of Eden will become the bane of your existence and in the fullness of time shall be wielded by the hand of a mortal in defense of this kingdom's realm. And one day you shall bow before its salvific power."

In defiance Satariel spat, "The humankind are weak. Yours is a fool's hope." Casting a detestable look over at Adam and Eve, Satariel continued, "They are pathetic and will only know weakness, fear, confusion, despair, pain, and unbearable suffering. By the time I'm finished with them, they will deny their Creator's existence and in time the Light will be snuffed out in them replaced by the Darkness."

A surge of dark energy opened a fiery portal next to the Tree of Knowledge of Good and Evil. Paimon stepped through first and then Abaddon. Satariel approached the threshold pausing just before crossing over gazing back at Metatron, "Blindly you follow the Light. Never questioning, ever obeying. Do you really believe these creatures of flesh and blood are worth the effort? They are weak and inferior to our kind."

Not able to resist one last barb meant to inspire dread, Satariel spewed more venomous words, "The days of humankind are numbered. The Age of Light fades into the Darkness." Satariel's hate-filled eyes mirrored the crimson energy encircling the black portal. "We will meet again, brother. And when we do, you will witness the harvest of what I have begun here." Turning he stepped through the black void vanishing from sight as the dark energy dissipated, leaving Metatron in the eerie silence that pervaded Eden.

After scanning Eden for any vestiges of the rebel angels, Metatron looked to Nikiel who was approaching from the jungle's interior. "Return to Empyrean with the others. I must finish what I was sent here to do."

"Yes, my Lord," Nikiel answered. "What of the couple?"

"I will take care of them. Be watchful. Satariel is emboldened by his latest conquest. Empyrean needs you now. But the time will come when you will return to this kingdom's realm."

Nikiel wasted no time following Metatron's command. Gathering the other warriors of Light she ignited a portal that shimmered with light. Stepping through they all vanished into the Light beyond.

Confident that he was alone with Adam and Eve, Metatron sheathed his sword. His compassionate eyes gazed upon Adam and

Eve who had not moved, paralyzed by fear. Removing his cloak the two appeared to be confused and terrified by all that they had just seen and heard.

The light that radiated from Metatron's countenance was so blinding that they reflexively closed their eyes putting their faces into the bends of their elbows. Adam spoke first pleading for their lives, "Please Great Light, have mercy on us. We were deceived by the Dark One who encouraged us to eat of the forbidden fruit promising knowledge that would empower us to rule as gods."

Moved with compassion, Metatron bent down on one knee gently raising their faces while gazing into their eyes. Placing his right hand on Adam and then Eve, he imparted a calming serenity that enveloped them both.

"I come in peace and mean you no harm. The emotions you now experience are a result of the forbidden fruit infusing you with the dark energy. Death now springs forth from the womb of Eden. You must go until such a time that you are summoned by the Light. But beware of the false light that shouts in your pain and whispers in your pleasure. Satariel is a cunning deceiver and his dark power has marked you for death. Deny the Darkness and welcome the Light. We will meet again."

Sensing their confused state of mind and the limitations of their flesh, Metatron stood signaling for them to rise and follow. He walked with them directing their thoughts to the beauty of Eden and providing nourishment that would sustain them for the journey away from Eden's garden paradise. Curtailing the immediate threat from

Satariel's dark disciples and their contingent of rebel angels known as the Dark Ones, Metatron walked with Adam and Eve to the eastern border of Eden.

Overlooking a vast land mass that continued as far as the eye could see, Metatron stood with Adam and Eve gazing out over the great vista of an untamed and uncharted world. The last vestiges of light from the setting sun gave way to darkness. "You must go now but always know that even in the darkness there is a light that still burns bright," Metatron said feeling so helpless as he watched Eden's first created among the humankind walk off dejected and afraid.

Departing, Adam and Eve began their long and arduous journey into the great unknown taking the first steps toward an uncertain future for the humankind.

Metatron made his way back into the jungle interior until he reached the crescent-shaped interior that fronted the Tree of Knowledge of Good and Evil. An electrically charged wind eddied around him, as the colossal tree began a rapid acceleration of decline. The leaves scattered in the wind, the energy fruit evaporated and vanished, the tree limbs recoiled and withered, the trunk petrified and fossilized before eventually crumbling to dust. The wind carried away the remains as nothing but a darkened stain remained; a foreshadowing of a future that had been set in motion by a growing evil unleashed by choices made and promises forsaken.

Standing alone in the midst of Eden, Metatron closed his eyes and breathed deeply the air that was stirring around him. Becoming one with the Light, he tried to reconcile his mind to the dawn of darkness that had now infected the once pristine Kingdom of Eden. He could sense the awen of death that was attaching to the life force of Eden beginning its slow, debilitating malignancy.

Opening his eyes, Metatron unsheathed the sword at his side igniting a tremendous fiery energy illuminating the darkness quickly descending on Eden. Metatron knelt on one knee bowing his head in a prayer-like posture with both hands gripping the sword with the blade facing downward just above the ground's surface. Like a surgeon preparing to make an incision, Metatron made a mental scan of the boundaries of Eden summoning astonishing power as the sword blazed in emerald fire.

Rising to his feet, Metatron spun the blade heavenward and then with tremendous force propelled the blazing sword in a downward arc driving it deep into the earth with a force of energy that began the separation of land masses isolating the borders of Eden from the rest of the earth by great bodies of water. He set into motion a continental drift that shifted the tectonic plates beneath Eden, which in time, split and divided the garden paradise of Eden into separate and distinct island land masses.

With the geological chain of events set into motion, Metatron had one final task to complete before returning to Empyrean. Knowing Satariel's dark desire to obtain the Sword, Metatron dared not risk returning it to Empyrean. Treachery and deception by the Dark Ones posed a real danger. The sacred prophecy was tied to the sword's true power and the Light within directed him to bury the sword within the bowels of Eden's sacred womb.

Metatron placed a cloaking device beneath the emerald stone encased within the circular crest of the sword's hilt preventing its detection by the angelkind. In a firestorm of terrific energy the sword cut downward into the earth descending deep into the lower mantle of the earth's mesosphere.

As the earth quaked, Metatron rose to his feet and opened a portal that shimmered a brilliant sapphire blue and glistened like the surface of ocean waters. Casting a solemn look back at the garden paradise of Eden, Metatron turned and stepped through the ethereal portal vanishing into the light beyond.

Chapter 1

MANA

Kaua'i, Hawai'i - Present Day

Rising early to get a head start on a busy day ahead, Dalton Orion rolled out of bed at 5:45 am and headed for the bathroom to begin his daily ritual of shaking the sleep off with a cold splash of water to invigorate the senses. Looking into the mirror he noticed a few more gray hairs adding natural highlights to his dark brown hair.

Stepping into the shower, Dalton immersed himself beneath the showerhead while pulling his hair back enjoying the cool sensation. The cold water ran freely over well-defined muscles and an athletic frame that evidenced the physical demands of his profession and personal lifestyle and diet consisting mainly of fruit, vegetables and healthy portions of protein. Dousing himself with an energizing body wash, Dalton felt exhilarated igniting a mental edge that kept him on top of his game. After leaving the shower and drying off he put on a pair of Asics, his running shoe of choice. He could still hear Lauren's voice in his head, "Why do you always shower before you go running?"

The smell of macadamia nut greeted him as he strolled out onto the lanai to pour himself a steamy cup of coffee that had been percolating in the coffee maker. After pouring himself a cup, Dalton scanned the panoramic vista of the majestic Na Pali Mountains and picturesque Kaua'i coastline. Taking a sip of his coffee, he found himself deep in thought as morning's first light began to crest the sky making Kaua'i the closest thing to heaven on earth.

A painful flash of memory fleetingly surfaced only to be quickly suppressed by Dalton who had become adept at shielding himself from the memory. Like the repetition of pounding waves crashing against the seashore, the psychological erosion had carved out a persona that was a mere shadow of his former self.

Shaking off the insufferable memory, Dalton breathed deeply the Hawaiian air reviving his senses with the intoxicating aromas of Plumeria and Pikake flowers, the very scent of paradise. After a few more sips of coffee, Dalton began his daily three mile run maintaining a rhythmic pace that kept him at optimal physical condition for his field of work.

Jogging down Weke Road along the Hanalei Bay shoreline, Dalton cranked up his cardio mix on his smart phone settling into his fitness zone. Focusing on nothing but the inspiration he often drew from music and nature, he derived a natural high from inhaling the Hawaiian air. The Coconut Palms swayed in the tropical breeze as Dalton jogged past the Hanalei Pier toward the Hanalei Beach Park.

Jogging had a therapeutic effect helping him cope with the grief he carried inside. Kauai was Dalton's paradise, not primarily because of its natural beauty but because of its seclusion, affording an escape from a former part of his life that had been eclipsed by tragedy and trauma.

Upon returning to his Hanalei home he quickly showered and put on a pair of khakis, a navy polo shirt, and his favorite Toffee colored Olukai shoes. Dalton grabbed the keys to his Jeep Wrangler and headed off to the Princeville Airport to meet up with his field research assistant Sommer Palekaiko. With the top down and the cool morning air blowing freely through his hair, Dalton leaned over and cranked up one of his favorite tunes, *Patriarch* by Delta Spirit.

Pulling into his usual parking spot at the airport, Dalton spotted Sommer as a smile swept across his face. With long, flowing bronze-colored hair and penetrating dark hazel green eyes, Sommer was an exotic Hawaiian beauty with a firecracker of a personality to boot. Possessing a keen intellect that demonstrated a masterful understanding of the elemental forces of nature matched only by her dauntless spirit, Dalton found Sommer to be an invaluable assistant in archaeological research both above and beneath the ocean's surface.

Dalton first met Sommer nine years earlier when he was the keynote speaker at a Symposium delivering an address on *The Awen of Life* at the University of Hawai'i on Oahu. Having only audited courses, Sommer proved astute in matters pertaining to the earth's oceanography and geosystems. Dalton was drawn to Sommer's uncanny grasp of the natural sciences and especially her knowledge of the many legends, myths, and lore surrounding the Hawaiian Islands. Professional soulmates, the two had been nearly inseparable ever since.

Dalton graduated Summa Cum Laude from the University of Hawai'i with a PhD in Earth and Ocean Sciences As a chief field scientist in oceanographic research and exploration for the National Oceanic Research Administration (NORA) based out of Charleston, South Carolina, Dalton was a highly respected field researcher for NORA's Pacific Division stationed in Pearl Harbor, Hawai'i. Sommer's affinity for the earth's ecosystems and her passionate views regarding the spirituality of nature provided an alternative perspective that Dalton found refreshing and had come to value.

Dalton and Sommer shared a kindred spirit in their fascination and love for exploring the five elemental forces of life: earth, water, air, fire, and spirit. They especially loved to explore volcano seamounts and were often jokingly called Vulcans by colleagues, a name derived from Vulcano Island off Siciliy, named after the god of fire in Roman mythology. And the Hawaiian Islands provided the perfect environment to indulge their passion for volcanoes and subsurface seamounts.

Dalton got out of his Jeep and paused by the front hood somewhat amused by Sommer in a clay colored Hang Loose tee-shirt and khaki cargo shorts running around in hiking boots chasing a rooster. He couldn't help but chuckle as he watched her persistently chase that rooster around with such a cavalier spirit. Sommer had a way of letting the cares of this life roll off her like water off a duck's back. She was his drug, the calm abating the raging storm of grief that intermittently assaulted his soul.

Sommer didn't miss a beat as she out maneuvered the rooster scooping it up in her hands. Turning around she wore a triumphant look on her face grinning ear to ear while holding her prize aloft in the air and then pulling it close to her bosom with beaming pride. The rooster, which had previously been squawking profusely began to settle into her arms as if she had a calming effect upon it.

Dalton hollered her way, "Hey, great stop and go reflexes!"

"Chasing roosters keep the reflexes sharp. Catching roosters builds confidence," Sommer said while putting the rooster down and watching it strut off without a care in the world.

Stepping away from the Jeep, Dalton walked over and tossed Sommer a writing pad, "I was talking to the rooster."

Pulling her hair back and looping it through her black NORA hat, Sommer looked at Dalton and teasingly replied, "Short legs certainly has its advantages but the slim, tone, and sun-kissed legs on this 5'10" Hawaiian gal, you must admit, make the stop and go look a heck of a lot more sexy than that rooster over there."

Dalton rolled his eyes, "Oh, the vanity of young women. Those slim, tone, tan legs of yours are going to develop wrinkles one day and you might as well begin making peace with it now. No amount of chasing roosters is going to change that."

Dalton enjoyed their back and forth bantering usually around the subject of his middle-age deterioration and her youthful prime of life bodily vigor. It offered just the right measure of playfulness that kept their professional camaraderie engaging and fun. Neither took themselves too seriously and enjoyed sharpening each other's professional prowess and making light of the more disconcerting realities of life. Sommer lived by the maxim, "No thrill! No deal!" While Dalton had come to embrace the maxim, "A good lie finds more believers than a bad truth."

As Dalton and Sommer began walking toward his 2002 Cessna 182 Sea Hawk, Dalton's cell phone began ringing. Answering he was greeted by the husky voice of Captain John Armington of the *Kanaloa* ("god of the ocean"), NORA's 274 foot research vessel boasting some of the most sophisticated ocean exploration equipment.

"Dr. Orion, you're needed aboard the *Kanaloa* ASAP. Kent has picked up an unknown anomaly on the latest sonar imaging feed along with some mild quake-like tremors. The *Sky Nene* is already enroute to Princeville to bring you out."

An exploratory dive was not scheduled for another day but the mere possibility of a potential earthquake along a seamount was not a matter to be lightly brushed aside. "Sommer and I are at the airport. As soon as the *Sky Nene* touches down we'll be on our way."

"Roger that," Captain Armington confirmed ending the transmission.

Cresting the mountainous terrain of the Na Pali coastline, NORA's research chopper the *Sky Nene* named after the Hawaiian state bird, began its descent at the Princeville Airport. Easily recognizable upon approach, NORA's colorful logo consisting of three interlocking spheres of sapphire blue, emerald green, and baked terra cotta were visible upon the *Sky Nene's* cabin doors. The *Sky Nene* painted in the traditional nautical colors of blue and white, touched down on the helipad. Feeling the rush of wind from the rotors, Dalton and Sommer jogged out ducking low beneath the spinning blades while boarding.

Dalton eased in next to the pilot quickly putting on his headset. Sommer jumped in the back, strapping herself in and grabbing the headsets hanging to her right. Jim Pearce, NORA's Pacific operations helicopter pilot light-heartedly spoke over his headset, "Good morning Dr. Orion. It's a beautiful morning in paradise. Buckle up and we'll get underway."

Dalton quipped, "Did you spot any promising swells rolling in?"

Jim smiled, "Surf is definitely up along Anahola."

"Too bad I didn't bring my board," Dalton quipped.

"Sommer, you ready back there?"

"Oh yeah. Rotate at your leisure."

Opening up the throttle to increase the speed of the rotor blades, Jim slowly pulled up on the collective control lever to his left working simultaneously the foot pedals. Upon gaining sufficient lift he pushed forward on the cyclical stick between his legs and with a slight forward pitch the *Sky Nene* took to the air gaining altitude and speed while climbing over the towering Na Pali Mountains and then dipping down toward the coastline heading out to the *Kanaloa*. The views from the air were absolutely breath-taking with the lush green mountain side, cascading waterfalls, and a school of dolphins below breaching the blue ocean swells of the Pacific.

Twenty-five minutes into the flight the *Kanaloa* came into view beneath a picture perfect cloudless sky as cresting white caps swept across the ocean's surface rhythmically moving toward the Kaua'i coastline.

Coming into view, the *Kanaloa* was anchored off the small crescent-shaped island of Lehua located only 0.7 miles (1.1 km) north of what is known as the "The Forbidden Isle" of Ni'ihau, approximately 17.5 miles due west of Kaua'i across the Kaulakahi Channel. Serving as a State sea bird sanctuary, Lehua is 284 acres of uninhabited island and famous for: its sea crater, world-class snorkeling and scuba diving, and an unusual geological formation called "The Keyhole" which is a tall, thin notch in one of the narrowest arms of the crescent island that cuts through to the other side. Underwater sea caverns abound as Lehua is part of the extinct Ni'ihau volcano.

Landing on *Kanaloa's* landing pad, the *Sky Nene* touched down on the helipad. As Jim shut down the rotor blades, Dalton and Sommer stepped out and were met by Dr. Ryan Fields the Seismologist aboard the *Kanaloa*.

"Good morning Dr. Orion, we've detected an anomaly on the most recent seismic data reading. We've also discovered what is believed to be a recently formed hydrothermal vent not formerly recorded on any of our charts. The developing formation appears to be caused by an aberrant source just beneath the seafloor."

Dalton noticed the dark clouds gathering in the distance and the swells gaining intensity and height cresting nearly six feet above the ocean's surface. "What is the latest weather report? Those are some mean looking clouds heading directly for us and the ocean seems to be getting temperamental by the minute."

"We're already on top of it," Ryan replied. "It's an unforecasted weather pattern. The Captain has engaged the dynamic positioning systems to stabilize the ship."

After descending stairs to the second of five lower decks aboard the *Kanaloa*, Dalton stepped through the doorway entering the Research corridor consisting of ten research rooms. He headed directly for Research Room 1 used for seafloor topography observations as well as meteorological and hydrological observations. The room was replete with all the latest in research related computer and software technology providing NORA's marine scientists and technicians with everything needed for oceanography research and exploration.

Akamu Paradis, a Hawaiian native and geophysicist aboard the *Kanaloa*, having just finished printing the latest data report, swiveled in his chair and jumped up quickly to debrief Dalton. "We're picking up what seems to be the emergence of a hydrothermal vent just off the northern tip of the Lehua Island cone. Looks like a white smoker at a depth of only about 200 meters. But even more perplexing is the unexpected subsurface behavior we're detecting posing the possibility of an imminent eruption and fast magma ascent."

Dalton looked back at Akamu incredulously quipping, "You really need to lay off the Hot Tamales."

"That's not the half of it," Akamu said excitedly reporting the latest findings. "We're also detecting what appears to be a subsurface sea cavern that is uncharted. It's almost as if the sea cavern recently breached the wall of the seamount. There is a possibility of an existing air pocket based on water oxygenation readings located close to the entrance of the sea cavern."

Processing the latest information while scanning the trace response data from the hydrophone read outs, Dalton sat back looking reflectively at the monitor. While transfixed to the supercomputer visual monitor Dalton asked Akamu, "What is the sparker picking up?"

"That's just it, there's no refraction coming from the trace. It's as if the sonar pulse and all related energy are simply being absorbed by some type of undetected anomaly."

"Interesting," Dalton said thinking out loud. "So we're dealing with a non-normal incident with an acoustic impedance source."

Instinctively Dalton continued, "We need to go down and extract the anomaly to see what we're dealing with. Who knows, maybe we've found the mother load," Dalton quipped.

Speaking into his two way Dalton said, "Sommer, ready the Namaka. We're going down in five."

"Roger that. I assume you realize we've got a pissed off sea pitching a fit with the currents?"

Dalton responded, "Then go ahead and suit up meet me at the *Namaka* . We need to get bottom side ASAP."

The *Namaka* ("water spirit"), a twenty-foot submersible with advanced underwater explorations systems for observing changes in geological formations, boasts the latest in underwater exploratory technology including ambient pressure capable of maintaining the same pressure both inside and outside the vessel.

Dalton and Sommer climbed inside the *Namaka* quickly strapping in before being lowered by the *Kanaloa's* wench over the side of the ship and released into the ocean. Dalton radioed topside, "*Kanaloa*, this is the *Namaka*. I have the controls and beginning our descent."

"Roger *Namaka*. You have the controls."

As the *Namaka* submerged beneath the surface the skies overhead were completely shrouded by dark storm clouds. The descent to 200 meters below surface was like descending into a black abyss. The *Namaka's* flood lights were beaming into the dark void offering only close range visibility within ten meters.

Looking out the observation window, Sommer commented, "The great mystery."

"What was that?" Dalton replied looking over at her.

"The great mystery. It's what the natives call the ocean. And what a wondrous mystery it is."

A sloping seawall suddenly came into view commanding their attention revealing a volcanic seamount possessing a steep decline along a large rift zone. Dalton strained to look further down searching for the opening to the sea cavern. Descending another seventy-five meters Dalton spotted what he was looking for nearly twice the size of the *Namaka*.

Concentrating the floodlights on the cavern entrance, Dalton spotted a luminescent green light coming from inside the cavern's interior. "What do we have here?" Dalton said as he began manipulating the Acoustic Positioning System (APS).

Navigating the *Namaka* for a better approach vector, Dalton looped around seeking a possible entrance into the sea cavern.

Wide-eyed, Sommer glanced over at Dalton, "You're not actually considering what I think you're considering are you?"

"I wouldn't dream of disappointing our onboard thrill-seeker," Dalton replied with a wry grin.

"Yes, but I'd like to live a bit longer to enjoy a few more thrills."

Dalton chuckled while allaying her anxiety, "The Acoustic Positioning System (APS) feedback is giving us plenty of room to maneuver. I can't believe we've not come across this cavern before on any of NORA's existing topographic maps of the area. We are definitely in uncharted waters my friend."

"Story of my life," Sommer replied matter-of-factly not taking her gaze away from the approaching seamount cavern.

While drawing closer to the cavern entrance a very large object began to move toward the *Namaka* quickly registering on the APS. Sommer was first to pick up the ping. quickly turning on the Fox eye exterior lighting feature while zeroing in on the fast approaching object.

"I've got visual," Dalton said. A large twenty-five foot great white shark swam up to the *Namaka* briefly lingering before rolling in an evasive maneuver. Reflexively pushing back, Dalton had the strange sensation that the shark paused to make visual contact with him before turning aside.

Sommer quickly said, "Whoa! Did you see how huge that shark was?!"

"I'm glad we're in here and he's out there."

"And you still want to proceed into his lair?" Sommer asked. "You may have awakened a slumbering Leviathan."

"We only live once. Besides, this is what we do. We brave the depths, the dangers, and the odds to explore and discover. Speaking of which, I saw a green light beaming from inside the sea cavern. I want to get inside and check it out. Maybe the air pocket Amaku detected is large enough to allow us access."

While Dalton was navigating the *Namaka* and positioning the submersible for entrance into the cave, Sommer's thoughts turned to an old Hawaiian shark legend. Gazing out the observation windows as if vaguely aware of Dalton's close encounters with narrowing seawalls, Sommer began to share her thoughts.

"Hawaiians believe sharks are not to be feared but respected. Many natives believe the shark to be an 'aumakua' or guardian spirit. One legend tells of how a woman was captured by a shark and negotiated her release by addressing the shark as her 'aumakua'. The shark released her but not before leaving teeth marks on her ankle to serve as a sign that she was under the shark's protection. So even to this day some Hawaiians tattoo their ankles to serve as a sign of their protective bond with the 'aumakua'. We would all be the better for pursuing harmony between human life and sea life and respect for that matter, all living things among nature."

While making minor adjustments to the lighting, beads of sweat began forming on Dalton's forehead as he continued to meticulously navigate within the close confines of the sea cavern while taking in

Sommer's every word.

"The 'niuhi' (NEE-OOH-HEE), the Hawaiian name meaning man-eating shark or powerful warrior, is also revered by many native Hawaiians as a sacred guardian and protector of the island people. Many Hawaiian legends surround the 'niuhi' but one in particular tells of how Kekūhaupi'o battled a great 'niuhi' shark to pass the final test with his lua master. Kekūhaupi'o fought so valiantly and with such cunning that he was able to defeat the great 'nuihi' shark in its own deep, dark lair returning to the surface unscathed by the battle. Believed to have acquired something of the 'nuihi's nature and power, Kekūhaupi'o went on to become the trainer and fellow warrior of the future Hawaiian King Kamehameha I."

Dalton shuddered at the thought of having to engage face to face out in the deep, what just swam by the *Namaka*. "If Keku papio or however you pronounce his name defeated anything remotely as close in size to what just swam by us, he would've also had my vote to rule as king."

Laughing Sommer quipped, "Yeah. I hear you. Reminds me of the scene in the movie, *Mutiny on the Bounty*, where the character named Christian keeps saying over and over to himself, 'Either you eat life or life eats you.' But in the end I think Kekūhaupi'o was honored with the position most suited to his unique disposition and resilient fighting skills. And besides, King Kamehameha I was a great warrior and ruler in his own right."

"Wasn't he something like an Alexander the Great of the Hawaiian Islands?" Dalton said ever fascinated by Hawaiian history and legend.

"I guess you could probably argue that point. At the time, Kamehameha lived during a violent era in Hawai'i's history. Conflict and wars between the chiefs on each of the islands had become prevalent. Capitalizing on the western weapons that were brought to the Hawaiian Islands when Captain James Cook arrived in Hawai'i during 1778, King Kamehameha I was able to win fierce battles on the different islands. He lived to fulfill the prophesy foretelling his conquest of the Hawaiian Islands when in 1810, King Kaumualii of Kaua'i agreed to become a tributary kingdom under Kamehameha. And thus it came to pass that Kamehameha was finally able to unite the sparring islands into one royal kingdom becoming the first ruling monarch of the Hawaiian Islands, forever more to be remembered and revered as King Kamehameha I."

Manipulating the controls, Dalton directed the *Namaka* into unknown waters proceeding slowly into the cavern beyond. The *Namaka* illuminated the dark confines of the cavernous surroundings as small fish and other sea life scurried out of the way. "Up ahead about twenty feet there seems to be a surface area." Dalton said.

Manipulating the controls, Dalton meticulously maneuvered the *Namaka* initiating its ascent within the cavern until it breached the surface. A faraway look came over Sommer as she took in a sweeping view of the cavern's interior.

Directly ahead, Dalton spotted a rocky outcropping which offered a natural docking area for the *Namaka*. Reversing propulsion, Dalton brought the submersible to rest next to the rocky ledge that looked like a dais about 30 feet in circumference.

"I'm going to check out the area. Keep the *Namaka* steady and give me plenty of light," Dalton instructed. Sommer took the controls as Dalton equalized the internal pressure with the exterior before opening the hatch whereupon they were greeted by dank air that smelled like rotten eggs.

Dalton stepped off the lip of the *Namaka* out onto the rocky outcropping. Exhilaration swept over him as he scanned the natural platform with his flashlight. His eyes followed the nearly thirty feet high vaulted cavern walls roughly hewn by ages of trickling water leaking in from the outside. A greenish yellow glow suddenly appeared about twenty feet from where he was standing illumining an entryway.

As Dalton approached the entrance into the mountainous cavern the glowing light began to intensify. Stepping into the light beyond, Dalton was stunned by what greeted his eyes. A divine being looking every bit a Hawaiian god with glistening light brown skin that was refracting the lambent flames blazing in a fire pit. The otherworldly stranger was sitting as if in deep contemplation while gazing into the flames. The fire was being fed by water and air as the flames danced amidst a steamy mist that drifted upwards as if ascending to an open sky. The peaceful glow filled the cavernous space with a purity of air that quickened the senses.

Dalton felt his heart beginning to pound in his chest as he froze in disbelief. His instinct was to turn back, to flee the fear that was welling up inside him. As if reading his thoughts, the otherworldly stranger who was staring stoically into the flames broke the awkward silence, "Don't be afraid. Come and please sit."

The spirit being possessed golden eyes like that of a lion's. Almost entirely naked, he wore only a loin covering and an unadorned headdress intertwined with the leaves and fibers of exotic Hawaiian plants. The crown itself was made of Acacia koa wood embedded with smooth greyish black stones that shimmered in the firelight.

Dalton took a seat on a basalt (volcanic) rock across from the spirit being. Feeling his heart racing he tried to steady his thoughts allowing the curious part of himself gain the upper hand asking, "Who are you?"

"I am Lonomakua – one of the guardian spirits of Eden and keeper of the sacred fire sticks."

"Eden? You mean the mythical garden of paradise?" Dalton asked quickly reverting to his skeptical nature.

"Eden is more than the garden of paradise of which you speak. It is the entirety of the kingdom fashioned by the Creator. The garden paradise is the womb of Eden, the center from which everything sprang forth. We sit within the womb of life."

Dalton felt an inclination to pinch himself to awaken from what appeared so real. Quickening his senses, a stirring of cool air eddied around him although he was sitting only feet from flames licking nearly ten feet upwards and yet there was no heat emanating from it. The odd color of emerald fire glinted off the otherworldly eyes of Lonomakua that seemed to bore into the very marrow of Dalton's soul.

Beginning to feel strangely at odds with his surroundings, Dalton asked the question that had haunted him for nearly ten years, "Why?"

"You have been chosen to wield the fire sword – the divine weapon forged by the hand of the Creator for the preservation of Eden and entrusted to its protector. Only one other has wielded its power. Even now you draw upon the mana that encompasses these sacred rocks, this hallowed ground, this spirit fire, as well as the water and air. Mana encircles and envelops the five elements used to create all things infusing the heart and soul of Eden with spiritual power."

The volcanic rocks upon which fiery flames leapt and danced began changing hues assuming a distinct emerald pigmentation as a blade made of emerald fire began to ascend within the midst of the flames. Dalton felt an incredible surging of emotions overwhelming him with a mixed sense of awe, fear, doubt, and then anger.

Rising in curious awe and wonder before the sacred flames that were surprisingly devoid of heat, Dalton was transfixed by the divine sword that was aflame with emerald fire. The shaft of the sword appeared to be made of earthen clay with a cross hilt that was animated by small angelic wings. There was an organic nature about the mythical sword as if it were somehow spiritually connected to the sacred fire. Dalton felt a strong tugging sensation within compelling him to reach out and take the sword.

Lonomakua sagely gazed upon Dalton and said, "Step into the sacred spirit fire and continue the healing that was begun in you by the one bearing the gift of the 'long breath'."

Dalton made to comply but then balked at the invitation as if paralyzed by fear and doubt suddenly feeling destitute of faith. Every carnal impulse in his body fueled by an upwelling of anger from nearly ten years of grief surged violently within. Pangs of internal suffering fought back against the mere thought of healing. The healing he needed would only be realized by confronting a God who had abandoned him and those he loved most long ago. Dalton resisted the invitation to step into the fire as he gave himself over to the rage within his spirit.

Lonomakua spoke once again in a prophetic tone, "Eden calls to her protector. Now release your grip on fear and embrace who you truly are, Dalton Orion. Only the healing fire can purify and prepare you to wield the fire sword. Only faith can unleash the energy within empowering you to walk the spirit path while embodying Eden's power. Only when the sacred fire burns within you the Sword of Eden will ignite in fiery wonder."

Dalton could feel the quickening of the blood coursing through his carotid artery setting his brain afire. The last time he took a leap of faith he witnessed those he loved most blasted into eternity by a fiery explosion from a terrorist bomb. He winced as the memory pierced his consciousness. *Why flames?* He thought seething inside.

"What kind of God would mock and try my soul in such a way?" Dalton cried out. The air suddenly became thick, hot, and humid as if mirroring Dalton's emotions.

Giving himself over to the upwelling of anger within, he gazed defiantly at Lonomakua feeling nothing but hatred and detest. "Who do you think you are? You expect much but only deliver pain. Why do you harass and hound my soul? I do not ask for any gift except that which frees my soul of you."

Acting on a surge of dark fire within, Dalton found his legs reaching out with reckless abandon into the midst of the flames seizing the handle of the flaming sword. Intending to bring it to bear upon Lonomakua, his effort proved futile. Upon gripping the shaft, Dalton felt a surge of energy rifle through his body feeling a supernatural heat that ignited his spirit. He had never felt more alive and consumed by such intense energy.

Seized by an overwhelming vision, Dalton found himself standing within a tropical setting looking at two fierce angelic beings; one dressed in black wielding a sword blazing in crimson fire and another in pristine white gripping a sword blazing in emerald fire. The two angelic titans were slowly and calculatingly circling one another; one a paragon of Darkness and the other a paragon of Light. The Dark Lord possessed crimson eyes filled with hatred. The Lord of Light possessed brilliant sapphire blue eyes filled with peace.

As if drawn into a tornado-like vortex, Dalton began spinning rapidly around the two towering titans and after a period of time found himself stopping abruptly before the Dark Lord, who with cold, hate-filled eyes, gazed intently at Dalton fixing him with a murderous glare. "Do you believe in the power of evil?" And then as if someone suddenly flipped the switch off, Dalton lost consciousness.

Chapter 2

FULL LIGHT

Lehua, Hawai'i

Emerging from the shallows and bathed in pale light, a lone figure donning a swimmer's physique with skin as smooth as polished marble waded toward the rocky shoreline of the Hawaiian Island of Lehua. Stepping onto the shore, there was a fearlessness about his gait as he carried himself in a manner of one given to a high purpose. Impervious to the cool night air, he gave a nod signaling to his companion up above. Perched upon a rocky overlook, his nod was acknowledged in kind.

Leaping effortlessly two hundred feet from the shoreline up onto the rocky perimeter of the island's rocky fortress just above the key hole, he walked over alongside his companion Soren who was keenly alert to any potential land or aerial threats. Standing in rapt attention, Soren continued scanning for any signs of the Dark Ones.

Emrick turned and gazed out toward the *Kanaloa* as the *Namaka* was being hoisted to its resting place upon the deck of the ship's fantail. The cool tropical trade breeze swirled around him, as he retrieved a dark tee-shirt from its resting place slipping it over his long, muscular torso. Collecting his thoughts he gazed out over the crescent-shaped bay at the dark foreboding storm clouds trailing off over the Pacific.

The winds began to subside lessening the stinging bite of the rain slapping against his strong, prominent facial features. With dark golden blonde hair cropped close to the crown, piercing blue eyes, a high forehead, taut jawline, and dimpled chin, Emrick possessed striking masculine features.

Looking toward the west across the Pacific, Emrick witnessed the descent of light as the sun fled before the encroaching darkness. His heightened angelic senses pierced beyond the natural veil of life as his keen angelic vision scanned the darkness for any signs of the Dark Ones. It would only be a matter of time before they would gather in force. *And so it is,* Emrick pondered to himself. The cycle of Light and Darkness. One rising and the other falling.

The radiance of his skin dissipated as he crouched in contemplative thought. Rising from his perched position, his young apprentice Soren walked over and with a flick of his finer ignited a fire within a circle of rocks. With dark brown hair pulled back in a braid, hazel green eyes, and hard body like granite, Soren commanded the respect of both friend and foe. A couple of scars were visible across the left side of his face. Tall of stature with a couple battle scars across the left side of his face, Soren relaxed his posture giving the all clear.

Approaching the small burning fire upon the rocky outcropping of Lehua just beyond the crescent perimeter of the island, Emrick continued to gaze out towards the Pacific preoccupied in thought.

The tropical breezes stirred around him as he pondered the implications of what had transpired beneath the surface. Forged by God, the ancient Sword of Eden was now in the hands of a mortal. The mere thought, even for one such as himself with unyielding faith in the Light, stirred a sense of unease.

Emrick was keenly aware that much was riding on the success of their mission. Those faithful to the Light were pinning their hopes on the wisdom of the Light and the Dark Ones desired nothing more than to seize the sword and crush the soul of the mortal chosen to wield it in defense of Eden.

Emrick believed in the ancient prophesy. He never challenged it as many of his kind had and some still did. Walking in the will of the Light was the discipline of an angel. And even more so since the Great Rebellion. It's what separated those loyal to the Creator from those loyal to Satariel. Dalton was the chosen one, of that Emrick had no doubt. He witnessed the exchange in the cavern. The intensity of energy that was elicited from the sword would've eviscerated a mere mortal instantly upon contact. But to the contrary, the reverse had happened. Some type of connection had been formed between Dalton and the sword although the confluence of Dark and Light energy flowing within him arrested the sword's power.

Pondering the implications, Emrick knew the Dark Ones would seek to snuff out Eden's hope before Dalton became a viable threat. Breaking the silence, Emrick said, "It has begun. The words of the prophecy are now clothed in mortal flesh."

The enormity of his words settled upon them both. The die had been cast. The fate of Eden, now hanging in the balance, was dependent upon the success or failure of their mission.

Emrick plucked a rock from the ground tossing it up and down in his right hand. "The sword beckons to him but he does not hear the call. Darkness pangs his soul and the Light wanes within him."

Soren weighed his words drawing his left hand back through his closely cropped brown hair. "Then we must draw him back to the Light."

The crashing waves pummeled unmercifully the rocky islet. Emrick drew back and effortlessly threw the rock with no visible sign that it ever hit water. "We are fortunate to be chosen for a time such as this. Only by the power of the Light will we triumphantly subdue the Darkness that so tightly holds Eden in its grip."

"Well, I was hoping you brought me along for a higher purpose than mere sightseeing," Soren quipped while resting his hand on the pommel of an energy dagger at his side.

The tropical air began to stir about fifteen yards to the south of where Emrick stood as a mid-air vortex consisting of earth, air, water, and fire began to materialize. A rapid swirling motion formed a shimmering pool of light that intensified by the moment. Crackling energy broke the silence as a mystical portal linking two worlds enlarged nearly fifteen feet in diameter forming a perfect circle with a fixed intensity of light as bright as the sun. The portal remained suspended in the air about a foot off the ground.

Turning toward the portal, a broad smile swept across Soren's face as the shimmering surface began to ripple as an angelic being tall of stature stepped through. Donning a breastplate of platinum with golden accents and a spiraling golden torque with the heads of two eagles flanking the nape of his neck, the angelic warrior sized up his surroundings with an unyielding gaze. Accompanied by five others dressed in similar fashion, each fanned out around the perimeter of the make shift camp along the rocky outcropping of Lehua assuming defensive positions.

Uriel, one of the seven lords of heaven and a formidable archangel had long flowing silver hair, prominent facial features and pale green eyes like that of a wolf's. Walking over and standing before Emrick, a smile creased his face as he raised his right hand to his left breast. Emrick followed suit slightly bowing his head in a gesture of comradery and respect.

Having fought alongside Uriel in the never ending Angelic War, Emrick had witnessed firsthand the significant role Uriel played in repelling Satariel's attempt at overthrowing the Creator during the Great Rebellion when the rebel angels laid siege to Emyprean, the celestial city of Heaven. Emrick's celestial hide had been saved more than once by Uriel whose deeds are often recounted among the Council of Light to inspire faithfulness, courage, and perseverance among the Faithful.

Known as the angel of vengeance, the Bright One who commands both thunder and terror, Uriel came into his own as a warrior who took pleasure in thwarting the efforts of the rebel angels. He desired nothing more than to crash the brazen gates of Primora, the dark kingdom referred to as Hell among mortals, and bring all the rebellious, unrepentant, and arrogant souls to divine justice.

Speaking with a commanding voice, Uriel broke the silence addressing Emrick, "The Creator has given the go ahead for Full Light." Soren's eyes opened wide with uncertainty realizing the implications. He gauged Emrick's reaction which betrayed no hint of anxiety or fear. Emrick accepted the message in good faith replying, "The Creator's Word is our Light. The Creator's Will is our duty. The Creator's Wisdom is our guide."

Walking over and placing his right hand on Emrick's left shoulder, Uriel replied, "May your efforts brighten Heaven's hope, inspire Eden's faith, and ignite Primora's despair."

Emrick responded in kind saying, "We kneel as one in allegiance to the Creator, stand as one in honor before the Creator, and prevail as one in love for the Creator."

Soren along with the other immortals all placed their hands over their hearts and responded, "One in Allegiance. One in Honor. One in Love."

Uriel touched the cylindrical-shaped medallion displaying the symbol of an eagle's head as a portal materialized. The angelic warriors stepped through the shimmering portal glistening like sunlight off a pool of water. Uriel paused before crossing the threshold glancing back at Emrick evidencing a war-hardened face, "Satariel is no fool. But neither are you. Eden's aura reeks of the Darkness. Ignite the Light my friend." Then turning, Uriel stepped into the shimmering portal which vanished behind him.

Soren had many questions racing through his mind as he looked to Emrick weighing the implications of their new mission status. "Full Light? I'm only aware of one other instance in which Full Light was employed and that was soon after the Great Rebellion."

Emrick perceptively looked at Soren replying, "I see you've been reading the *Book of Light*. Yes, the last time it was employed was at the Fall of Eden. It's a calculated risk like stepping into a black hole. The outcome is not assured. And in this case, all hinges on the faith of a mortal or lack thereof. Satariel is about to unleash a darkness in Eden unparalleled in human history. If successful this kingdom will fall into oblivion and along with it the hope and promise of our Creator. So, there is much to lose if our efforts prove futile. Not a time for fear but faith, we must draw from its energy and focus on what will be achieved when our efforts prove successful."

Soren wrestled with his thoughts and was not as inclined to optimism as Emrick. "Your thoughts betray you," Emrick said while gazing off into the distance.

Soren hated it when Emrick read his thoughts. He tried to give a defense for his reservation. "Full Light is predicated upon variables that we have little control over. The most obvious is that the one sure weapon designed to stop Satariel in his tracks is worthless if the hand of the one called to wield it doesn't do so while exercising faith in the Light. If Dalton is the one chosen by the Light to wield the fire sword, then we have a serious problem. Dalton's faith is messed up. He's messed up. And quite frankly our mission seems doomed to fail from the start. In all due respect master, he is far from a blazing light ready to ignite the darkness as the ancient prophecy foretells. How can we even be sure he's the prophesied one?"

"Are you finished, O soul of faith?" Emrick said sarcastically turning to face his young apprentice. "You seem to know much about fear. What do you know of faith? The path that leads the Faithful to Darkness begins with fear. And the dark harvest is sown by seeds of doubt. You rely too heavily upon what your eyes see rather than on what your faith knows to be true. You're not that different from the current disposition of Eden's Protector. Walking in Full Light will require you to unreservedly exercise faith in: the Creator's Word, the Creator's Will, and the Creator's Wisdom. And you must restrain yourself when events beckon you to question and deny your faith; the means by which you discern the truth of all things. Full Light is only invoked when something is amiss and the likelihood of treachery is highly probable. Now that the Sword of Eden is in mortal hands Satariel will seek to acquire it at all costs depriving the Light from using it to thwart Eden's demise. Pride and rebellion rooted in a wavering faith in the Creator was the catalyst for Satariel's fall and the eventual fall of Eden. His dark seed was sown in Eden's womb which gave birth to death. Only faith can restore the reign of Light in Eden."

Pondering Emrick's words Soren replied, "How is that even possible? Once faith is lost how can one stand against the Darkness? The sacred writings state, 'Faith is the shield from which we extinguish the flaming energy of the evil one.'"

"Yes, but you speak as if faith is something you lose. One chooses or rejects faith, it is never lost. You either place your faith in the

Darkness or in the Light. For the sacred writings also state, 'The victory that overcomes the Darkness is our faith.' And so the flipside of this spiritual truth is that a catastrophic shift in faith away from the Light to the Darkness could result in the dethronement of the Creator by the power of free will. And so this Angelic War and the battle for the very heart and soul of Eden is a battle of attrition. What Satariel is seeking to achieve is essentially an epidemic of doubt that creates a catastrophic crisis of faith. Eden will stand or fall depending on whether mortals choose or reject faith in the Creator."

Soren quickly retorted, "But this is impossible! The Creator can never fall. His rule is absolute. And how could Satariel possibly achieve such a crisis of faith?"

Emrick answered, "If our own history has taught us anything it's that the power of thought can change reality. Anything is possible with the power of faith; Satariel's rebellion being a case in point. Many incorrectly assumed that Satariel lost his faith. Nothing can be further from the truth. On the contrary, he rejected faith in the Creator and instead placed his faith in the dark energy. He will seek to achieve no less in Dalton?"

"I don't mean to be flippant master, but how can one person make such a difference in the larger scheme of things? He is but an insignificant pebble compared to the sea of darkness that envelops him. What possible difference can he make? He's a mere shell of his former self."

"Your frustration and lack of patience clouds your judgment," Emrick cautioned sensing the fear and doubt gnawing at Soren.

Picking up a rock with a small slit in the side, Emrick made a drop of water appear and fall into the hairline crack. "You speak of faith as if it is something to be quantified or measured. The seemingly impenetrable fortitude of a towering mountain can be eventually laid low by an insignificant trickle of water that finds its way inside the cracks and crevices within the rock. And when the cold freezing breath of Eden begin to stir, the water residing between those cracks and crevices freeze and then shatter the rock from within. Over time the mountain is laid waste. What began as a few insignificant cracks became the opportunity by which trickles of water established a foothold eventually bringing about the ultimate collapse of the mountain. Never underestimate the influence of a single trickle of faith that can find its way into the crevice of a mountain of darkness. A trickle of faith has the power to shatter doubt. And that is why we continue to fight the good fight of faith."

The rock in has hand broke apart dissolving into mere dust. Emrick blew the remnants of dust outward which were quickly carried away by the wind. Gazing toward the Pacific, Emrick mused, "Eden is Satariel's playground. As goes Eden so goes the Kingdom of Heaven, at least according to Satariel's malevolent thinking. Our task is to give him a wake-up call. And we're going to do so by taking the fight to him."

Soren bowed his head and laid his right fist across his left breast as a sign of respect and acceptance of the wisdom of his master's words. They both looked off in the distance at the *Kanaloa* as a helicopter lifted off the helipad turning toward the island of Kaua'i. Along its flight path a few lights across the scarcely populated surface of Ni'ihau dotted the forbidden isle off in the distance. Noticing a few lights go out on the island, Soren fought back the tempting thought to view it as an ominous sign of Eden's inevitable plunge into darkness. The hush of the evening, the diminishing lights, and a starless night sky, all served to cast a pall of foreboding doubt over Soren as he wrestled with the conflict raging within.

Emrick sensed his struggle and said, "All will be revealed in good time. The future of Eden will be determined for better or worse by the choices of the one aboard that helicopter. Our present task is to ensure that he lives long enough to have the opportunity to become what I know he is; Eden's Protector."

Soren quickly interjected, "But what if those choices are for the worse? Would we not be inadvertently aiding the cause of Satariel when we could simply take the sword and remove it from Eden?"

"Now, you're beginning to experience what it is to walk in Full Light. Just be careful that you're not blinded by its intensity. Measure your thoughts, question your doubt, and exercise your faith. Hold true to the Light. For redemption is won in the Light but is wrought in the Darkness. And to sojourn there you must hold fast to your faith or more than just your soul shall be lost."

Lightening the mood, Emrick added affably, "So yes, I've brought you along for more than mere sightseeing."

Chapter 3

PREYING EYES

Dalton arrived via the *Sky Nene* at Wilcox Memorial Hospital on Kaua'i and immediately rushed into an examination room before being transferred to a hospital room. Slowly regaining consciousness Dalton surveyed his surroundings trying to ascertain where he was. Sommer was standing over him with a caring smile across her face, "Nice to have you back among the living."

Dalton started to sit up but dropped back to the bed feeling very weak as if all the energy in his body had been drained from him.

"Hey, just relax," Sommer said standing by his bedside. "You need to regain your strength. You've been out for most of the day and the Doctor wants to keep you overnight for observation."

Dalton stubbornly brushed her worry aside, "Hey, I'm fine. It was a simple black out. There's no need to stay overnight for more tests."

Sommer was quick to counter, "I don't know what happened to you in the cavern but I found you out cold on the ground. And I don't recall you having colored your hair with silver highlights prior to your leaving the submersible."

"What?" Dalton said as he forced himself up slowly making his way over to the sink. Gazing into the mirror he beheld the silver highlights and a face staring back at him that appeared fifteen years younger without the slightest hint of aging for someone in his forties.

"That's some highlight treatment. And I've got to get some of whatever facial cream this is?!" Dalton quipped.

"That's what I'm saying," Sommer replied.

"A bit envious are we? Sort of levels the playing field now, don't you think?" Dalton joked giving Sommer a wink.

"But do you have the youthful energy to go along with it old man?" Sommer was quick to retort.

"I guess we'll find out soon enough," Dalton said gazing back at his reflection in the mirror, Dalton's memory of the events in the cavern was spotty at best. He remembered an otherworldly stranger, an emerald fire, and reaching out into flames for a fire sword. He felt as if there was more but all he could recall was a phantom memory.

"Man, I've got a craving for some…red wine." Dalton said chuckling at the thought. "How odd is that?"

"About as odd as this," Sommer said retrieving the hilt of a bladeless sword from behind her shirt.

Turning away from the mirror, recognition swept over Dalton's face. He was about to respond when Dr. Blake Kealoha walked into the room greeting them both with a warm smile, "Aloha!" Walking over to Dalton he added, "How are we feeling old friend?"

Sommer quickly put the hilt of the sword behind the small of her back while returning Dr. Kealoha's smile.

Dalton had known Blake since he was boy when he used to spend a lot of time on Kaua'i during his early years with his parents. Dalton and Blake enjoyed snorkeling the Pacific blue and surfing the North Shore swells together. Those were good years.

Dalton gave Dr. Kealoha an enthusiastic response, "Never felt better Doc! How about a clean bill of health so I can get the heck out of here."

Dr. Kealoha continued smiling while flipping open Dalton's chart. "Everything appears in perfect working order based on your vitals. But almost too perfect. I'd like to run more blood work. Nothing to be alarmed about but initial results are off the charts. You look as if you are in your twenties. What have you been doing to achieve such extraordinary physical results?"

"Doc, I jog, surf, and eat lots of fish and veggies. Nothing I haven't been doing since you've known me."

"Well, keep it up. I don't have a problem clearing you for release but with only one stipulation. If anything and I mean anything appears to be out of the ordinary or if you begin to have any further black out spells, I want to see you ASAP. Sommer has doctor's orders to be my eyes and ears alerting me to anything out of the ordinary. You got that?"

Dalton responded, "Got it. I owe you one Doc."

"Don't mention it. Take care of yourself out there. Let's hit Cannons Beach soon."

"You got it. We'll make it happen."

Dalton turned to Sommer after Dr. Kealoha stepped out. "Now let's get out of here. *Keoki's Paradise* is calling."

"You hearing the whispering makani also," Sommer said with a mischievous smile.

"When the winds blow, I listen," Dalton said excited to be leaving the hospital and heading to one of his favorite spots to grab a bite to eat.

Arriving at *Keoki's Paradise*, a popular restaurant and bar in Poipu on the south shore of Kaua'i, Dalton and Sommer headed inside for some sustenance and drink. Dalton was feeling unusually famished as he strolled up to the bar and sat down. Sommer made a slight detour and headed for the refresher.

Seeing Dalton taking a seat at the Bamboo bar, Naoki the bartender greeted him with a smile and said, "What kind of day has it been Dalton?"

"A glass of merlot kind of day."

"Not the usual Raspberry Lava flow?"

"Not tonight. I've got a hankering for some red wine."

"You got it. Coming right up."

The famous island restaurant was a favorite among both natives and tourists who enjoyed the ambience of seated dining surrounded by flaming tiki torches, lush tropical foliage, and the fragrant smells of the garden paradise. A live band was singing Hawaiian tunes as tourists and locals drank and dined.

Two young females approached the bar area and sat down next to Dalton. One of them, a green-eyed brunette gave him a flirtatious grin and asked, "Do you want to get lei'd?"

Dalton about choked on his drink before replying, "Excuse me?"

The sexy temptress rubbed the lei around her neck suggestively and repeated herself, "Do you wanna get lei'd?"

"Oh honey, I'm all lei'd out but a good conversation is always welcome," Dalton quipped back. "And who might you be?"

The brunette beauty replied, "I'm Jill and my friend here is Kate. We both hail from the great state of Maryland."

Kate, the blue-eyed blond seated next to Jill extended her hand across to Dalton with a wicked smile on her face. "And to whom do we owe this delicious pleasure?"

"Dalton."

"Well, Dalton aren't we just the lucky ones to find you sitting here all alone."

"Looks can be deceiving."

Walking up just as Dalton glanced over eagerly awaiting her return, Sommer plopped down next to him while quickly sizing up the two young women engaging Dalton in conversation. Jill and Kate nodded with a curt smile turning their attention to the bartender.

Sommer leaned over and whispered in Dalton's ear, "Just a heads up, seated at your ten o'clock are two men that seem to have taken a special interest in you."

Dalton took a healthy sip of his wine shifting his body toward Sommer as if engaging her in intimate conversation, "Then I guess you will just have to be my eyes."

One of the things Dalton had come to appreciate about Sommer, was her keen observational skills. He had worked with many researchers and interns in the field but none possessed the eyes of a hawk like Sommer. Not much slipped her notice especially if something seemed amiss.

Naoki the bartender came over and asked, "What you having Sommer?"

"I'd love a Mai Tai."

Dalton quickly interjected, "Can I get a Grilled Veggie Sandwich and whatever else Sommer would like to have."

Sommer declined, "Just the Mai Tai, thank you."

Feeling something slithering around his ankle, Dalton looked down and saw a red, white, and black striped coral snake recoiling with fangs laid bare as if ready to strike. Quickly jumping off the bar stool clearing about seven feet, Dalton nearly landed on top of a couple dining close by near the lighted tropical pool.

Sommer had no idea what spooked Dalton nor did she remain seated long enough to ask as she followed his lead hopping up onto the bar nearly hitting her head on the Bamboo canopy above.

Everyone seated at the bar and in the restaurant stopped their chatter and looked over at Dalton. Glancing back to where the snake had been, Dalton only saw a lei consisting of red and white carnations intermixed with black beads on the ground.

Leaning over to pick up the lei, Jill returned his confused gaze with serpentine eyes appearing to glow maniacally. Cackling over Dalton's reaction she said, "Oh my God, you're a jittery one. Spunk with a whole lot of funk."

Dalton was embarrassed more than amused. He was certain he saw a coral. Fully aware of the fact that the Hawaiian authorities go to great pains to prevent snakes from being brought onto any of the

Hawaiian Islands to preserve and protect Hawaii's fragile island ecosystem, Dalton felt as if he were starting to lose his mind.

Naoki ran over from around from behind the bar to help Dalton stand up. "Dude, you ok?"

Regaining his composure and reluctant to share what he saw, Dalton grabbed Naoki's extended hand and stood back up. "Yeah, I'm ok. I thought I saw a coral snake."

"A coral snake? You're losing it brah. We don't do snakes in Hawai'i. You know that. And besides, coral snakes are native to Central America."

"Spare me the Ophiology lesson," Dalton said suddenly feeling a desire for fresh air. Looking over, Dalton noticed the two young girls leaving the restaurant. Glancing back over her shoulder, Jill gave him a wink as she teasingly ran her finger around the black beads on her lei.

Sommer jumped down from the bar top and stood next to Dalton. Glancing over she watched Jill and Kate leave. "Those two are a bit on the strange side," Sommer said. "That's enough excitement for one night. Let's get out of here."

"You won't get an argument out of me," Dalton said. After settling up with Naoki, he walked back over and saw Sommer gazing over to the table in the far corner where the two strangers had been sitting. They were gone.

"You ready to roll?"

"I see our two friends have left," Sommer answered as if deep in thought.

"Who knows, maybe they're afraid of snakes too," Dalton said breaking up the tense moment. Sharing a laugh at their own expense they walked out and jumped into Dalton's topless Jeep. Firing up the engine, Dalton said, "Let's go chase the moonlight."

"What you waiting for? Let's roll!" Sommer said while tying her hair back in a ponytail.

In hot pursuit of the moonbeams dancing over the Pacific waters and a few tunes later, Dalton pulled over off the Kuhio Highway just north of Kapaa coming to a stop at an overlook parking area along Kealia Beach which offers some of the best views for whale watching on Kaua'i. Sitting for a while in silence listening to the crashing of the waves on the rocks below, Sommer sat quietly not desiring to disturb Dalton who seemed to be lost in thought.

The moonbeams seemed to float upon the surface of the water eliciting a peaceful calm. "I remember now what happened inside the cavern," Dalton said while taking in the mesmerizing beauty of the night. "There was someone in there who referred to himself as Lonomakua, a guardian of Eden."

Dalton glanced over at Sommer to gauge her reaction. Gazing out over the Pacific, Sommer had a faraway look in her eyes. Continuing, Dalton recounted all that he saw inside the cavern. When finished he said, "It all sounds so preposterous. Who in their right mind would even believe it? I'm not even sure I do."

"There are many legends surrounding Lonomakua," Sommer said arresting Dalton's attention. "A visitation by one of the sacred spirits of Hawai'i is not something to be taken lightly. For there is meaning and purpose behind such an encounter. It would seem that you have been chosen for a great purpose and yet mystery surrounds the path that it will take you down. Fire sticks were gathered by the natives to prepare offerings to the gods. The sticks were used to feed the element of fire. But the true spirit energy resided not in the offering or even the fire itself but in the sticks. The wood contains within its very fibers the elements of earth, water, air, and spirit – the awen of life. And when added to the sacred fire an energy is elicited that provides tremendous mana or spiritual energy."

"I'm not following," Dalton said struggling to understand.

"Great souls were believed to be sacred fire sticks called upon by the gods to even make the ultimate sacrifice, if necessary, to serve a higher purpose in feeding the sacred fire that purifies all life. To recall one's true self and divine purpose one would sacrifice the sticks to feed the sacred fire to be cleansed and empowered by the resulting mana. Dalton, based on the vision you had in the sea cavern it would seem that you have been chosen and marked as one of Eden's sacred fire sticks. You have been chosen as a guardian of Eden. Guardians are called and arise during times of great evil to protect Eden from the threat of an impending apocalypse. Your life no longer belongs to you but to Eden."

"So basically, I'm a piece of wood to feed the flames of the gods," Dalton said sarcastically. Recalling the anger that welled up within him Dalton continued, "What is this some kind of sick joke by the gods meant to torment my soul even more? I lost my wife and son to a raging inferno. Were they fire sticks as well? If my divine purpose is to feed the flames for a psychopathic God, then he better have a contingency plan. If I couldn't even protect Lauren and Kaden, then how the hell does he expect me to protect Eden from some coming apocalypse?"

Sommer sensed the tempest of emotions raging within Dalton and felt it wise to let the matter rest for the time being. "It is what it is. I'm just glad you're ok. So what do you want to do with this?" Sommer said holding up the gleaming sword hilt as the moon rays refracted off the pommel.

Looking at it and weighing his options Dalton said, "Let's get it to the *Kanaloa* and see if we can ascertain its composition. I've never seen anything quite like it. I need some answers to the questions that are swarming my mind and the last thing I'm going to do is take the word of a spirit being that is probably only the figment of my overactive imagination."

"Then let's go find some answers and settle that mind of yours," Sommer said with a gleam of adventure in her eyes.

"That's what I love about you," Dalton replied with an affable smile.

"I know."

Chapter 4

MOVES AND COUNTERMOVES

Zurich, Switzerland

Peering out the top floor executive office window of the fifteen story charcoal gray high rise featuring black tinted windows, Devin's gaze was transfixed upon Grossmünster, a nearly thousand year old magnificent Romanesque-style Protestant church that loomed like a lone bastion of Light over the Zurick cityscape near the banks of the Limmat River. *Your efforts will prove futile,* Devin thought, eliciting a burst of cool malevolence telepathically to a distant adversary across space and time. *Eden is mine and too far gone for a return to the Light.*

President and CEO of Dominion Global Corporation (DGC) and mastermind behind DGC's rise as a global defense conglomerate, Devin Sinclair possessed an affinity for warfare technology including: Advanced Weapons Technology, Defensive Systems, and Space & ISR (Intelligence, Surveillance, and Reconnaissance) Systems. But his clandestine work and passion was in the area of Superintelligence, the new frontier in Artificial Intelligence (AI).

As a corporate anthropologist, Devin had achieved global star power and viewed as the epitome of success with a philanthropy reputation for making sizeable financial contributions to political campaigns, academic and field research, and humanitarian relief organizations. He had been awarded several honorary doctorates from world-renowned universities for distinction and eminence in his contributions toward advancements in Molecular Biology, Biophysics, and Computational Neuroscience.

Boasting flawless facial features framed by a chiseled jawline, dimpled chin, slender, athletic build and close clipped salt and pepper hair, Devin possessed photogenic good looks enhanced by a debonair persona; the essence of masculinity. When stepping into a room, Devin wielded a grace and presence that commanded attention. Refined, intelligent, and articulate, he possessed a magnetic and winsome personality, the kind of person people are drawn to and readily take into their confidence. And he knew how to work it for all its worth.

A popular draw for television interviews, Devin enjoyed celebrity status on the speaking circuit. Brilliant and far exceeding the intelligence of some of the world's top scientific minds, Devin's proclivity for tapping the brightest and best was key to his master plan. Very much a self-made entrepreneur and considered one of the top five wealthiest in the world, money was never an obstacle for Devin. If he wanted it; he acquired it with or without cash.

What many of his competitors viewed as the height of unparalleled arrogance, those within Devin's close inner circle viewed as the embodiment of self-confidence galvanized by vision and determination. Devin viewed obstacles as opportunities and setbacks as stepping stones. He inspired the pursuit of greatness in others by his proclivity for success.

The streets of Zurich during rush hour were littered with motorists and pedestrians hurrying along the curb sides, all clamoring for right of way. Peering down upon a sea of humanity scurrying about like rats fleeing rushing water, Devin found humor in the fact that their ignorance was shielding them from the evil about to be unleashed; an apocalypse of epic proportions that would trigger an extinction level event for humanity.

Watching the mundane human ritual below, Devin found himself speaking recounting words from one of his favorite Shakespearean plays, "What a piece of work is a man. How noble in reason. How infinite in faculty. In form and moving, how express and admirable. In action how like an angel! In apprehension, how like god. The beauty of the world. The paragon of animals. And yet, to me, what is this quintessence of dust?"

"I see we are quoting Hamlet again," a confident sounding female voice said entering the room. "The preceding line is also worthy of note, 'this goodly frame, the earth, seems to me a sterile promontory; this most excellent canopy, the air—look you, this brave o'erhanging firmament, this majestical roof fretted with golden fire — why, it appears no other thing to me than a foul and pestilent congregation of vapors.'"

Gracefully walking across the large executive office, the room was infused with the aroma of bergamot, orris, sandalwood, natural gum resin, vanilla, and ylang ylang extract. Breathing in deeply the aromatic perfume, Devin said, "Clive Christian No. 1. How you wear it so well."

"Am I supposed to be flattered?" Aeron asked with a teasing smile as Devin turned to face her.

"That and more," Devin replied affably.

A tall, striking beauty with nearly perfect feminine features, Aeron Trevil wore her radiant blonde hair short and chic, perfectly accenting her penetrating blue eyes, a slim figure, and shapely rear, the epitome of feminine beauty. She possessed a sexual appeal quickening Devin's pulse. Her intelligence, confidence and mesmerizing beauty were powerful intoxicants that Devin enjoyed and valued at his side.

Welcoming the sight of her sensuous and full lips and feeling the fire of desire beginning to ignite within, Devin warmly welcomed her, "I trust your flight aboard the Relentless was uneventful and relaxing."

"Yes, and I must say the black with red accents are most appealing to the eyes," Aeron said with an alluring smile. Devin had sent over his personal corporate helicopter, the Bell 525 Relentless, his preferred means of luxury flight between his corporate office in Zurich and the DGC's clandestine research facility located in a remote area of the Black Forest in Germany.

The current Division Director of Artificial Design and Intelligence (ADI) for the DGC, Aeron graduated egregia cum laude ("with outstanding honor") earning a dual PhD in Biophysics and

Nanoscience from Dresden University of Technology in Germany with a concentration in Emerging Technology. She had shown herself to be far superior to her counterparts in the field of artificial intelligence.

The Division of ADI, a covert division within the DGC was Devin's brain child with no traceable records due to clandestine genetic experimentation in Synthetic Biology, Cyber Intelligence, and Nanotechnologies. Known as Project Dark Halo, Aeron was the lead scientist overseeing the research, design, and experimentation with advanced intelligent humanoids conducted within the DGC remote facility deep in the heart of the Black Forest.

Devin created a culture of creativity within the DGC inspired by his premise, "If you can imagine it, you can create it. The only limit to creative design is the limit of one's intellect. Unleash your imagination and you unleash creative power."

The DGC's contributions and successes in the field of superintelligence and advanced weaponry made Devin a coveted keynote speaker for corporate gatherings and commencement addresses at university graduations as well as a person heavily courted by the political elite from around the world.

Returning Aeron's greeting, Devin extended his hand directing her to take a seat. He could not help but admire her beauty, grace, and poise. To have such a loyal executive and confidante only served to captivate his imagination with the limitless possibilities of what the two of them could continue to accomplish together.

Devin placed his utmost confidence in Aeron and empowered her as an extension of himself. He possessed a deep abiding affinity for her because of the narcotic-like effect she had over him. She was the stimulant that inspired his imagination and quickened him. But she also was a woman of many talents, the kind of which were quite lethal when employed.

Devin stepped out from behind his desk and walked over to take a seat across from Aeron which he would often do in private one on one meetings, especially with those he held in high regard. Although a beauty, Aeron's keen intellect was what Devin valued most.

Possessing a charm that didn't smack of pretense, Aeron found Devin very appealing as she often found herself ensnared by the captivating and sexual appeal of his steely black eyes. Intelligent, resolute, and in command, Aeron found in Devin a kindred spirit that she highly respected and to whom she was fiercely loyal.

Devin turned to the mega screen that dominated the wall opposite the office windows overlooking million dollar views of Zurich. "Global," Dalton said. Responding to voice command, the video monitors came to life with a high definition video feed from various locations around the world.

"What is the latest with Project Dark Halo?" Devin asked turning his attention to Aeron.

"Our shadow agents are positioned and actively inciting mayhem and chaos among major world religions."

Speaking to the far right video block, Aeron said, "al Jazeera". A breaking news caption cut across the screen as an image of an Islamic militant dressed in black with a hooded mask revealing only his eyes and mouth. Aeron pause and interjected commentary, "The Islamic military leader goes by the name Razeen Demian likened to Tamerlne, the great Turko-Mongul conqueror of the fourteenth century who was one of the most powerful rulers of the Muslim world and considered by many within the faith of Muhammad to be a modern day 'Sword of Islam'. Many Arabs view him as the personification of the myth of Sekhmet, the lion-headed deity Leo in the Egyptian pantheon who represented the age of chaos and destruction that enveloped the end of the Ice Age. Others refer to the Jihadist leader as Abu al-Hawl meaning 'Father of Terror' after the Sphinx of Giza in Egypt. Although his real name remains a mystery, the Jihadists believe the Lion of Leo is born again in Razeen and destined to bring about the end of the Age of the Infidel."

Standing behind a defiant American humanitarian aid worker who was kneeling before the camera, Razeen held a twelve inch razor sharp knife in his right hand. The aid worker was flanked by six other humanitarian aid workers, three to his left and three to his right. Addressing the United States President Douglas Franklin, Razeen spoke with disdain in his voice, "Franklin, you have played the fool's hand. These will meet the fate that awaits America. We will bleed the blood of infidels as a sacrifice to Allah and rid the earth of all vestiges of the Great Satan. Allahu Akbar!"

Razeen then proceeded to ruthlessly and without reservation slit the throat of each bound aid worker as blood spurted from the severed jugular veins. The grisly image faded to black as the monitor powered off.

A smug smile broke across Devin's lips as if he were cat playing with a mouse. He listened a few moments more to the arrogant ramblings of Razeen before adding, "How passionately these radicals pursue Jihad and all in the name of their precious God. No doubt. No reservation. Just unfettered hatred that unleashes chaos and death. It really is a beautiful thing to behold. I'll give mortals their due. They are keenly adept at death and destruction. Religion has a marvelous way of lighting them up."

The middle monitor came to life as CNN carried live coverage of another breaking news piece in Rome providing assassination coverage of Cardinal Pedro Ferdinand of Spain who was killed by a sniper's bullet on the steps of the Vatican. The Cardinal's scarlet biretta laid in a pool of blood. Weeping and panic were readily apparent on the faces of gawking bystanders.

The bulging crowds were being pressed back by the Polizia di Stato, the State Police of Italy who were assisting the Corpo della Gendarmeria dello Stato della Citta del Vaticano, the gendarmerie, or security force of Vatican City. The gathering throng of people were rife with anger, fear, and grief. The television reporter continued reporting live, "Cardinal Bernardo Ferdinand Adolfito is the third Cardinal to be killed in the past month. And we still have no answers to who is behind the killings or why. The growing fear is that the killings are serial in nature being perpetrated by a lone wolf killer. Vatican sources are tight lipped providing very little insight into a possible motive behind the killings. The slayings are being attributed to the evil nature of humanity. Some fear that the assassination of the

Spanish Cardinal could be the work of a Jihadist assassin invoking fears of the fall of Spain to Muslims in the year 711. At this point, the Vatican says it has no evidence to attribute the murders to a larger plot directed against the Seat of Christian Power in Rome."

Another video monitor sprang to life as Fox News was covering a developing story along the Gaza Strip in Palestine. The television reporter, wearing a black flak jacket and protective helmet was nervously reporting the news as explosions were seen and heard in the background. "Jihadists invoking the name of Allah and Razeen are rallying around the Palestinian cause and gaining ground in their pursuit of a broad coalition to include Middle Eastern and Eastern powers to stand up to Israel and the Western powers. The rallying cry is, 'To Hell with the Infidels! Our Rise their Demise!' The bloodlust of Razeen seems to be wetting the appetite of moderate Muslims who are also rallying in surprisingly large numbers to the Jihadist cause."

Another video monitor flashed to life as a BBC television reporter was providing coverage, "A late night raid by Israeli Police has busted a messianic sect for running a prostitution ring alleging to its members that 'sex among Christians and Jews will create a purifying connection with the Messiah and will save both Jew and Christian bringing about their ultimate redemption'. It seems that the dire situation in which Israel finds itself has digressed to a haven of religious prostitution that is cashing in on the fear and uncertainty that now pervades the NOT so Holy, Holy Land."

Devin walked over to the window and looked out while adding his own assessment, "As goes the Holy Land so goes the rest of the world. Religion is and has always been our most powerful weapon in bringing about Eden's destruction. The mortals are like clay in our hands. All we have to do is facilitate the means and how eagerly they oblige."

Aeron interjected, "And that day will soon be at hand."

"I know. Isn't it a wonderful feeling," Devin said as he pulled her hungrily into his embrace. "How are the ARCHs coming along?"

Aeron shifted in his arms giving him a sensuous kiss on the lips inflaming the passion within him. "Must we always go from arousal to business," Aeron said whispering seductively in his right ear as she allowed her tongue to stroke his ear lobe. Pulling back she lightly caressed his neck with her finger.

"The ARCHs are coming along masterfully. Eden's Creator pales in comparison to your creative brilliance. Our bioengineers have worked around the clock ensuring that the synthetic organs as well as intelligent algorithms are functioning at optimal levels. The nuclear powered nanocells are nearly perfected. We're currently prepping for testing among diverse eco-systems."

Devin walked over and poured two glasses of Brandi offering one to Aeron. "We have waited for a long time. Good fortune smiles upon us." Taking a sip of his Brandi, Devin continued with contempt in his voice, "Together we will launch a master race of Artificial Regenerative Cybernetic Humanoids (ARCHs) far superior in intelligence than that of a flawed and pitiable humanity. Once we introduce our Special Ops line of ARCHs we will have the global powers salivating on their knees. A strategic blow to the second in command to Razeen will accomplish two important things. It will hold Razeen's ego in check reminding him of who is in charge. And secondly, it will garner the press needed to launch phase two of Project Dark Halo. In the meantime, a visit to the *Lycaon* is in order so I can see with my own eyes the fruit of your creative oversight."

Aeron lifted her glass in response, "To the ARCHs and the destruction of the humankind."

Before Devin could respond, his arrogant smile quickly gave way to a look of rapt attention as he dropped his Brandi glass to the floor leaning back against the mahogany desk. His coal black eyes changed in coloration to a dark crimson as his countenance assumed a faraway gaze. After a few moments his eyes morphed back into their normal hue.

"We have a situation that will require special attention."

Putting her glass down, Aeron assumed a vigilant posture as if anticipating his directive.

Turning slightly the crimson ruby stone dial encircling his Rolex watch facing, Devin activated a sequence of numbers. Devin then turned inward and telepathically spoke to Samael, who belonged to the Archein and one of his most lethal generals in the field. "Samael, I've sent you coordinates. Seize Oblivion. Be vigilant. Guardians of Light will be present."

"My Lord, did I hear you correctly? Oblivion?" Samael asked.

"Yes, and time is of the essence."

"What about the mortal?"

"Your priority is Oblivion. The mortal will be closely protected. The Guardians will always choose a human life over an object of worth even if it puts their mission in jeopardy. Use that to your advantage."

"Yes, my Lord."

Devin walked back over to his grand office window with a sweeping panoramic vista of Zurich. "The fullness of time is upon us," Devin said ever cognizant of the subtle fluctuations and shifts in power between the Darkness and the Light. "The Sword of Eden has now passed to the hand of a mortal. It's almost laughable and yet pitiable."

"It's a desperate move," Aeron replied. "Their chosen vessel has been so spiritually demoralized that he is impotent to wield Eden's Sword with any real threat. What fools. A pathetic last ditch hope of the Light in placing the fate of Eden in the hands of a mortal. I could use some vacay time. I can finish what Samael began ten years ago," Aeron said cooly, feeling the assassin's itch.

"No. Not now. I may have need of your special gift but not at this time. We must remain focused and not allow the annoyance of the Light to distract us from our higher objective. It's prudent to be aware of the Light but never guided by it. For once you're drawn to its enchantment, reason gives way to faith and we both know where that will lead."

"As always, your words point to our dark hope; Eden's destruction and an end to the Creator's hope of uniting the seven kingdoms into ONE Kingdom of Heaven."

Devin drew in a deep breath as he looked down upon the miserable rodents of a humanity scurrying about on the streets below, "A hope that will die along with humanity."

Walking up behind Devin and putting her arms around his well-toned and muscular chest, Aeron placed her chin on his right shoulder peering out to the distance beyond. "What is so wickedly ironic is that the Creator's creative DNA flowing in you will ultimately bring about the death of Eden. How poetic. No other created being whether angelic or mortal has ever come close to surpassing your aptitude for creative brilliance. All that the eye beholds is the direct result of your imagination and influence. Eden's fate has always been yours and yours alone to command. Everything else is mere special effects."

Chapter 5

AN ANCIENT MYSTERY

Dalton and Sommer arrived back on board the *Kanaloa* to the cheer of the crew glad to see Dalton still in one piece. The sea breeze was as inviting as the reception. The starry sky above shown bright in the night despite the cloud banks that were drifting in from the north. Dalton couldn't help but gaze in awe at the magnificent beauty of creation.

"There's not a cathedral anywhere that can match it," Sommer said gazing up at the heavens while walking with Dalton to the door leading to the lower decks.

"Why would anyone want to build a religious habitation when you have this?" Dalton said.

"The smell of rain is in the air. Maybe that would be one reason," Sommer wisecracked trying to get a rise out of Dalton.

"You're such the weather hound," Dalton said.

They both made their way down to the main research room where Dalton pulled out the sword hilt laying it on the table. Standing over the mythical object, his thoughts returned to his encounter with Lonomakua in the sea cavern. A chill swept down his spine at the recollection of the confrontation.

Akamu swiveled around in his chair to see what Dalton had lain on the table. "What do we have here?" Akamu asked excitedly.

"I'm not sure," Dalton answered not letting on more than he knew. "Run a metallurgical examination on it. Let me know when you have something. I'm heading back topside for a few."

"On it boss."

Back on the main deck, Dalton felt a restlessness tugging inside. He stood alone in silence as the *Kanaloa* gently rocked in the Pacific. It had been awhile since he'd allowed himself to sense the presence of God. Wrestling inside with the possibility he was undergoing a spiritual awakening, terrified him. It was not a place psychologically or spiritually he was prepared to return nor did he desire to.

His late wife Lauren was the spiritual one with a special connection and affinity for the spirituality of creation. Dalton met Lauren at Duke while working on his PhD in Theology. Lauren was also a student working on a PhD in Pneumatology, a relatively new field of academic study focusing on the defining nature of spirituality among world cultures.

Lauren was intelligent, adventurous, and passionate. While he engaged his mind in the academic side of spirituality, Lauren immersed her senses in the experience and practice of spirituality. Looking upon the surface of the deep Dalton recalled her words, "The Spirit is the life force that animates creation."

Dalton and Lauren were kindred spirits deeply in love with each other often sitting and ruminating together about God, heaven, and angels cultivating a deep spiritual bond. She had encouraged Dalton to accept an interim stint as a parish minister believing in his spiritual giftedness. She would often prod Dalton by saying, "You can't be true to God or anyone else if you're not first true to yourself." Her passionate faith and simple spirituality ignited his soul as he felt there wasn't anything that he couldn't accomplish with her at his side. She was the spark that enflamed his passion for love, life, and God.

After successfully defending their dissertations and graduating from Duke Divinity School they moved to Sullivan's Island, South Carolina one of Charleston's historic island towns, where Dalton spent many of his early years dividing his time between the Holy City and Kaua'i due to his father's work with NORA.

It was on Sullivan's Island that he and Lauren tied the knot with a romantic beach wedding and moved into the harbor front home that was given to them as a wedding gift from his parents. The breathtaking views of the Atlantic and Charleston Harbor was a divine experience in and of itself.

Stirred from his restlessness, Dalton felt the first droplets of rain like a light mist upon his face. He recoiled not sure if from the rain or the echo of memory. Sometimes he felt as if two opposing forces were at war within depriving him of a peace that seemed so elusive. He had come to expect in life nothing less than grief and disillusionment; the faithful companions of his redefined existence. The promise of the Spirit had failed him; a fact made palpable by the deaths of Lauren and Kaden. The reminder was a daily torture only abated by giving himself fully to his research among the Hawaiian Islands, the closest thing for him to paradise on Earth. It's where he felt removed, distracted, and safe from the life he once knew back in

Charleston.

"Intoxicating isn't it?" Sommer said walking up to Dalton who was leaning against the rail unfazed by the lightly misting rain.

"Quite."

"I'm reminded of a Hawaiian legend surrounding the Ohia tree which grows on new lava flows. The Ohia tree produces the most beautiful red Lehua blossoms. According to legend, Ohia and Lehua were young lovers: he was handsome and she was the most beautiful girl on the island. But, one day Pele the goddess of volcanos encountered Ohia and desired to have him for herself. When he rejected her advance, she worked her dark magic by turning him into a twisted, ugly tree. Lehua pleaded to no avail for Pele to change him back. The other gods took pity on Lehua and although they could not undo Pele's magic, they found a way around the dark magic which would require love's sacrifice. Without reservation, Lehua chose to be transformed into a beautiful red flower that would bloom on the tree ensuring the two young lovers would never be apart. It is said that as long as the flowers remain on the tree, the weather is sunny and fair. But when a flower is plucked from the tree, rain falls like tears since Lehua still cannot bear to be separated from her beloved husband Ohia."

Dalton's eyes glistened as tears mixed with the moisture accumulating on his face. Sommer had a knack for knowing when Dalton was wrestling inside especially with grief. She had a way of speaking healing to his turbulent soul, almost as if she felt a kindred connection.

"I experienced something down in that sea cavern," Dalton said while gazing up at a half moon that had reached its zenith, veiled by tatters of clouds.

"The seeing mind is often awakened by the feeling heart," Sommer replied as she turned and faced Dalton sensing his readiness to talk about what he saw and experienced in the cavern.

"Then my mind has definitely been aroused from its slumber," he said. "The emerald fire that flamed forth from the lava rocks within the fire pit was alive with such energy that seemed to pervade the entire cavern. I have never felt so alive before in my entire life. It was like an out of body experience that was so intense and mesmerizing. It was as if I were in the presence of a power and beauty that captivated and yet repulsed at the same time. And the sword. When it hummed to life with such intense power, I felt as if a part of me that had died with Lauren and Kaden came back to life. More than an awakening, it was like a resurrection of sorts. And then I felt a torrent of fear as all the anger that I have been carrying around inside, suddenly and unreservedly erupted as if some uncontrollable power had been unleashed taking hold of my thoughts and emotions urging me to seize that sword and strike God down. And then I felt incredibly weak as everything just suddenly went dark."

"Anger rooted in fear, can become an emotional leech sucking the very life force out of you. It often impairs sound judgment," Sommer said. "It's the dark gift. Intoxicating, a surge of energy, and then rapidly depleting once your purpose has been served. Once sown in the soul it often reaps death and destruction."

"Sometimes, I get the uneasy feeling that you were put in my way to lead me back to the Light," Dalton said proffering a smile.

"Now wouldn't that be a wonder to behold?" Sommer replied with a soothing smile.

Opening the main deck door, Akamu stepped out and walked over to join them. "I'm curious. What's your hunch on what you've found?"

Dalton shook his head and said, "I really have no idea." Not desiring to appear as if he had lost his marbles, Dalton looked to Sommer feigning a mystified expression on his face asking, "Any thoughts?"

"You're the expert," Sommer replied.

"It really defies logic considering where you found it and in such pristine condition," Akamu said.

"Were you able to isolate a metallurgical dating?" Dalton asked Akamu.

"Yes, which is why I asked for your thoughts because the initial data findings are perplexing. The artifact which appears as you suggest to be sword hilt predates the Bronze Age."

Challenging the notion, Dalton responded, "That's impossible. There are no known swords that predate the Bronze Age especially made with a metal other than bronze."

"That was my thought as well. So I ran an alternate analysis to rule out any potential internal breakdown with the first analysis and the results are consistent. According to the metallurgical finding, we're dealing with an archeological anomaly that predates any known sword-related finding in known existence. The hilt is in pristine condition without any signs of corrosion. It's as if the hilt was recently crafted."

Akamu excitedly continued, "I tested the hilt for sources of metal used and metallurgical analysis turns up no known source traces of metal such as steel alloy, iron, or even bronze. The type of metal used to fashion the hilt is not found on the current periodic table."

Dalton cut in, "What about traces of chromium which would explain the lack of corrosion?"

"Negative. We've even examined the strength of the hilt and find no detection of Martensite which leaves me even more befuddled."

Dalton lifted the cylindrical device noticing how light it felt in his hand. The hilt was exquisite, with an emerald stone inset within a diamond-shaped encasing just above where the fiery blade had appeared. Flanking both sides of the earth tone hilt were ancient markings. Ascending from the base of the hilt to the pommel of the sword was a superbly crafted tree with trunk and branches made of jasper and leaves made of emerald. Running along the base of the hilt were accents of turquoise with strange symbols he had never seen before.

Recalling the vision he had of the blade humming in blazing power, Dalton couldn't help but admire the craftsmanship that looked every bit that of a mythical weapon. But a weapon forged by the actual hand of God was a bit much for his mind to wrap around.

Akamu was beside himself with excitement as his scientific wheels were spinning gaining no traction without a logical rationale to make sense of the mysterious artifact.

Dalton's thoughts were reeling from the possibilities as he turned his attention to an interpretive analysis of the symbols hoping to garner any clues that could shed light on the sword's origin, still not accepting the veracity of his vision.

"Akamu, I want close up digital images taken of every detail and then prepare for an encrypted transfer to Dr. Lyle Hudson, a colleague back in Charleston who is an expert in ancient writing systems and symbols. Take extra precautions to ensure no images are leaked to the media."

"I'll send the images via high encryption and secure the digital images in the vault," Akamu replied.

"Is the sword hilt secured in the vault," Dalton asked.

"Of course. Not going to leave that thing of beauty laying around. Who knows what master thief could be lurking in the shadows," Akamu joked.

"I see we're getting close to the port at Nawiliwili?" Dalton said.

"We should be arriving within 30 minutes."

Dalton inhaled the refreshing sea air as he looked out upon the approaching Kaua'i coastline. He noticed a couple of deck hands with their hair drawn up in a pony tail that he did not immediately recognize descending to the lower decks. Figuring they were new hires, he didn't think more of it.

Akamu stepped up next to Dalton by the deck rails and sighed, "What a day brah."

"Keeps you young and alert," Dalton quipped.

"I'm so needing a tall one right now," Akamu said.

"Two brewskis on me when we get to port."

"Make that three!" Sommer chimed in.

"Little too much excitement for one day have you desiring the liquid of the gods?" Dalton smiled teasingly.

"Yup. Some of us have to maintain full functionality when others go lights out," Sommer joked making light of Dalton's blacking out in the cavern.

Akamu shook his head and said to Dalton, "Ooh, she just busted the proverbial coconut on you brah."

"Go easy on the smack," Dalton joked to Sommer with an easy smile.

No sooner were the words out of his mouth when an explosion erupted below deck rocking the *Kanaloa*. Multiple explosions began to break out throughout the ship. Screams could be heard below deck as the ship began ripping apart from bow to stern. The concussion from the initial explosion violently slammed Dalton, Akamu, and Sommer into the ship's rail. Fortunately they were spared the nightmare many of the ship's crew were experiencing below deck. One technician was ablaze as he frantically emerged from the stairway screaming desperately as he blindly ran into the deck railing, flinging himself overboard to the water below.

Feeling an adrenaline rush, Dalton hollered above the raucous, "Sommer, you ok?"

"Yes. I'm fine. Don't worry about me."

"Ready the life boats!"

Looking around, Dalton noticed Akamu was slowly getting up and shaking his head in an attempt to regain his composure.

"Hey, you ok?!"

"Yeah. I think so," Akamu said as he felt around his body to make sure everything was still intact.

"We need to get below and lend some assistance," Dalton yelled as another explosion shook the ship.

Running to the stairway leading below deck, Dalton glanced up and noticed Tommy Dillon, one of the bridge crew appearing dazed. Briefly making eye contact, another huge explosion ripped through the bridge raining down shards of glass and shrapnel all around them.

Dalton instinctively lifted his arms over his head struggling to maintain his balance. When he looked back up he saw no sign of Tommy. The flames were putting off heat like an unfettered wild fire. Looking around for Akamu, he spotted him nearly twenty feet away bent down on his knees looking at what remained of Tommy; a burnt torso less his head, arms, and legs. Akamu had the look of horror in his eyes as Dalton quickly ran over to pull him away.

"There's nothing more we can do for him. He's gone," Dalton said not allowing himself to be overwhelmed by the emotions that were roiling within him. "We've got to get below. Come on," Dalton said grabbing Akamu from behind while lifting him to his feet. Succumbing to the stark reality of Tommy's fate, Akamu shook off the shock looking around as Dalton hauled him to his feet. Joining Dalton, they both rushed to the stairs leading down below.

A huge billow of fire and smoke mushroomed upward as more

explosions violently rocked the *Kanaloa*. The heat was almost unbearable as they quickly descended to the research level deck. Flames were pouring out of the research room. Dalton grabbed a fire extinguisher from off the wall but the flames were searing hot and the smoke heavy in the air. They both began coughing and feeling the burning sensation in their lungs. Assessing the situation, Dalton held out little hope that any survivors would be found alive on the research deck as only sounds of angry flames could be heard spitting and crackling through the interior walls like a crazed fire dragon.

Dalton felt the ship beginning its death roll as water was quickly ascending from the lower decks. He yelled to Akamu, "We need to get back topside and see if we can gain access from the stairs on the port side. There's nothing further we can do here!"

Running back up to the main deck, Dalton noticed Sommer was busy helping several crew members onto a lifeboat struggling to get them launched as quickly as possible. Dalton quickly ran over trying to keep his balance as the ship continued lurching like a five story building turning over on its side.

"The ship is going down fast! We're close enough to shore with life vests to swim for it. Get everyone who can swim, overboard and into the water immediately," Dalton said.

"Dalton, you need to get off the ship as well. There's nothing more you can do," Sommer anxiously implored.

"I'm not far behind you. I've got to get back down below. Akamu, help Sommer with the survivors."

Dalton quickly ran off leaving Sommer and Akamu to assist with getting the remaining survivors off ship. Sommer watched Dalton descend below deck through the aft stairwell.

Tossing a life vest to Akamu she said, "Get this on and in the water with the survivors and make sure they get to shore safely. I'm going to go help Dalton."

Akamu started to object but thought better when Sommer gave him a firm look. Quickly donning his life vest, he jumped into the ocean joining the remaining survivors.

Sommer frantically ran to the aft stairwell and tried to descend but was pushed back by a torrent of water rushing up from below. Pushing her way forward, she found herself waste deep upon reaching the bottom of the stairs. Desperately she looked for any sign of Dalton. She yelled down the corridor but the only reply she received was the rushing roar of water laying siege to the ship pulling it downward into the belly of its dark abyss.

The ship suddenly lurched violently causing Sommer to slam her head on the corner of the corridor hallway as blood gushed from her head. Dazed and struggling to maintain consciousness, the last thing Sommer saw was a figure approaching; a silhouette of light. Her vision narrowed until only the blackness of nothingness claimed her. Wrapping its liquid talons around her, the violent current pulled her under within the watery mausoleum.

Chapter 6

THE DARK ONES

While awaiting the arrival of the *Kanaloa* dockside at Nawiliwili on Kaua'i, Emrick witnessed a huge fireball billow up from aboard the research vessel lighting up the night sky. With his keen angelic site, Emrick scanned the exterior and interior of the ship spotting what he was looking for. Discerning the work of the Dark Ones, he and Soren immediately sprang into action.

So it begins, Emrick thought to himself.

"Save as many as possible. I will cover Dalton and ensure the sword is not compromised. Remain vigilante. Satariel's elite assassins, the Dark Ones have been employed. Beware of the dark powers at work around you. Faith is your greatest weapon against fear. Use it."

"I'm on it," Soren said before vanishing from sight like a flash of lightning.

Flames were quickly engulfing the listing ship as a series of explosions ripped open the ship's hull claiming the lives of a number of crew members who were decimated in the initial blast.

Emrick spotted Dalton entering the aft stairwell with one of the angelic assassins dressed as a NORA deck hand approaching from behind brandishing an energy dagger. Emrick was upon him in an instant. Another explosion coincided with Emrick's assault with the concussion blast propelling Dalton down into the aft stairwell below.

Emrick quickly regained his footing seizing the forearm of the angelic assassin who was drawing his energy dagger. Twisting his arm in an upward motion the dagger dislodged and careened across the deck and into the Pacific. The assassin instinctively rolled his body into Emrick's chest and then flipped up, over, and down behind whereupon he place a choke hold on him. Anticipating the maneuver, Emrick quickly stepped back dropping to one knee while gripping the dark angel's forearm and with a tremendous force of strength pulled him over slamming him down upon the deck.

Momentarily dazed the rebel assassin slithered back into a defensive posture with a wicked grin upon his face. "You're the best the Light has to offer?"

"Appears enough to get the job done here," Emrick said parrying his opponents over confidence.

"Fool! Your dalliance with the Light is no match for the superior power of the Darkness," he spat in contempt. "Blinded by the Light, your incompetent master has played the fool's hand choosing a half-baked mortal to wield the power of Oblivion."

Powering his energy sword, he quickly lunged in a miscalculated attempt to take out Emrick. Avoiding the lethal jab at his chest, Emrick executed an aerial somersault landing lightly on his feet striking his assailant with a crushing blow to the head. In rapid successive fashion, Emrick pinned the assailant to the ground with his knee dislodging the energy sword which went dark. Placing his hands on the assailant's head, he unleashed blinding-white energy causing the rebel assassin's mortal body to spasm jettisoning the vile spirit that possessed it. Emrick noticed on the right side of his pale neck, a black orb with daggers extending outward in all directions.

Meanwhile, Soren alighted upon the Kanaloa's bridge only moments before it erupted into flames. Captain Armington was severely dazed and in shock when Soren picked him up leaping down to the surface deck. Placing a life vest around Armington's neck, he leapt back up to the bridge which was engulfed in smoldering flames and billowing smoke. He scanned for possible survivors detecting only eight souls who were beyond mortal assistance.

Soren quickly made his way down to the lower decks making it as far down as the second level where the water was nearly chest high. Trapped behind a door due to the flooding water, Soren heard desperate cries for help. He immediately bent back the latch on the exterior door releasing a flood of water and several bodies, two of which were still breathing. Soren placed one person on each shoulder wasting no time returning to the surface deck. Soren was met by Sommer who assisted with putting life vests on the two unconscious survivors. When she turned back to thank him, Soren was nowhere in sight.

Sensing a dark presence toward the bow of the ship near the helipad, Soren turned his attention to those responsible. Stepping around highly flammable refueling tanks, he caught sight of an angelic assailant prepping the fueling tanks with an incendiary device. Soren couldn't risk using his energy dagger in such close proximity to the fuel tanks so he opted to engage the enemy the old fashioned way. Leaping through the air, he delivered a withering blow from behind catching the assassin off-guard pummeling him to the deck whereupon he twisted and spun before hitting the unforgiving hard steel of the ship's bulwark. The angelic assailant quickly recovered and alighted upon his feet with cat-like reflexes turning to face his attacker. With shoulder length black hair, the Dark One possessed eyes black as onyx hardly distinguishable from the black attire he was wearing if not for his pale white skin. He flexed his left forearm bearing a tattoo of a black sun with daggers pointing outward in all directions. His eyes narrowed giving Soren a murderous glare.

Wasting no time in re-engaging, Soren leapt in the air with a lethal tornadic spin move in an attempt to place a strangle hold around his adversary's neck but was greeted by a well-timed kick that dealt him a crippling blow sending him violently crashing into the steel bulwark.

"You're outmatched and fighting a futile effort for the wrong side," his combatant menacingly bellowed. "Join us or I'll end your sorry excuse of an existence right here and now," the Dark One challenged arrogantly.

Soren slowly stood realizing he was facing a skillfully adept, lethal angelic warrior with a mastery of the dark powers. Knowing that time was not on his side he couldn't risk the peril of his higher objective. He quickly analyzed the situation ascertaining he could be in for a lengthy duel expending precious time and energy he didn't have the luxury to waste. His options were clear; either risk a lethal strike, which if unsuccessful, could prove fatal or could count his losses and create a diversion to buy him more time to retrieve the sword while saving as many lives as possible.

Quickly scanning the below decks for signs of life while ascertaining the doomed fate of the ship he quickly made his decision to ignite the incendiary device to the shock and dismay of his opponent. While spinning and dropping to one knee with his back to the incendiary device, Soren ignited his energy dagger sending a force of energy charged particles toward the closest fuel tank igniting it with a powerful force which propelled Soren toward his life-saving objective while the concussion from the blast sent the angelic assassin over the bulwark out into the Pacific.

On the other end of the doomed ship, Emrick spotted Dalton treading water toward Research Room 1 where the sword hilt was being held in a secured location. Suddenly a violent blast rocked the ship whereupon it further lurched upon its side. Dalton lost his balance as the force of the water accelerated and swept him under as he thrashed wildly trying to regain his sense of orientation. Debris beneath the surface pelted his body disorienting him as he spun and kicked not knowing if he was swimming to or away from the surface. He was struck upon the head by a fast moving object beneath the surface arresting his struggle. Before losing consciousness, he felt someone grab him from behind pulling him upward as everything went black.

Emrick swam through the watery corridor like a salmon swimming upstream while holding Dalton from behind swiftly ascending the aft stairwell. He met Soren at the main deck doorway as he placed Dalton over his shoulder.

"Quick, grab the sword and meet me on the shore."

Soren wasted no time diving down into the rapidly flooding research deck hallway swimming into the research room sensing the orbing energy of the sword within the secured vault. With all power on the ship lost, he used a small round atomizer which he placed on the digital lock mechanism releasing the lock. Retrieving the sword he swam back through the flooded corridor hearing a female voice crying out, "Dalton," as another explosion rocked the ship.

Instinctively he swam toward the direction in which he heard the voice finding Sommer drifting unconsciously with blood trickling in the water from a bad gash above her right temple. Reaching the stairwell, Soren pulled Sommer up over his shoulder while trying to maintain a semblance of balance as the ship began its final death roll in the water. With a lurch, he jumped up and over the deck rail and into the Pacific.

Awakening with a massive headache, Dalton rolled over on the sandy beach gazing up into the starry night sky. Suddenly the full weight of what had just transpired hit him like a freight train. Sitting up on the beach a little too quickly, he felt a massive pain shoot through his head. Wincing he looked around catching sight of Sommer lying unconscious about ten feet away.

Feeling a bit queasy Dalton tried to stand only to fall back to the sand in a moan of pain. He waited for the excruciating ache in his head to subside so he could make a second attempt to stand. Successful the second time around he rose more slowly finding his legs and making his way over to Sommer. Relieved to find a distinct pulse, he glanced back toward the Pacific seeing no trace of the *Kanaloa* above surface. Rescue boats were beginning to converge upon the area where the doomed vessel formerly occupied.

Looking down the beach he noticed some survivors beginning to stir. Hearing the sound of an approaching helicopter he looked up and spotted the *Sky Nene* descending trailed by a medical helicopter from Wilcox Memorial Hospital. As soon as the *Sky Nene* touched down at a safe distance, an EMT and a member of NORA came running over.

"Dr. Orion, thank God you're ok! We feared the worst upon hearing the news."

With a placid look on his face, Dalton responded, "I think the worst is what we got. Don't worry about me, I'll be ok. Please see to Sommer and the others first."

The EMT went over to Sommer and found her beginning to stir moaning from obvious pain. Medical personnel began arriving at the remote beach area to lend assistance. The whole beach head was quickly turning into a make shift triage.

Dalton slowly rose to his feet and worked his way down the beach where other survivors were awaiting medical attention. He also came upon six bodies laid out on the beach waiting to be covered. Akamu was assisting an EMT carry a stretcher with a survivor on it to a nearby medical chopper.

Dalton noticed movement by the water as a man in shorts and a dark tee-shirt clinging to well-defined pectoral muscles emerge from the water with a body in tow. The man immediately placed the body on the shore and provided CPR as the individual coughed up water and sputtered back to life. Dalton quickly strolled over and knelt down beside Pattie Jo Mandrake, one of the research technicians. "Pattie Jo, can you hear me? It's Dalton." Slowly blinking her eyelids regaining consciousness, she gave Dalton a slight smile before lapsing back into unconsciousness.

Dalton looked up at the gentleman and said, "Thank you for saving her life."

"I wish I could've been more helpful to others."

Looking over Dalton's shoulder, Emrick spotted Soren down the beach perched upon a rock jutting out over the Pacific. Walking over a few paces, Emrick pointed to a sword hilt lying in the sand. "Is this yours?"

With an incredulous look on his face, Dalton walked over and picked it up. A bit perplexed as to how the sword could've been dislodged from the secured vault, Dalton replied, "Yes. I thought it had gone down with the ship."

As Emrick turned to walk away, Dalton called out, "Hey, thanks for the help. What is your name?"

"Emrick."

Hearing Pattie Jo groan again, Dalton turned and bent down, "Hey Pattie, you're going to be ok. Just take it easy. We'll get you out of here as quickly as possible." Casting a quick glance over his shoulder, Emrick was nowhere in sight.

A couple of EMT's came running up to assist with Pattie Jo.

Stepping aside Dalton allowed the medical technicians space to do their work. He heard a voice call his name from up the beach. It was Sommer making her way over with an ice pack to her head.

"What are you doing out here?!" Dalton said concerned. "You should be in an ambulance heading to the hospital."

"I'm a tough gal and there's no way I'm going to go lay in a hospital bed while others in worst condition are in need of one more than I. And besides, I'll be unable to rest until we find out what just happened out there."

Seeing the sword hilt jutting out from Dalton's pants, Sommer asked, "How did you manage to retrieve that from the vault during all the chaos?"

"I didn't. When I awoke on the beach it was laying close by on the sand. I have no idea how it landed there."

Dalton looked back toward the Pacific at the emergency boats and personnel trolling the waters. "I don't know how many but lives were lost and God knows how many others are severely burned and in critical condition. With the light of morning, I'm sure some answers to our questions will begin to emerge. Until then, let us see if we can lend any further assistance."

Taking one last look around the beach for any sign of Emrick, Dalton rejoined the efforts to assist those who were wounded and in need of medical attention.

Chapter 7

DARK HALO

The Black Forest, Germany

A sleek, black Bell 522 Relentless circled above on approach whipping up a whirl of snow before setting down within a narrow clearing of trees just outside the entrance to a small mountain fortress carved out of Alpine stone. The fresh smell of clean mountain air greeted Devin and Aeron as they stepped out from the Relentless. After they cleared the threshold, a retractable subterranean platform upon which the Relentless resided descended into the ground. A cover closed over the platform, blending with the elements providing a natural camouflage.

Located within a remote area of the Schwarzwald (Black Forest) in Germany, the DGC's research facility enjoyed off the grid concealment offered by the forested slopes and shady valleys. Known as the *Lycaon*, the remote research location was the base of operations for Project Dark Halo where Aeron lead a team of scientists designing the superintelligent ARCH's.

Sparing no expense, Devin ensured that the state-of-the-art research facility remained undetected from prying eyes. Any who wandered dangerously close mysteriously disappeared as angelic assassins known as *Lycaonian Sentinels* stealthily covered a large swatch of the surrounding alpine forest enforcing the restricted ground space. Radar jamming technology and image cloaking devices kept eyes in the sky from detecting actual ground movements.

Scanning the area, Draven's eyes swiveled covering the perimeter along a dense thicket of Conifer trees that wrapped around the narrow clearing where the Relentless had touched down. Leaping down from a rocky outcropping above the entrance to the *Lycaon*, Draven landed on all fours before rising to his feet. Towering in the freshly fallen snow, his pale skin blended darkly with a full head of black hair as a loose strand fell down across his face. His all-consuming golden-yellow eyes glowed beneath dark brows as he watched Devin and Aeron approach.

Draven nodded in deference allowing them to pass as two large twenty feet entryway doors retracted allowing access inside. Three unusually large black and gray wolves with narrow chested bodies flanked both sides of the entrance while one remained above on the rocky outcropping. Clearly the alpha leader, Draven remained vigilant while the entrance way remained open before closing behind Devin and Aeron. Nodding at the three lupine guardians, Draven watched as they immediately leapt off through the tightly packed snow disappearing into the densely forested mountain side.

Devin and Aeron walked down a corridor with walls made of granite and a walkway made of black onyx. Ceiling energy crystals projected crimson light illuminating the interior. Entering an elevator at the end of the walkway, they descended nearly four hundred feet.

As the doors peeled back they both stepped out and into a large infrastructure housing several research chambers where much of the advanced biosystems for the machine superintelligence was being conducted. Each chamber had lab technicians and scientists busily conducting tests and monitoring data screens.

Devin was particularly interested in the research chamber devoted to the engineering of Cybergenetics. Entering the room he walked over to a life-like simulant that was encased within a housing unit with tubes providing chemical infusions necessary for the development and sustainability of the synthetic skin tissue. The housing unit was resting in a vertical position. Devin looked into the fixed dilated pupils of the simulant that appeared in every way like a human being within a perfectly engineered male body.

"How is our progress with the irreversible animation?" Devin asked.

Aeron came alongside him and answered, "We're still working on maximizing the capacity of the artificial neocortex to far exceed human intelligence by ensuring 100% cognitive functioning and instantaneous upload of information and date."

"And you're confident that all organ functions will perform at optimal levels?"

"Very," Aeron answered confidently. "Soon we will have achieved what none other has; superintelligent beings with intellectual, emotional, and moral intelligence. Biological humans will in time become obsolete; a species of the past. The ARCHs will become a potent threat to the humankind finishing off any survivors of the coming apocalypse."

Aeron knew Devin settled for nothing less than perfection. The ARCH systems were critical to Devin's plan to lay waste to Eden. He detested the human race and although he viewed humanity as infinitely weaker and inferior to its spiritual and vastly more superior angelic counterpart, Devin was prudent enough to recognize that mortals were a necessary means to achieving an ends. Once the mortals were out of the way he could achieve the critical blow needed to ultimately take Empyrean by storm imposing his will and ultimate rule.

Everything was falling into place perfectly. His lips parted in a malevolent grin as he calculated his next move. Devin's analytical wheels were churning. He had waited nearly an eternity to accomplish what none other among the angelic kind had dared; the creation of a new creature far superior in every way than man and who would destroy and supplant the Creator's pathetic humankind who were fashioned in his image. He could almost envision the end result. But now wasn't the time to drop the ball and lose the winning edge. Too much was at stake.

"Beyond the functionality of motor movements, sensory perceptions, and physical strength we must achieve superior intelligent algorithms and cognitive processes combining language ability and knowledge with perfect recall. An intelligent invasion of all existing AI systems will in essence take out the core pillars of human civilization. Shutting down the core systems of human civilization such as finance, communication, transportation, manufacturing, and global defenses will give way to chaos, disease, and death. Optimal performance of the ARCH systems equates to total domination. With the US Presidential election only weeks away we need to be ready for our first real test with the ARCHs. I will be leaving for Dubai soon to meet with Aziel in the Middle East to ensure everything is in place for the rise of the Great Caliphate. Ramiel is leading the apostates in rebellion in Rome. Soon there will be a new Pope more amenable to our, how shall I put it, better judgment for the future of Christianity. Israel as always, remains in turmoil and is a powder keg waiting to be ignited. At a time of our choosing we shall provide the spark."

Walking out of the ARCH chamber, Devin approached a concealed entryway built into a stone wall undetectable by the natural eye. An energy sensor device camouflaged to blend into the wall quickly scanned Devin's retina which elicited a modicum of crimson energy. The entrance door suddenly activated and opened into a large inner chamber with state of the art holoimaging enablers for screenless viewing.

Devin strolled over and took a seat in a high back black leather chair with a large "D" monogrammed in the center behind a desk made of black diamonds. The chair immediately conformed to his physique providing lumbar support and comfort. As if reading Devin's thoughts, Aeron walked over to the global monitoring enabler and activated it. A CNN breaking news report came on with aerial footage of a research vessel that had just sank off the island of Kaua'i.

Devin felt a stirring within as his eyes glazed over to receive a telepathic message from Samael. In his mind's eye he could see Samael kneeling down on the ground as if in prayer. "I'm looking at your handy work. Do you have the sword?" Devin asked.

"No. We were unable to do so due to unexpected resistance from two of whom I believe belong to Metatron's elite forces."

Devin's black eyes narrowed and brows furrowed at the mention of Metatron's name. "Then my suspicions are confirmed. Any idea regarding their rank among the angelic order?"

"Not sure but my sense is that they belong to the Guardians of Light. Both were highly skilled in close contact combat and proficient in their mastery of the Light."

"And what of the sword? Was it activated?" Devin asked.

"No trace of the sword's energy detected. I have cause to doubt it is Oblivion. Could be a decoy."

Devin took a moment to process the information before responding, "I don't think so. Shadow the mortals for now. If an opportunity presents itself, seize it. Keep me posted. And Samael, do not underestimate the Light."

"Yes my Lord. And they would be wise to do the same," Samael replied in an arrogant and confident tone.

Devin swiveled in his chair and looked over at the global map and through voice activation called up DGC satellite imagery of Kaua'i, Hawai'i. "Zoom in on Nawiliwili Harbor in Lihue." The 4D imagery quickly adjusted and gained clarity giving Devin a live close up of Nawiliwili Harbor and the surrounding rocky beach area on the southern tip of the Lihue airport runway not too far from where the

Kanaloa sank.

Scanning the area, Devin looked intently along the shoreline for any sign of the two Guardians. He voiced an alternate command to recall satellite imagining of the beach area following the explosion at 2100 hours. He quickly accelerated the imaging until his eye caught what appeared to be a sword lying on the beach among a few individuals.

"Stop!" Devin commanded. "Zoom in."

The satellite imagery presented a clear image of a woman lying on the beach with a male leaning over her and a third individual standing with his back to the prying eyes of the DGC's satellite. Devin's attention was immediately drawn to the individual standing. He manipulated the various angles of the imaging feed unable to get a clear frontal image necessary to identify the individual.

Devin sat back in his chair and thought to himself, *You're a clever one aren't you?* Looking over to Aeron he said, "If the Sword of Eden has indeed surfaced then an opportunity presents itself. He who possesses the sword wields a nuclear power a thousand times more powerful than that of the Sun with enough nuclear fusion to infinitely power an entire army of ARCHs for infinity."

The implications were not lost on Aeron. "An army of ARCHs wielding the Sword of Eden would be virtually unstoppable able to easily obliterate Eden and triumphantly march on Empyrean."

Devin felt the surge of dark energy quickening within. "Remain here until further notice. Heighten security and remain vigilante. We can't afford any slip ups. We've accomplished much and waited a long time. Now is not the time to have the fruit of our efforts picked off by the Light. I will keep a close eye on our friends in Hawai'i."

Devin dismissed Aeron and remained within the solitude of his office. His thoughts turned to the individual standing on the Kaua'i beach. *Who are you?* Devin thought to himself as he approached the image for a closer look. He examined the physical stance of the individual for any sign of familiarity or recognition that would betray his identity. The Darkness within him recoiled at the mere sight of the image.

Speaking to the holoimager, "Remove person of interest." And just like that, the angel vanished. *Were it so easy,* Devin mused to himself.

Chapter 8

FLIGHT OF SOULS

The peaceful cadence of life was shattered – suddenly and without warning. Thirty-one friends and colleagues lost their lives and ten others received second and third degree burns as a result of the deadly explosions and subsequent sinking of the *Kanaloa.*

Dalton couldn't help but think of the emotional aftermath for the family, friends, and loved ones left behind forced to pick up the pieces in a futile effort to make sense of it all. Reminded of his own abiding sense of loss and the lingering grief, Dalton felt numb and subdued. One minute life is a very paradise on earth and the next it becomes a living hell, a tomb filled with grief, anguish, and suffering. He knew more than anyone that there are no gracious heartaches that come with the loss of a loved one.

The *Kanaloa* tragedy hit too close to home for Dalton. Having moved to Kauai'i nearly ten years earlier in an effort to assuage the pain of losing his wife and son to a deadly terrorist attack, the haunting memories were now awakening from a dark slumber. It was the day that his world went dark as if the inner light that once burned so bright was snuffed out. Everything changed in a breath-taking moment when a senseless act of religious extremism radically altered the trajectory of his life.

The pain of his loss ignited a crisis of faith that burned strong within as he questioned everything he once held to be sacred and true. Dalton knew only two truths since that day. One was a quote by Homer's Iliad, "Life and death are balanced on the edge of a razor." The second truth was that he would never be whole again. And if he had to listen to one more religious nut say, "things happen for a reason", or that "it was God's will", he would go mad with blind rage.

Hawai'i had a way of calming Dalton's festering soul. Among the remoteness of the islands, he remained comfortably numb with a heart hardened by a deep seated anger toward a God who rests idly as evil incites hopeless misery. And now, the safe haven Dalton had made for himself in paradise was proven vulnerable by the long reach of evil; the one constant that plagues humanity like a terminal cancer.

Dr. Blake Kealoha approached from behind putting a hand on Dalton's back stirring him from his thoughts. They both stood on Blake's sprawling six thousand square foot Poipu estate with an ocean side lanai running the length of the home. The well-manicured oceanfront lawn just to the north side of the pool was flanked by a couple of tall Coconut Palms gently swaying in the tropical breeze. The lush tropical foliage and fragrant gardens along with the unobstructed views of the majestic Pacific, made the perfect natural setting for a memorial service.

Dalton had found solace among the peaceful Garden Isle of Kaua'i. He left his personal tragedy behind fleeing to paradise to:

escape, hide, and heal. The company of the ocean and the refreshing trade breezes had a way of lifting his spirit. The waves were gently and melodically rolling upon the shore providing a rhythmic cadence serving as a healing balm to Dalton's troubled soul. And now, once again tragedy found him helpless and powerless to stem the tide of death and destruction. Feeling responsible for the loss of life as if somehow he could've prevented it, the *Kananola* tragedy nagged and berated him as accusing thoughts pricked his psyche like pins to the body.

As a physician who was all too familiar with death and dying, Blake had come to believe that a comforting presence was more effective during times of emotional grief and pain than a cacophony of lofty thoughts and trite platitudes. Dalton appeared distant and absorbed. Looking drawn and exhausted, Blake couldn't imagine what Dalton was feeling inside much less thinking.

The absence of truth leaves us devoid of hope, Dalton thought becoming more sullen by the moment. *Truth is the foundation of theology, but if truth is devoid of love then the very underpinnings of theology are a farce. So, where does love fit in the grand equation? Einstein's famous equation for special relativity; e = mc2 holds more truth than much of the empty religious formulaic hope of world religions; d = ec2 (dogma equals extreme confusion squared). How can one make sense of the insensible? What formula actually equates in making sense of humanity's age old conundrum, WHY?*

Dalton sighed before pulling away from his disparaging musings. Drawing in a deep breath he turned to acknowledge Blake's presence, "Thank you for hosting the memorial service. You're a good friend with a big heart. The world could use more like you."

"Anything for you, Dalton."

Seeing the mourners gathering on Blake's lanai Dalton muttered, "Looks like the ceremony is about ready to begin."

In keeping with Hawaiian funeral tradition all attendees were dressed in colorful attire as opposed to black which is often the color of choice for funerals on the mainland. The interfaith memorial procession trailed behind Rabbi Josiah Abrams, Father Ron Kekoa and Reverend Penelope Freitas.

Reaching the ocean's edge the long procession of people formed a crescent shaped perimeter around the ministers. Father Kekoa began the ceremony addressing the gathering of mourners with a brief word of centering, "Death is but a flowing field of constant transformation." Then turning and facing the Pacific, he lifted a Pû (Hawaiian name for conch shell) to his lips and began to blow, symbolizing a call to the Divine.

Reverend Freitas followed with an opening prayer. "Creator and sustainer of all life, we gather in our time of grief to remember, celebrate, and give thanks for the lives of our friends and loved ones who were tragically taken from us. We look to you for comfort and peace, beseeching you to untangle the mysteries that often confound us during tragedy and loss. While we celebrate the human spirit in all its resilience we are also ever mindful of the fragility of life. You are the dawn of life and the twilight of death. Bring to full glory the resurrection of our loved ones to eternal life. Amen."

Following the prayer, Rabbi Abrams provided a short reflective homily in which he closed with a quote from Norman Cousins, "Death is not the greatest loss in life. The greatest loss is what dies inside us while we live."

Dalton felt as if the Rabbi had released an arrow that found its mark within his soul. Standing to his left, Sommer noticed a tear trickle down his cheek beneath the concealment of his black sunglasses. Reaching for his left hand, she gave him a gentle squeeze trying to ease the emotional storm beginning to break over him like angry waves crashing upon a battered shore.

The memorial ceremony concluded with family and friends of loved ones placing leis in the ocean in memory of the victims. There was a solemnity to the occasion as Dalton watched the leis drift out with the tide as if the lives of those who perished were being swept out to sea, forever lost to the silence of eternity.

Taking a deep breath, Dalton redirected his thoughts toward those gathered around him. Sommer stepped up and gave him an empathetic hug as they just clung to each other for a lingering embrace. Dalton felt such comfort and strength emanating from her, he almost didn't want to let go. Catching his eye over Sommer's shoulder was an 'akeke'e bird that had alighted on a nearby Naupaka plant growing along the beachfront. On the endangered species list, the 'akeke'e was rarely spotted so close to the shore usually preferring the branches of an Ohia tree.

A peace came over Dalton as he said, "Thank you Sommer for always being there for me. It means more than you know."

Sommer responded in her carefree manner pulling back with her arms still around Dalton's back, "I'm ready to free my soul with a Mai Tai. How about you?" Like air escaping a balloon, Dalton's pent up tension escaped in much needed laughter. "Free is good."

Dalton glanced over to the lanai area and noticed that Dr. Dan Rutledge was walking in his direction. The President and CEO of NORA, he had flown to Kaua'i from Charleston, South Carolina to offer condolences and look into the criminal investigation. Approaching and extending his hand, Dan offered a friendly southern greeting, "Dalton, it's good to see you ole friend. How are you holding up?"

Dalton held Dan in high regard and found him to be a most gracious southern gentleman. It was Dan who made it possible for Dalton to come on board with NORA and relocate from Charleston to Kaua'i after the death of Lauren and Kaden. But Dalton also had an unsettling suspicion that Dan had another agenda for being on Kaua'i.

"Good to see you again, Dan."

"Dalton, do you have a moment so we can speak in private?"

"Sure."

Looking to Sommer with a casual smile Dalton said, "Go get that Mai Tai and bring me one too."

Sommer smirked, "I must warn you. When it comes to Mai Tai's they don't last long in my hands. So don't wander off too far."

Akamu walked up and chimed in, "Don't worry Dalton, I'll make sure one finds its way to you." The four of them shared a chuckle as Sommer and Akamu headed off for the lanai area.

Dan led Dalton back down toward the beachfront offering some casual conversation. "What a very paradise on earth. I've often wondered how anyone would want to live on a remote island such as this but the beauty of this place is intoxicating and possesses a magnetism that draws one in."

"The land and sea certainly has a way of bringing much needed respite from the travails of life. But something tells me you do not simply want to make small talk about the solace of paradise," Dalton added.

"You have a way of cutting to the chase," Dan said with a casual grin. Knowing that Dalton would most likely not, at least initially, respond well to what he had to say, Dan decided to just put it out there. "Dalton, I know you've been through a lot. The entire NORA family is coming to grips with the horrible tragedy surrounding the *Kanaloa*. The media storm is not going to subside anytime soon especially as the investigation moves into full swing. I could really use you back in Charleston, at least until we can clear the investigation, put a team back together, and regain our sea legs. I'm worried about the toll all this has taken on you and thought maybe it would be a good time for you to maybe spend some time with old friends back in the Holy City."

"Dan, I really appreciate your support but I don't know that now is the best time for me to return to Charleston. I just lost a lot of great colleagues and close friends and feel like I should be here to help pick up the pieces."

Sensitive to Dalton's feelings but also concerned about his frame of mind, Dan persisted, "There is going to be a criminal investigation to determine if there was any foul play involved. NORA also will be doing an internal investigation for liability reasons. The Administration feels strongly that you need to at least be temporarily assigned to Charleston."

"Look Dan, I think you're making a mistake by recalling me back to Charleston. I totally disagree…"

Dan quickly interjected, "Dalton, the decision has been made. It's a done deal. The Administration feels you're too emotionally compromised to be part of an internal investigation."

Dalton knew he had one of two choices. Either he could quit and remain on Kaua'i or suck it up and accept reassignment to Charleston.

"Ok. But I'd like at least enough time to tie up a few loose ends here on Kaua'i. Also, I want Sommer assigned as well if she'll consider it."

Dan was all smiles, "Consider it done. Dalton, trust me on this. We have your best interests at heart."

Dalton retorted, "Well, it's not like I have a real say in the matter. But I do trust your judgment Dan and you've been there for me in the past. And for that I'm grateful."

Walking up with a couple of Mai Tais, Sommer brought much needed levity to the moment. "Ok gentlemen, I've got just what the Doc ordered. Literally."

"Sounds like my kind of doctor," Dan quipped while reaching out to receive a glass from Sommer.

Dalton took his glass and lifted it up toward Blake who was smiling from back up on the lanai, "To the good Doc," and then looking out to the leis that were now drifting nearly out of sight Dalton added, "and to the flight of souls."

CHAPTER 9

MENACING MEMORIES

A full orange Harvest moon rose over the sleepy Kaua'i town of Hanalei situated beneath the majestic emerald green pinnacles that towered above the tranquil Na Pali Coast. Cascading waterfalls could be heard off in the distance plummeting down velvet green cliffs into the verdant rainforest and flourishing valley below. The Geckos were vocal with their chirping. The occasional tapping sound could be heard where a Gecko had seized a prey in its mouth and was hitting it against a solid object. The stridulating of crickets and katydids joined the evening chorus.

The symphony of night sounds stirred Dalton from a restless and fitful sleep. Lying on his back in bed he just stared up at the ceiling fan listening to the whirring of the blades watching them spin round and round while feeling the swirling of the cool night air. The rhythmic droning of the blades was almost hypnotic but failed to lull Dalton back to sleep. He rolled over gazing out the window making out the dark violet peaks of the four thousand foot high Namolokama Mountain. The wall of darkness appeared ominous in the distance. From a distance the mountain range looked like a sleeping giant laying on its back cutting zzz's.

Glad at least one of us is getting some sleep, Dalton thought to himself.

A myriad of thoughts began to invade his mind panging his consciousness as menacing memories were beginning to awaken. Ever since the *Kanaloa* went down the flashbacks were becoming more pronounced and disturbing. He had disciplined his mind to keep his grief stored in a mental vault locked away from the new life he had made for himself on Kaua'i. And now like an emerging leviathan from the abyss traumatic memories began to claw at the surface of his consciousness.

After years of mental walls to keep out the post-traumatic memories his defenses were laid waste in less than an hour with the sinking of the *Kanaloa*. The harsh reality of mortality settled upon Dalton like a funeral pall. Lives fade like a passing shadow as death moves ever closer one step and one heart beat at a time preparing to claim its next victim. Cynically, he had come to believe that premonitions, precautions, or praying were powerless to make a difference in preventing the inevitable. It was just a matter of time when someone you love will be ripped from your embrace. The only way to guard against the inevitable is not to allow oneself to get close to anyone.

Dalton had grown up the son of a hot-tempered and strong-willed geologist. Growing up in the shadow of a father who was highly respected and devoted to his field of work was certainly a motivating factor behind Dalton's decision to pursue a career in a similar field in the natural sciences. But Dalton's real passion was in ancient esoteric writings. It was at Duke Divinity School where he pursued a PhD in Theology with a focus on the spiritual forces that shape religions, religious traditions, and world cultures. He developed an affinity for Spiritual Ecology after meeting Lauren who helped him to look at his father's work in Geology and the field of Earth and Ocean Sciences from a different perspective. Never developing a close bond with his father he turned instead to a faith sculpted by a relational understanding of God that filled the void he never experienced as a child; mainly the love of the Creator. But all that came to a screeching halt with Lauren and Kaden's death.

Jettisoning his idealistic notions of faith in God, a higher purpose, and that all things work out for good in the end, Dalton became a realist adopting an existentialist view of life. Like wielding a sledge hammer, Dalton reduced his imbecilic notions of God to nothing but dust and rubble. Now after nearly ten years, the walls of his interior life were supported by a carefully laid foundation of faith in the natural sciences. Only a skeletal remainder of his former convictions remained, a mere specter of his former beliefs.

Stirred from his depressing thoughts, he got up from bed and walked over to the armoire and opened it. Sliding his shirts to the side he reached out and depressed the number combination to an electronic vault built into the wall. With a click, the vault door opened revealing an intricately crafted sword hilt. Upon removing it, a moon beam from the nearby window refracted off the inlaid emerald stone. A semblance of energy shot through Dalton as he touched it dissipating as quickly as it surged.

Lifting the shaft with his right hand and turning it over while studying the ancient artifact, Dalton got the distinct impression, as absurd as it seemed, that it somehow was studying him and peering deep into his soul. Drawn to the emerald stone that was inset within the hilt, it began to swirl until Dalton's attention was arrested and transfixed by the luminous orb.

A sudden flash of memory ignited within him of a time in his life when Lauren and Kaden were running along the beach where they stumbled upon a rare albino bottlenose dolphin that had washed up on shore. Dalton, who had been hanging back from a hard run began to pick up his pace when Kaden began yelling for him to hurry. Finding the rare albino dolphin in a lifeless state on the beach, Dalton felt nothing but compassion for Kaden who was obviously shook up by the lifeless creature on the shore. Judging by the size it was a fairly young dolphin.

"Is he dead, Dad?" Kaden asked sounding somewhat distressed.

"I don't know son. Let me check." Bending over Dalton placed his ear close to the blowhole of the dolphin. "I think I hear something," Dalton said excitedly. "There just may be life in him yet," Dalton said. "Hurry, let's get the dolphin back into the ocean."

"Dad, shouldn't we say a prayer first," Kaden asked with childlike faith and innocence.

"You bet," Dalton said. "But we better make it short."

"God, help this dolphin get better. Amen." Kaden prayed fervently.

Together they helped lift and carry the young dolphin back into the water. Standing waste deep with the dolphin buoyed by the water, Dalton whispered, "Fight little fellow. Fight and live!" And with those words the dolphin jerked to life thrashing its tail in the water before slipping out of Dalton's grasp swimming with fervent desire into the depths beyond.

Live again, a voice boomed inside his head wrenching Dalton from his trance-like state of mind. A cold chill caused him to physically shudder. A fresh hope surged within but was quickly extinguished as he regained his mental faculties writing off the sound of the voice as nothing more than a memory flash from an overcharged brain.

Walking over to his desk and firing up his laptop computer, Dalton typed in biblegateway.com and pulled up Genesis chapter three and read its entirety finishing with verse 24 CEV, "Then God put winged creatures at the entrance to the garden and a flaming, flashing sword to guard the way to the life-giving tree."

Leaning back in his chair, Dalton assumed a reflective posture staring blankly at the screen for a few moments. Although he had taken a seminary course on Angelology, he never really stopped to consider what it would be like to stand in the presence of an angelic warrior. A divine being whose primary existence is devoted to serving at God's behest as a messenger, guardian, protector, and assassin. Hairs raised on the back of his neck as Dalton looked at the sword hilt lying in front of him. Each beat of his heart felt like a dull, hollow thud of fear as the thought of the possibility of the veracity of his vison was unnerving.

Disrupted from his frightful thoughts, Dalton's attention was arrested by a fleeting shadow that passed across his window. A spine-tingling sensation shot down his back as goose bumps raised along his forearms. He quickly put the sword hilt back into the hidden vault sealing it shut. Walking over to the window he looked out straining at the darkness trying to detect anything amiss. In the intense stillness, he could hear his pulse quickening and feel his blood coursing through his veins. The moon was hanging full and hazy casting its incandescent light upon the surrounding valley. Dalton fixed his sight on a swaying coconut palm across his yard and waited watchfully trying detect any possible movement with his peripheral vision.

After the tension of the moment had subsided, Dalton turned his attention to assuaging a dry mouth from the mounting tension that had gripped him. Strolling into the kitchen, he poured himself a glass of cool water gulping it down in an attempt to quench his rising thirst. Pouring himself a second glass, he walked out onto the lanai. Gazing up at the autumn moon, Dalton found himself scanning the starry night sky as if seeking an answer to the questions that were burning within; trying to fathom the elusive mystery behind his vision that confounded as much as it astonished. *What a vast universe,* he thought to himself. *If you could but speak, what stories you could tell, what lies you could expose.*

Other than the sounds of nature stirring at night, all seemed peaceful and quiet. But something didn't feel right. He could sense it deep in his bones. Something was out of place although everything around him dictated otherwise. Maybe it was the spell of the moon with its tantalizing stare. And then it happened. Accosted by a menacing memory that rushed his mind with a great thunder of vengeance, Dalton felt caught up and carried in the clutches of a winged bird of prey, up and away, over oceans and continents to a place and time he wished to neither remember nor revisit.

It was a place that forever changed the core of his existence. Like a radical shifting of the tectonic plate within his soul, his grounding in reality would become a slippery slope into a dark hungry abyss of death and grief that devours without thought or mercy. He wanted to escape that painful place and time but it was as if Death itself like Dickens' ghost held him transfixed to a front row seat of that terrible day. How could he ever forget it or escape it? Foolishly thinking he ever could, it was seared within his psyche like a branding; destined to forever hound him.

He went to Israel as a young interim pastor who had a knack for motivating and inspiring faith in others. But he returned home to Charleston as an agnostic questioning everything he once held to be sacred and true. The so-called Holy Land was anything but. It was a land characterized predominantly by ethnic divisions, religious strife, and sectarian violence.

Leading a Holy Land tour of Israel, Dalton arrived in Tele Aviv with Lauren and Kaden along with thirty one others from The Rising Church based in Charleston. What began as a faith-inspired pilgrimage ended as a living nightmare.

A tour guide met Dalton and his tour group at Ben Gurion Airport in Tele Aviv helping them quickly navigate through customs and baggage claim before boarding a luxury motor coach. Stepping on board the bus, Dalton greeted everyone with a twinge of excitement in his voice. "Folks, we're here. The Promised Land!"

With eager anticipation and excitement, everyone erupted in cheers and clapping.

Giving Lauren and Kaden a wink, Dalton continued. "Everyone has prayed hard, worked hard, and believed hard to see this two year journey come to fruition. Folks, this is the stuff that faith is made of!" The tour group was feeling the passion in Dalton's voice and responded once again with jubilant excitement. Dalton rounded out in typical fashion, "God is good!" to which everyone responded, "All the time!" Smiling Dalton continued, "And all the time?" To which the collective response was, "God is good!" Everyone laughed reveling in the sheer ecstasy of the moment. Life was good. So they thought.

Dalton wished he could edit his memory for he would stop everything at that moment in time. How he wished he could go back and just tell everyone, "Get off the motor coach now! God is not good and definitely not all the time. Enough with this foolish babble, it's time to get back on the plane and never look back."

"Hindsight is always twenty/twenty," Dalton mused to himself.

At the time, little did Dalton or any of the other traveling passengers aboard the motor coach realize they were sitting on a ticking time bomb. While mentally traveling through downtown Tele Aviv again everything seemed as if it were moving in slow motion. The tour bus had just made an unscheduled stop in front of a local food court. The tour guide said that he needed to pick something up and would be right back. Upon opening the bus door a rush of wind swept through the interior.

Dalton looked outside the bus window trying to see what was up with the weather. Catching his eye was a young lady bent over grabbing her throat as if she were choking. Not wasting any time, Dalton quickly jumped up speaking over his shoulder to Lauren as he rushed to get off the bus, "Someone needs help, I'll be right back."

Within moments of stepping off the bus, the last thing Dalton remembered was an incredible blast and the force of searing hot air that catapulted him across the food court and into occupied tables and chairs. When next he awoke it was in the Tele Aviv Sourasky Medical Center.

After several days in a comma, Dalton finally regained consciousness. The first thing Dalton asked the nurse was, "Where is my wife and son?" The nurse left the room with a reassuring smile as the attending physician entered and broke the news to him.

"You were fortunate to survive a very violent explosion. It's a miracle you stepped off the bus when you did otherwise you would not be with us now."

"What about my wife and son?" Dalton asked more adamantly.

Reluctantly the doctor continued, "Unfortunately, you were the only survivor. I am so sorry. May God's peace comfort you in your loss." The words were like a bayonet driven into his heart crushing his hopes, dreams, and faith.

Now, nearly ten years later, Dalton still found himself being assaulted by the menacing memory that terrorized his consciousness. He took another deep draw of water from his glass draining the remainder and setting his glass down on the front lanai railing. He looked at his watch seeing that he still had about an hour before dawn. Walking back inside Dalton put on his jogging shorts, tank top and a pair of running shoes.

Dalton jogged down to the Hanalei Pier as he often did especially when he was dealing with anxiety. He slowed to a walk as he stepped onto the board walk as air rushed in and out of his lungs. He found the transition between the darkness of night to the breaking dawn to be therapeutic always putting his soul at ease.

Staring out over the expanse of the Pacific illumined by the moon's light, his thoughts where interrupted by a silvery voice, "Quiet remarkable isn't it?"

Startled Dalton quickly turned toward the source of the question. Much to his surprise sitting quietly and leaning back against a piling beneath the canopy, was a figure partially concealed in the predawn shadow just out of reach of the moon beams. With close cropped blonde hair that seemed to glisten in the moonlight, his glinting eyes were intense commanding attention and yet he wore an ingratiating smile that disarmed.

"Excuse me?" Dalton asked a bit unnerved.

"Creation. Its beauty and splendor is quite remarkable. I never tire of appreciating its grandeur and design."

"This place does inspire," Dalton said feeling a bit awkward and uncomfortable in the moment.

"I cut the stars out of fire, and I decorated heaven, and put it in their midst," Emrick said pondering aloud the ancient words.

"The Second Book of Enoch," Dalton replied becoming

cautiously intrigued by the stranger.

"You know the ancient writings," the stranger said as the moon beams now illumined his face.

The dawn of recognition settled over Dalton. "I know you. We met on the beach, the night the *Kanaloa* went down. Your name is Emrick, right?"

"You have a sharp memory especially in light of the unfortunate circumstances."

"Are you from around here?" Dalton asked.

Emrick rose to his feet standing a little taller than Dalton. He walked toward the center of the pier canopy drawn to the panoramic view of the Pacific expanse before casually turning toward Dalton in response. "I guess you could say I'm sort of a native."

Pressing further adopting an interrogative tone, Dalton replied, "I've lived here off and on a good part of my life but I don't recall ever seeing you before."

Somewhat amused Emrick responded, "I've been away for a while but you would possess a remarkable memory indeed if you recalled everyone with whom you ever crossed paths."

Still not feeling comfortable in the moment, Dalton followed with another question, "What do you do for a living?"

"I'm a life guard," Emrick replied as his eyes seemed to shimmer a pristine blue unusually noticeable in the shadow beneath the canopy almost as if the light that appeared to be refracting off his eyes was actually emanating from within. *If eyes are windows to the soul then this guy is definitely full of illumination.* Dalton thought. There was something familiar about Emrick's glinting eyes but Dalton couldn't place it.

"Really? Have you been life-guarding here on the island for long?" Dalton asked.

"Oh, I've worked on and off Kaua'i over the years."

"I didn't realize life guards could actually make a sustainable living from saving lives."

"It has its perks."

Redirecting the conversation Emrick asked, "How are you holding up?"

Dalton turned his head toward the majestic Na Pali coastline and responded flatly, "Fine." After a lingering moment it just felt natural to speak how he really felt. "Well. Not really. Not sleeping very well here of late."

"Who would in your position? You carry a great burden of responsibility. As if a storm of grief has battered your soul."

Dalton sighed, "You have no idea."

"And if I did? Would that change your frame of mind or ease your suffering?"

Dalton felt his eyes beginning to mist over forcing down the raw emotions welling up inside. "Do you know the pain of loss? What it feels like to lose someone close to you? Bone of your bone and flesh of your flesh. Then you will begin to understand the weight of the burden I bear. And nothing can ease that kind of pain."

"I too, know the pain of loss of someone close to me. But death is something that can be reframed."

Dalton scoffed, "There is absolutely nothing about death that can be reframed. It would be like leaving a house filled with memories realizing that you will never be able to touch, feel, or speak to those you love ever again. All that is left are haunting memories from which there is no escape, no safe haven, no lasting peace. The only certainty in life is that nothing is certain. In the end it all comes crashing down on you. No mercy, no partiality, no light. Just depressing darkness mocking you in the night hour."

An awkward silence lingered for a few moments as Dalton almost dared Emrick to respond. But then Dalton thought he saw a glint of light emanate from within Emrick's eyes or maybe it was a reflection of light, but from where he couldn't readily discern, for the night had still not released its grip. And yet, at that moment the Pacific horizon was cast in the soft morning light of sunrise filling Hanalei Bay with its radiance. Looking back at Emrick, his eyes appeared to shimmer as blue as the sapphire ocean. There was a mystique about him that was evidenced in his eyes.

"It's always darkest before the dawn. An enduring truth that hounds the darkness," Emrick said matter-of-factly. "And of course, the sunrises seen from this vantage point are always the best," he said rising to his feet with a mirthful look about him. "It is good seeing you again Dalton. I'm sure our paths will cross again soon."

Dalton watched Emrick walk away almost envious of his peaceful countenance and the carefree nature of his gait. He had felt a stirring within when Emrick spoke but Dalton refused to allow himself to trust once again in that part of himself that was prone to faith. It was safer to just ignore and not give credence to that which could only bring more pain. And so Dalton chose to batten down his emotions and cling to the part of his life he had come to trust and believe over the past ten years. He had learned to survive and cope with his grief by distrusting the God voice in his head. It was his way of shielding himself from disappointment and grief. To believe otherwise was to play the fool and cling to a fool's hope. And this grief-born belief had become the unyielding truth of his life. But one that would soon be put to its greatest test.

Chapter 10

MASTER OF SHADOWS

New York, New York

The Challenger 605 Business Jet touched down on the runway at JFK International airport in New York. Flaunting a bold black D on the vertical stabilizer and sporting in crimson across the platinum fuselage the slogan, *The Future of Civilization*, the Bombardier luxury jet taxied to a stop outside the General Aviation area.

An attractive flight stewardess with fiery auburn hair dressed in a black business skirt with a white button down blouse slightly revealing a tanned and toned upper body, approached Devin with a flirtatious smile, "Mr. Sinclair, is there anything I can get you before you deplane?"

"No thank you, Neira. You've been most delightful in ensuring my utmost comfort on the flight over from Zurich."

"The pleasure was all mine sir," she said lightly brushing her hand against his as she stooped to remove his wine glass. A tantalizing surge of dark energy rifled through his body. His pupils briefly flashed crimson as he gazed upon her near perfect feminine form. Devin appreciated created perfection. It was one of the few acknowledgements he conceded to the Creator. Although it was Devin's influence that was responsible for empowering the female kind to exploit their bodies in ways that made them sexually irresistible. It was a wicked perversion he was quite proud that served him well.

Devin along with two of his personal attendants who were dressed in black Armani suits and wearing dark sunglasses stepped down the boarding ramp where a black limousine awaited. Dressed to the nines, Devin presented in a Giorgio Collezioni thin striped grey colored suit with a solid black Gucci silk dress shirt accented by a platinum and crimson colored striped tie. On his right ring finger he wore a black diamond ring in the shape of the letter D with a crimson colored ruby in the center.

John "Jack" Stirling stepped out of the limousine, the Republican Senator from South Carolina and Chairman of the US Senate Armed Services Committee. As the shining star of the Republican Party and the Republican Presidential Candidate in a close campaign against the Democratic incumbent President Douglas Franklin, Senator Stirling was eager to tap Devin's monetary resources as well as endear himself to Devin's global connections.

Several Secret Service agents wearing black suits and black sunglasses were flanking the Senator. With brown wavy hair slightly graying on the sides and a fit physique, Senator Stirling exuded an air of confidence and power enhanced by a winsome personality. With lots of fight left in the engine, lofty ambitions, and a colorful personality, Devin found in Stirling the kind of grit and lofty ambitions that played perfectly into his own plans for humanity.

The Senator enjoyed the favorable appeal that his association with Devin Sinclair engendered among his Republican constituents and a large number of the American voting electorate. With global unrest and world powers on the brink of all-out war, the US Presidential election was being pitched by many political pundits as either a precursor to world peace or Armageddon, depending on the outcome of the election.

The current tension among global leaders was palpable reminiscent of the 1960's nuclear standoff between America and Russia. As a die-hard Republican, many viewed Stirling as the ideal candidate who would advance America's burgeoning Artificial Superintelligent Warfare Systems. Many pinned their hopes on Stirling's leadership in giving the United States a strategic advantage in modern warfare and thus by flexing the American muscle help avert a nuclear apocalypse.

Senator Stirling greeted Devin with a firm handshake and affable grin. Raising his voice above the whir of the jet engines the Senator yelled, "Welcome to New York, Dr. Sinclair!"

"Jack, it's always a pleasure."

After exchanging a few pleasantries, they both got into the limousine for the drive over to the Plaza, a very posh and luxurious hotel located off Fifth Avenue. Senator Stirling wasted no time in sharing the latest news on the most recent special ops mission, "I just received word regarding Operation Paranoia. It's all over the news. Razeen's number two in command, Khalid bin Yousef was killed by the Operative. They are assuming it was an inside job and chaos is rifling through their ranks. If the Operative is also as successful in taking out Razeen then we are dealing with a game changer. Your creative brilliance is unsurpassed and will pave the way for a powerful America boasting the most formidable military in the world. Do you know what that means?"

"Opportunity, Senator. Opportunity. War equates to dollars. With regional upheaval in the Middle East, tension in the South China Sea between China and Japan, Europe watching Russia's every move, and the highly unstable North Korean regime, public opinion will become more favorable and supportive of our Superintelligent Operations Soldiers (SOS)."

"Yes, Operation SOS is coming along nicely, thanks to your brilliant team of scientists," Senator Stirling replied excitedly.

Stroking the Senator's ego, Dalton added, "And you will go down as one of the greatest Presidents in American history. Which means, after this latest news hits the airwaves, you stand to cash in on a golden opportunity to assure your election as the next President of the United States of America. As long as you play your cards right."

"And I have you to thank for all of it, Devin. If elected, I will certainly leverage my significant influence with the Senate Armed Services Committee ensuring that Dominion Global Corporation enjoys the lion's share of our defense spending budget."

"Not if, Senator, but when elected. Never leave room for doubt or defeat in the pursuit of victory."

"Spoken like a true conqueror," Senator Stirling smiled. "These are times that require your kind of, shall we say, resolute attitude. I'm glad to have your invaluable support. It's going to be a packed house tonight. There will be lots of media coverage."

"I'm here to ensure you achieve your political goals," Devin said enjoying the fact that everything was unfolding as planned.

The Senator desperately needed Devin Sinclair's deep pockets and his political clout in America. Worth in the billions, some jokingly said that Devin Sinclair was the first person to create genetically engineered trees that grow money. Appearing recently with the Senator in a Fox News special called *RPG: The Role of Religion, Politics, and Guns in Global Culture*, Devin was a hit among the conservative and moderate viewership. The special enjoyed a viewership that topped the Nielsen ratings due to the growing anxiety among the populace with the global state of world affairs inspiring a renewed interest in the role of superintelligence in modern military weapon systems.

The conservative elites in power unreservedly embraced Devin and the DGC which had mushroomed into a global military defense conglomerate. One of Senator Sterling's campaign promises was to ensure a more powerful America and that would only happen if it wielded the most powerful military in the world with the very latest in advanced weaponry. And healthy relations with Devin and the DGC was key to ensuring that campaign promise.

Devin found in America's populace the kind of political passion and tendency to divide itself along party lines a means to achieving his own diabolical ends. He appreciated all the fire and brimstone that both major parties threw at one another. It was quite entertaining and made for great public theater. Politics like religion could prove socially explosive when handled rightly. "Passion is good, making people more pliable and susceptive to manipulation," Devin would often say to those within his inner circle.

Stepping out of the limousine, Devin and the Senator were greeted by an enthusiastic crowd of media, paparazzi, and bystanders. Easy on the eyes with a debonair persona, Devin was a media sensation. He waved at the throng of people with a winsome smile while walking out of his way to shake the hand of a young political columnist he recognized who had been favorable regarding Dominion Global Corporation's pioneering work in the field of burgeoning field of superintelligence.

Although many viewed the creation of intelligent machines as essential to world peace by gaining a leg up on rival super powers others viewed it as akin to opening Pandora's box with a strong likelihood that intelligent humanoids with an emerging consciousness would rebel and destroy a weaker human counterpart. By setting up a potential survival of the fittest humanity would be put at a huge disadvantage.

Intelligent machines presented a clear and present danger that many feared once sanctioned by the government would be the beginning of the end for the human race. But many feared that the alternative would be just as bleak with global powers teetering on the brink of all out nuclear war. The temptation for political powers within the American government was too great to resist the opportunity to steer the course in superintelligence by assembling a military force that would be the most powerful in the world guaranteeing that if war should come America would prevail. And Devin was counting on the most powerful nation in the world to lead the march toward Eden's ignoble demise.

Walking into the Plaza Hotel they were greeted by representatives of Senator Sterling's presidential campaign and escorted to the Grand Ballroom where the fund-raiser dinner was being held. The who's who among business moguls and political dignitaries including wealthy donors from around the country were mingling in the ballroom.

The Grand ballroom was exquisite with floor to ceiling white marble pillars and overhead chandeliers creating a sophisticated and elegant ambiance complemented by soft lighting. The gold accents on the ceiling and pillars with ornate artwork in each of the four ceiling corners around the room was the perfect setting for American royalty. Everything was presented in exquisite fashion as the Senator spared no expense in selecting the finest venue in an effort to inspire donors to open their pocket books and give generously.

Walking into the ballroom the Senator was greeted by Pastor Ted Ransky, the lead minister of the World Nation Church (WNC), the largest evangelical church in America boasting over 250,000 local members from the Dallas/Fort Worth areas with satellite churches spread around the world consisting of over 2.7 million members globally. In his mid-thirties and above average height, Ted possessed a swanky, charismatic appeal along with Hollywood good looks.

Ted's personality along with thick brown hair styled with a full tousled silhouette, mid length side burns and a tapered neckline were a huge part of his popular image appeal. More looks than substance, Ted knew how to play to his audience, a fact not lost on Devin.

Religion was nothing but a cult of personality that all major world religious leaders enjoyed. And Ted was a perfect pawn in Devin's plan to leverage his considerable influence among evangelicals as well as a majority of mainstream Americans who shunned organized religion considering themselves spiritual rather than religious.

Ted liked to be called by his first name without any associated religious titles, which was his way of letting people know that he was personable and not overly religious. He was very intentional about casting himself as down to earth and without religious pretense in an effort to win over those turned off by organized religion. The Senator viewed him as a potential diamond in the rough in his bid for election as the next President of the United States due to his considerable appeal among the conservative electorate. A partnership between the WNC and the RNC made for a very powerful alliance and Senator Stirling aimed to keep it strong.

"Ted, I'm delighted you were able to come. I know you stay very busy doing the Lord's work." Standing just to the Senator's right, Devin could feel the dark energy coming from the pastor and mused to himself, *Now here is one who craves power and longs for religious supremacy.*

"Senator, thank you for the invitation. It's an honor to be on the guest list."

Turning to Devin, the Senator rejoined, "Let me introduce you to Dr. Devin Sinclair, President and CEO of Dominion Global Corporation."

With a beaming grin, Ted extended his hand, "Nice to meet you Dr. Sinclair. I enjoyed what you had to say on the recent Fox News Special."

"Thank you Ted. I'm flattered by such affirmation coming from a religious heavy weight such as yourself. But please, call me Devin."

"Not religious Devin. Spiritual."

Smiling Devin replied, "A spiritual soul with a personal touch. A man after my own heart. Pardon my oversight. I tend to forget you evangelicals distinguish yourselves as spiritual as opposed to your Catholic and Protestant counterparts who are, shall we say, more tepidly religious."

Ted's face radiated, "Spoken like a true believer."

With a jovial laugh Devin eased into the moment, "At the heart of every achiever is a believer. Where would any of us be today if not for belief."

Before Ted could respond, an announcement was made for everybody to take his or her seat. The gathered crowd of people began dispersing heading off to their assigned table. Devin and Ted joined the Senator up on the platform taking their respective seat as guests of honor.

The two-term Republican Mayor of New York Ron Cedillo greeted the gathered with a warm welcome kicking things off with gusto, "As I look around this room, I become excited about the future of our country. Sometimes we just need to abandon the road and forge a new path. Well, my good friends. We are the trailblazers who will begin the bold and arduous work of forging just such a path this very night. We ARE the future of the Republican Party and we ARE the future of America!"

An energetic applause erupted around the room.

"The Democrats have occupied the White House for far too long and I'm beginning to feel like I'm living in another country. It's time for the Republican Party to rise in power, prosperity, and prominence once again. It's time for us to pull out all the stops to ensure that Senator John Stirling becomes the NEXT President of the United States of America!"

Everyone in the room stood to their feet in ecstatic applause. The Senator delighted in the spontaneous and euphoric response to the Mayor's words which were having the desired effect.

The Mayor continued, "But before we get ahead of ourselves as we're sometimes prone to do in our political revelry." Cackles were heard around the room. "Let me introduce to you someone who really needs no introduction, the man many are calling 'America's Pastor', the one who will spiritually lead America to that Promised Land of great favor and abundant blessings from God above, the one and only Pastor Ted Ransky!"

The room erupted in welcoming applause as Ted stood and walked to the podium in obvious delight to the public acclaim all his hard work and efforts had garnered. Feeding off the electricity in the room, Ted took to the podium like a horse out of the gate at the

Kentucky Derby.

"Good friends, saints and sinners alike. I believe that this is going to be America's year! American's time! America's victory!" The crowd was mesmerized by Ted's larger than life charisma and persona hanging on his every word.

"Before we give all our love to the one and only, Senator John Stirling, let us seek the face of the One who will clear the path to victory for America." Let us pray.

"God of power, righteousness, and victory. We humbly come to you and ask that as we do your work, obey your will, and serve your purpose, remove the obstacles that lay ahead of Senator Stirling's new path for America. Grant your favor to Senator Stirling and may he rise in favor with all people taking his rightful place as the one who will wield the scepter of your righteousness for the world to witness. We ask for a shower of material prosperity to rain down upon him and his presidential campaign. May he lack for nothing and excel in everything as the instrument of your divine purpose. Amen."

"Ladies and gentlemen, the Senator of South Carolina and the next President of the United States, John Stirling!"

While approaching the podium the Senator paused to give Ted a warm embrace. Turning toward the crowd, Senator Stirling basked in the standing ovation and waited patiently as the extended clapping continued even as he gestured with his hands half-heartedly for everyone to be seated. Finally the crowd's supportive applause died down and everyone took a seat.

"My dear friends and generous supporters, YOU make possible

the bright future we shall build together for America. The good book says, 'Without vision the people shall perish.' Well, I'm here to serve notice to our political opponents in the White House, we ARE the party of Vision! And we see a POWERFUL, PROSPEROUS, and PROMINENT future for America! Step aside so we can step up. Make way for dynamic leadership for a time such as this. We will ensure that any country or religious militant group that questions our resolve to utilize military power and might will do so at a grave cost. And in regards to a weakened economy, we mean business and we WILL make business for America!"

The crowd was eagerly partaking of the Senator's words as if dining on caviar handed to them off a silver platter. Beaming ear to ear, Senator Stirling was astute at working a crowd knowing that when you loosen the tongues and hands of a crowd the greater the likelihood they will loosen their wallets. The Senator's words were intended as a financial laxative to relieve monetary constipation among donors.

After the room quieted down, Senator Stirling began his introductory remarks in welcoming Devin to the podium.

"Ladies and gentleman, just today we received the welcome news that Razeen's number two in command, Khalid bin Yousef was killed. I can assure you that the one indirectly behind the success of this mission is probably the most brilliant mind in cutting-edge advances in smart munitions and technological warfare. It's my distinct privilege and indeed honor to introduce you to a close friend, a transformational architect, and the intellectual genius behind the future of global civilization – Dr. Devin Sinclair, the President and CEO of Dominion Global Corporation!"

The Senator joined with the crowd in giving an energetic applause as Devin rose slowly with a charming smile walking over to the Senator receiving an enthusiastic embrace. In his element and basking in the worship-like adulation, Devin felt the dark energy swirling within as his power and hold over people began to intensify.

"Senator, distinguished guests, and friends one and all. I'm deeply honored and moved by such a reception. What is there not to like about America?!" The audience responded enthusiastically as cackles were heard around the room, a predictable response as Devin played to their sense of patriotism.

"Over the years, I've watched this country rise in prominence through adversity, travail, and triumph. You're a most resilient nation with strength of purpose, firm resolve, and passionate faith." Taking a brief moment for emphasis, Devin turned to Ted nodding in friendly affirmation.

"Sometimes it takes outside eyes to see things from a different perspective. Other nations struggling around the world look to America as the great hope inspiring optimism during the darkest of times. Like a phoenix rising out of the ashes of uncertainly, America has proven time and time again it doesn't yield to hardship, it doesn't surrender to a defeatist attitude, and it doesn't bow to terrorist demands." Everyone in the room rose as one and cheered in thunderous response.

"To achieve your vision of a more powerful, prosperous, and

prominent America you must dream, believe, and achieve. Long ago I dreamed of creating world-changing technology that would shape, define, and determine the future of human civilization. My dream gave rise to Dominion Global Corporation the platform for creating and achieving superintelligent technology that is making possible a reality that formerly has been only the fictitious stuff of Hollywood. We have come far as a civilization. Like many of you here, I grew up in the shadow of powers that sought to limit my imagination and creativity. I dared to believe that in liberating my mind, I could liberate myself along with others as well. Free the mind and you unlock limitless potential and possibilities. But first evil must be eradicated. There is an evil that enslaves lives but there is a far greater evil that enslaves the mind. And nothing is more evil than religious militants regardless of their religious persuasion, using a creed to brainwash and justify barbarism so their fanatics can with impunity be and do evil. It's time for a new creed, a new America, a new World. One in which the just rule and the brave flourish. Electing Senator Stirling as your next President will be America's finest hour as she positions herself as the greatest ruling power in the world."

Ted Ransky along with the Senator leapt to their feet in spontaneous praise and applause. The crowd eagerly followed suit with a standing ovation. Devin's short, yet inspiring speech was everything that the Senator had hoped it would be. Raising his hands to quite the room, Devin finished by saying, "Senator John Stirling has my trust, confidence, and full support. He is a man of unparalleled vision unafraid to make the tough decisions required to employ the necessary measures to assure that the dream of a better America, a better world is realized. The future of America could not be in more capable hands. And WHEN John Stirling is elected the next President of the United States of America, it will go down as a defining moment within the history of this great nation. Thank you for your hospitality Senator. And thank you for being a fantastic audience."

The Senator stepped up enthusiastically giving Devin a big old southern bear hug before they both turned and waved at those standing and applauding. The Senator leaned in and said, "I owe you one Devin."

To which Devin replied while waving never taking his eyes off the audience, "Yes, you do my good friend. Yes, you do."

Chapter 11

CANNONS BEACH

Blake had the windows down in his fuji white colored Range Rover Sport Limited Edition with the music cranking to Israel Kamakawiwo'ole's rendition of John Denver's *Country Roads*. Attached to the roof racks were several surfboards slicing wind. Sommer was riding shotgun up front while Akamu enjoyed the leisure space in the back.

Blake and Akamu orchestrated a day of surfing to help lighten the mood as Dalton and Sommer prepared to leave for Charleston. They didn't want them leaving without some fun in the sun. Pulling into Dalton's driveway, Sommer was hanging out the window sporting a nose ring yelling, "It's time to go surf our cares away!"

Kicking back on the lanai in a rocker sipping on some guava nectar juice Dalton's face broke out in a big ole grin. "Blake, you better reel her back in boy before she hurts herself," Dalton said rising to his feet to step off the lanai.

"Good luck with that brah. This crazy girl is ready for a surf rodeo and I don't think she's going to settle for anything less than a bull of a barrel to roll."

Approaching the vehicle, Dalton looked at Sommer and said, "A nose ring. Really?!"

"Oh, come on Dalton. You're starting to show your age. Live free and blissfully," Sommer replied playfully.

"You guys better not surf next to shiny, bling nose here cuz she's lining up to be prime shark bait," Dalton said ribbing Sommer.

"Then I guess you'll just need to come with us and watch my back because that's where you will be most of the time – in my wake," Sommer said ribbing him back.

Akamu chimed in, "The surf's calling, brah. I'm feeling the need to carve some waves."

Dalton shook his head, "Guys, I'd love to but I've got to get everything squared away for the relocation to Charleston."

Sommer not letting him off so easily said, "Look, if I'm leaving paradise behind to accompany you to Charleston then you can take a break to surf the pipeline. Or are you clucked?!"

Dalton laughed, "Who me? Clucked? Honey, when it comes to catching waves, fear is not on my radar."

Blake ready to hit the road interjected, "Enough of the smack. Change up and grab your board. The sets are rolling in."

"Ok, ya'll win. Hang loose while I transform to perform," Dalton said running back inside to change. Grabbing his board on the way out, he secured it on Blake's roof rack before jumping in the back with Akamu.

Blake wasted no time turning the Rover around as they headed out for Kuhio Highway enroute to Haena State Park for some of the best surfing on the North Shore at Cannons Beach aptly named for the powerful surf that blasts surfers like a cannon ball shot from a cannon. Only the most experienced and seasoned surfers dare to tempt fate at Cannons Beach.

The day was gorgeous with a few scattered powder-puff clouds in the sky. The temperature was nearly ideal at 79 degrees Fahrenheit with gentle trade-winds delighting the senses with the fragrance of vanilla-scented Maile and the Hawaiian Coconut Orchid Maxillaria Tenuifolia.

Driving along Kuhio Highway with windows down and Blake and Sommer trying to carry a tune, Dalton found himself enjoying the peaceful moment of just being with his closest friends. Looking out the window he noticed along the side of the highway someone he recognized carrying a surf board.

"Hey Blake, pull over!"

Turning the music down Blake spotted two guys walking alongside the road with surfboards in tow. "You know these guys?"

"At least one of them. He helped save a few lives when the *Kanaloa* went down."

"Then by all means let's meet and greet. Sounds like my kind of people."

With the Rover pulled over on the side of the road, Emrick and Soren walked up.

"Hey Emrick. Where you guys heading?"

"Soren and I are heading to Ke'e Beach to catch a few waves."

"We're heading to Cannons Beach. Why don't you both jump in and join us." Taking Dalton up on the offer, Emrick and Soren secured their boards to the roof rack and hopped in the remaining two seats in the far back of the Rover introducing themselves as they did so while Blake drove back onto Kuhio Highway heading for Cannons.

Akamu who was seated next to Dalton in the second row of seats turned to Emrick and said, "I understand you helped pull survivors out of the water the other night. What a God send brah."

"I'm just glad Soren and I were close by to assist."

Dalton turned around and said, "Thank you both for risking your own lives to help us. A lot of good people and close friends were lost and still many others are recovering from horrible burns and injuries."

Pulling into Haena State Park, Blake considered parking beneath a Coconut Palm but thought better of it less he risk a coconut dropping and damaging his new wheels. Driving down a bit further away from the path leading to Cannons Beach he found a spot next to a black Mercedes SUV.

Dalton suddenly felt charged by the close proximity of the water and egged on the group, "I'm definitely feeling amped and ready to take all you Barney's to school."

Akamu quickly responded, "Oh no you didn't. Sommer might be a Barney but I'm no amateur. You're about to eat those words."

"A Barney?! By the time I'm finished ripping through a few barrels you both will be left looking like a couple boogie boarding boogers caught in the impact zone feeling my spit," Sommer chaffed.

Laughing Dalton issued the challenge, "First one to catch an epic wave and ride the pipeline is wined and dined by the losers."

Emptying out of the Rover, everyone grabbed their respective board and headed down to Cannons Beach. A few surfers were out beyond where the waves were cresting. Seated and standing along the beach were less experienced surfers called "cluckers", those who were trying to muster the courage to brave the surf and the strong, swift, and deceptive currents.

For a brief moment Dalton along with Akamu, Sommer, Blake, Emrick, and Soren all stood and looked out toward the breaking swells. Dalton spoke first, "Well, from the looks of those swells it seems that old Pacific blue is napping lazily beneath a carefree Sun.

"Yeah, well it's time for old Pacific blue to wake," Akamu added.

Blake looked over at Akamu and jokingly said, "Akamu, what you doing out here today? Aren't you the church-going type? The man upstairs is going to slap you down in the water boy!"

Soren joined the playful banter, "Oh, I don't know about that. I imagine it would be more of an act of worship to have someone sitting on a surfboard thinking about God than having someone sitting in a church thinking about surfing."

"I love the way you think, brah," Akamu said.

Dalton glanced over at Soren as his words triggered an old memory.

Blake picked up on the nostalgic look that blanketed Dalton's face. "Hey, you ok man?"

Stirred from his thoughts, Dalton answered, "Yeah. Just a memory of when I said something similar to a few surfers in a youth group back in Charleston when I was helping out as an interim pastor. It was a conversation surrounding spirituality and religion. They pressed me on whether they had to go to church or not."

Sommer quickly interjected and said, "I like how you and Soren think. I always feel closest to God when I'm near the ocean."

"You were a preacher?" Akamu asked incredulously.

"It was just for a few years to help out a seminary friend."

"You been holding out on us. I would've never picked you to be the preacher type." Akamu said joshing Dalton.

"It's not really a part of my life I've desired to talk about."

Akamu picked up on the less than jovial tone in Dalton's voice and opted to jettison the subject.

Stepping over to the water's edge Sommer knelt down and swirled her hands around in the breaking surf while gazing back up at Dalton. "I think old Pacific blue is beginning to wake now. Check out the sets beginning to roll in out there."

Dalton and the others looked out seeing a few waves rising and falling beneath the surfers but nothing of significance. And then all of a sudden, the size of the waves began to dramatically rise in height.

"Dang girl! How did you see those party waves that far out?" Akamu asked incredulously.

"Sometimes it takes a female perspective to compensate for a male deficiency," Sommer said with a big smile breaking across her face. "Maybe you should spend more time feeling rather than seeing."

"Oh, she just took you to school brah," Dalton said losing himself once again in the bantering. "Taught her everything she knows about the science of surfing."

"Oh really?" Sommer said with a teasing grin.

Akamu soaked it up in good fun. "You definitely have the magic touch girl. Just keep those waves a-coming."

Adopting a more serious tone, Dalton added, "Today, we surf to celebrate life and to celebrate the memories of our friends and colleagues. We surf to keep their memories alive in us."

Blake, Akamu, and Sommer slapped their boards in a surfer's way of affirming words spoken. Emrick and Soren looked at each other and followed suit.

"And we surf beneath the blue dome of God's grand cathedral celebrating life that transcends death," Emrick added.

"Here! Here!" Blake responded, as everyone slapped their boards. Dalton simply glanced over at Emrick as he felt a stirring within at his words.

Soren was the first one to rush the treacherous surf and took a scaling leap over the first crashing break landing on the back side at which time he quickly hit the water paddling out into the breaking waves.

"Dude, no way he did what I just think I saw?! He just went vertical about ten feet and accelerated while airborne over that wave." Akamu said in awe.

"He gets his name honestly. He's ever soaring to the occasion. Dalton you may have some competition on your hands." Emrick said.

"Yeah, and it looks like we're all buying Soren dinner tonight if we don't start breaking some waves." Blake added before running and leaping into the surf.

Wasting no time getting wet everyone took off following suit. The ocean was roiling with waves cresting nearly twenty feet high surging toward the coastline. The current began flexing its muscle making it difficult even for the most experienced surfers to get out beyond the thunderous crashing waves. Huge sets were rolling in making the surfing conditions even more treacherous.

Soren was first to reach beyond the angry breaks and spun around on his board to quickly check to make sure everyone was still above water. Dalton reached the back of the breaks next and felt as if he'd just endured an hour long rowing session in the gym. Emrick intentionally remained behind the group to make sure all made it out safely beyond the breaks.

Akamu pulled up next to Dalton and sat up on his board. "Dude, these waves are hungry."

Dalton looked over at Sommer who just came up from duck diving beneath a wave. "You getting your adrenaline rush on ducking these half-crazed waves?"

"Omg, the current and waves are raging," Sommer said energized by the rush.

Soren drifted closer to Dalton keeping a keen eye on the sets. "Looks like the perfect party wave heading our way."

Dalton turned and said, "Where?"

"About four sets back."

"How can you possibly see a party wave that far back?"

Paddling out a little further Soren replied, "I can feel it in the water. Just be ready. It will be the ride of your life."

"You must some kind of sixth sense or just hallucinating,"

Soren laughed. "More like faith. Sometimes when you quit feeling you miss seeing the bigger picture. Trust me. The pictures about to get much bigger."

"Hey everybody, we've got a party wave heading our way. We got a surf hound over here picking up on a scent." Dalton said more so to put Soren on the spot than any sincere belief in what he was actually hearing.

Blake, Akamu, and Sommer quickly paddled out to the spot where Soren had pulled up and was awaiting whatever it was he was sensing. Glancing out, Dalton was incredulous by what he saw. Sure enough barreling right toward them while gaining strength and rising in height was a titan of a wave that had the appearance of a mini Tsunami in the making.

"You've got to be kidding me," Dalton said with a stunned look on his face as he glanced over at Soren. "You really are a surf hound."

A capricious smile broke across Soren's face as he replied, "The key to surfing begins beneath the water. It's all about feeling. Same in life. The rush begins within. It's not about what we see but what we don't see."

Blake and Akamu paddled up alongside Dalton and Soren. Blake hollered out, "Hurry up Sommer, we're getting ready to ride!"

"Don't worry about me, I'll be ready."

Dalton saw Emrick paddling toward them. Looking back at the quickly approaching wave Dalton yelled, "Hey Emrick, get ready to duck dive. We're coming your way!"

Sommer had just made the turn on her board when everyone began positioning on their board as the titanic of a wave scooped them all up catapulting them upward and onward before they began descending within the barreling pipeline.

Soren was first to take the drop as he caught the face of the wave and began his descent. The others followed looking down on Emrick as he quickly duck dived beneath the cresting wave. Dalton was feeling the adrenaline rush as he rode one of the tallest waves he'd ever surfed in his life. Sommer was riding high on exhilaration and cut her board toward Soren about twenty feet ahead of her position. Blake and Akamu were falling in just behind Dalton with each spread out about fifteen feet apart.

Beneath the surface, Emrick quickly spun his board and with a surge of energy began to jettison under the water like a dolphin beneath the wave. He shot out of the water and into the pipeline pulling up as the anchor. As if blasted like a cannonball out of a cannon, Emrick kept his board trim and took advantage of the power behind the blast of the wave pulling an aerobatic maneuver in which he kicked out above the wave and rolled in the air up and over Blake, Akamu, and Dalton landing just to the outside of Sommer. Akamu was so shocked by what he saw that he momentarily lost his balance allowing the wave to unsteady and overtake him.

Sommer was struggling to maintain balance and was about to go down when Emrick landed just at the right spot and moment putting her back on balance. Simply amazed at the display of aerobatic skill, it was all Dalton could do to stay abreast of the wave without succumbing to the watery spit of the barrel. Soren glanced back and saw Emrick gaining on him and pitched his board slightly downward to maximize his acceleration speed.

Spotting an adjoining wave, Emrick went airborne again and flipped up and back landing perfectly upon the cresting wave providing him with a straight downward acceleration until he took advantage of the optimal moment whereupon he quickly shot upward gaining tremendous speed slightly augmented by his angelic powers.

Soren with a triumphant grin on his face glanced back trying to locate Emrick. It was at that very moment when Emrick soared over him dropping down in the first place position before pulling up close to the shore. Soren pulled up and dropped into the water alongside Emrick.

"Show off."

Emrick laughed and said, "Haven't taught you ALL of my tricks young one."

Sommer, Dalton, and Blake pulled up shortly after. Everyone looked back out for Akamu and saw him catching a wave out of the break heading their way.

Dalton regarded Emrick with disbelief in his eyes. "You were ripping out there! I've never seen anyone pull an aerial like that."

"Dude, you defied gravity," Blake added excitedly.

Sommer was just stoked that she actually made it back to shore in one piece, "Thanks for the bounce out there, you kept me from becoming chum for the sea life."

"Nothing is more invigorating and motivating than the sight of a deep blue sapphire barrel rising to greet you," Emrick replied.

"Well, you rode that wave like a pro surfer who didn't leave anything out there," Dalton said.

Akamu, who was walking out of the surf excitedly said, "You were hovering over that wave brah. Been surfing my entire life and never seen a surfer pull a hurdle like that. That was just righteous dude."

Blake couldn't help but get a playful dig in on Akamu as he slapped him on the back saying, "It's amazing you were able to tread water long enough while grubbing to see him leap frog you."

"Hey brah, I didn't fall off my board until Clark Kent here went all Superman on me."

"If we're going to wine and dine Emrick here then we best find us a spot to set up a camp fire," Dalton said walking toward a more secluded stretch of the beach.

Blake walked up and put his hand on Emrick's shoulder, "You didn't think we were talking about a restaurant did you?"

"Yeah brah, around here we catch our food and put it on the spit," Akamu interjected while ribbing Emrick.

Sommer joined in, "But what about the wine? I'm not doing sea water."

"Go fill some jugs of water. Maybe Soren here can turn the water into wine," Dalton said jokingly.

I can do that, Soren thought to himself.

"Let's spear some fish and gather some fruit," Akamu said.

Blake turned to Emrick and Soren adding, "Hope you like gathering grub. We do it the old fashion way."

Emrick raised his right eyebrow, "Oh, we can grub. We can definitely grub."

Akamu jokingly said to Emrick, "Yeah, we can spear in the shallows while you provide an aerial assault with a drop dive."

Sommer walked up to Soren and asked, "Care to help me get a few things out of the Rover?"

"Sure."

Pausing to appreciate his closest friends on earth, Dalton just took in the moment feeling a sense of peace and happiness come over him. It would prove short-lived.

Chapter 12

DARKNESS RISING

Standing in the shadow of the lush green Na Pali Coastal peaks, Samael gazed down upon Cannons Beach at those gathered around a bonfire blazing brightly. A pinkish wash from the setting sun colored the horizon. Samael observed with disdain the two angelic guardians who were fraternizing with the mortals. Samael detested those who remained loyal to the Light and especially those who served as guardian angels over the mortals. He believed they were blinded to the true freedom and power that only the Darkness afforded. It was just a matter of time when like a supernova, the Light of Empyrean would be extinguished once and for all. And the Kingdom of Heaven would fall to the Darkness.

Detecting a low frequency warble Samael turned to greet a dark translucent portal that briefly stirred the air as a formidable Dark One stepped through and stood before him. Dressed in black with a tattoo featuring a black sun and daggers pointing outward in all directions on his neck just below his left ear, the angelic warrior donned his mortal form standing tall wearing a fierce glare on his face.

Samael nodded in a gesture of respect, "Andras, my dark friend. Welcome back to Eden."

Approaching one another they both gripped the other's forearm raising their free hand in the form of a fist to their forehead. The gripping of the forearm denoted the strength of passion and the clinched fist to the forehead denoted one in rebellion against the Light.

Wearing a loathsome look across his face, Andras spoke with a tone of sarcasm, "Eden, the flawed creation that God abandoned."

"Yes, disillusionment has a way of breaking us all. Even the Creator himself is not immune from such disappointment. But Eden has proven a great ally in that these pathetic mortals are drawn to the Darkness like moths to a flame. Makes our task here a welcome respite from the Kingdom Wars raging against Empyrean," Samael replied.

Walking toward the lofty edge of the Na Pali trail, Andras peered down and set his angelic sight on the human figures moving below around a bonfire. "So those are the mortals that require our special attention. Why are we even toying with them? We should just crush them now and be done with this place. Don't we have more important things to do like laying low the walls of Empyrean?"

Stepping next to Andras while placing his left arm on his shoulder, Samael said, "And miss out on the pleasure of making the humankind suffer? No, we must show restraint for now. There is a darker plan."

Andras scoffed, "There is always a darker plan. We are wasting our time and resources here tip toeing around these pesky mortals. We should be storming Empyrean, burning it to the ground and dethroning the One whom these mortals worship."

Samael knew the reputation of Andras very well. They had served together in a few covert missions into the Celestial city. Fierce in battle and unrelenting in his hatred directed at the Creator and those who blindly swear allegiance to the Creator, Andras had little patience in dealing with the trifling affairs of mortals. He viewed Eden as Satariel's playground and a waste of energy and resources. Andras was losing patience with Satariel's insistence that the mortals were a necessary inconvenience that must be dealt with before a new Dark order could rise to prominence.

"So, I see we have friends among the mortals," Andras spat in sarcastic contempt.

"Yes. One is standing next to the female on the right and the other is standing to the left of our target of interest. They go by the mortal names of Emrick and Soren."

"Which one is responsible for overtaking Renaud?"

"That would be the one standing next to the mortal called Dalton standing just left of the bonfire."

Andras' angelic sight sharpened and zoomed in on Emrick. "Have you seen this mortal persona before? Any idea who we're dealing with?"

"I've not personally dealt with him face to face much less in hand to hand combat. But Renaud was a lethal warrior as you well know. My suspicion is that he belongs to Metatron's elite Guardians of Light."

"What about the other one?"

"Not much to him. A simple annoyance," Samael caustically replied.

"And yet he bested you," Andras interjected with an annoying tone to his voice.

Samael bristled while brushing aside the comment. "A fortunate bit of luck on his part of which he will not enjoy when next we meet again."

"Sometimes luck is all it takes to best a combatant," Andras replied matter-of-factly. "You play around with these vermin long enough and they will bite you. Of all angelic warriors, you should know this. Have you forgotten your stand on one of Eden's mountain ranges against that mortal, what was his name? Oh, yes, Elijah I believe it was. How do you know that your simple annoyance down there is not another embarrassment waiting to happen?"

Samael felt the dark energy quickening within as he restrained himself from reaching to pull the dark heart out of Andras' angelic body. It was all he could do to resist and let the slight stand. "There will be no flaming chariot for this one. Of that I can assure you," Samael countered.

The sun began to set giving way to a shrouding darkness. As the twilight shadows lengthened the darkness was diminished by the shimmering moonlight off the Pacific Ocean. Andras gave a hellish glare as a couple hikers stumbled upon them heading back from hiking the Kalalau Trail. Samael quickly reached out and stayed Andras' hand as he lurched toward the young couple desiring to end their pitiable existence and speed them on to their eternal reward.

The young tourist couple quickly hurried along not daring to look back.

Finding humor in the moment Samael said, "Anxious for a snack are we?"

Andras with an impatient starkness in his voice replied, "I have more tolerance and appreciation for the blood-sucking mosquitos than I do for these inferior creatures. Satariel should give Eden to Draven and let him suck every mortal dry while we get back to the REAL business of taking down Metatron and his Guardians of Light. We pull that off and Empyrean falls."

"The time will come my dark friend. But first we must weaken the Light. Timing is crucial so when the opportune moment presents itself we strike fast and unmercifully." Spotting a couple of drug addicts meandering through the public parking area, Andras sized them up as ideal vessels to use for their bedeviling purposes. "And so it has," Andras said.

The wind began increasing in intensity around the Na Pali mountain range as the tropical trade breezes stirred the night air. Clouds began to blanket the gaze of the moon like an ominous omen warning of the encroaching darkness threatening to diminish the light.

Samael and Andras took full advantage of the dimming night sky and leapt to the roadside some one hundred and fifty feet below as their angelic wings spread outward slowing their descent. Approaching slowly from behind, they walked toward two young beach bums who were slightly staggering as they walked toward the beach. Both were scruffy looking with unkempt hair and tanned skin from the island life.

Andras leapt over them landing directly in their path. The beach bums looked incredulous and dazed from what they assumed was a hallucination effect from the synthetic cannabinoids called "Spice" they had just ingested. Walking around from behind them, Samael took up position next to Andras as they sized up their prey.

Both of the beach bums stood less than six feet tall and possessed sun-bleached shoulder length sandy blonde hair. The shorter of the two spoke first looking up at the two intimidating figures dressed in black, "Dudes, you been hanging out in coconut trees?" His companion nervously snickered while wobbling on his feet.

Stepping up in their personal space, Samael looked deeply into the young upstart's eyes. Speaking to Andras telepathically he said, *This one is a weak-minded fool who has wasted his youth on pleasures of the flesh and will provide little resistance.*

Andras walked up to the other bum and with soulless eyes fixed on his prey gave voice to his thoughts, "This one is filled with anxiety, anger, and uncertainty. A bit less reliable but too weak to resist."

Samael and Andras simultaneously placed a hand on the head of each unleashing a vexing, devilish spirit that quickly took control of their bodies and began assaulting and tormenting the mind of each. Both began to writhe in agony until Samael commanded the spirits to go down to the beach area and unleash havoc. The countenance of the two young men became dark and maniacal as they immediately turned with renewed focus heading down toward Cannons Beach.

While watching the two loathsome mortals walking briskly away, Andras said to Samael, "What of the one of whom the prophecy speaks?"

"The prophecy is but a desperate ploy of the Light to distract and splinter our forces. We do not leave without the sword. And if we end the sword bearer's pathetic existence then so be it."

Walking over to the Haena State Park parking area they approached a black Mercedes SUV. With a downward motion of his hand, Samael unlocked the doors. Before getting in, he recalled with a flick of his hand a miniscule size smart dust device from beneath the passenger's side of Blake's Range Rover. The tracking device doubled as a voice tap which helped to tip Samael off in advance that they would be heading to Haena State Park. He had the information he needed for now. Both of them got into their black Mercedes and headed to their next destination, Dalton's Hanalei home.

Chapter 13

THE VOICE OF CREATION

The last light of day began working its magic over the island as many who flock to the shores of Kaua'i are enraptured by the mesmerizing sunsets that have a way of diminishing the cares of life in a daily ritual of visual splendor. The bonfire on the beach burned brightly with a blaze that shot up several feet in the air as the wood and empty coconut shells fed the intensity of the flames.

Blake and Akamu had just returned from the Rover with a couple spearfishing guns. There was little activity on Cannons Beach from locals or tourists presenting a semblance of privacy making for an idyllic evening for chillaxing with friends by an enchanting fire. Everyone stood around just taking in the moment. The sounds of the spitting flames and the stunning visual over the Pacific filled the senses with the wonder and grandeur of creation.

Looking over at Blake and Akamu, Dalton quipped, "You both going to just stand there holding the fish or are you planning to put them on the spit?"

Jarred from the intoxicating wonder as the last of an apricot light sank beneath the horizon, Blake jokingly replied, "Oh, I thought the fire was just for ambiance and we were going to eat sushi."

Sommer quickly joined the conversation, "I love sushi! Especially

Mahi-mahi."

Walking over to the makeshift tripod used for cooking over the fire, Dalton said to Soren, "I've never seen someone catch Mahi-mahi so close to shore much less spear one."

"Give me a spear and a glimmer of shimmer and I can feed the island," Soren replied.

"Oh, a little cocky are we?" Dalton replied light-heartedly.

"I was feeling inspired when our dolphinfish swam nearby for a look and see. I had to insist on him STICKING around," Soren joked.

Erupting in laughter with the others, Dalton found himself appreciating the company of Emrick and Soren as well as the sense of levity they both brought to the day.

After gutting and slicing the fish into chunky fillets, Akamu impaled the fillets along a sharp-ended bamboo stick placing it over the flames. Sommer washed a few other fillets in the shallows prepping some sushi.

An intoxicating starry night sky began to intensify with the deepening of twilight. The entrancing sounds of the waves rhythmically breaking along the shallows provided a natural symphonic repose as the moon beams danced upon the ocean. Dalton couldn't help but feel a sense of calmness come over his troubled spirit. At least for the moment, although fleeting it may be, he found his soul being massaged by the scenic wonder of creation's enthralling beauty.

Noticing that Dalton had become distant and absorbed in

thought, Emrick walked over and bent down to pick up a conch shell. Picking it up from the sand and turning it over, he lifted the shell to his ear and smiled. "When a conch's life force has been expelled, only the shell remains. But though seemingly lifeless and barren from within, the shell captures the energy of the earth and magnifies it in unique whorls that get rotated clockwise in perfect synchronization with universal harmony. Thus the reason why one hears the sound of the ocean upon placing the conch shell to the ear. Also among some island cultures, the conch shell is blown during sacred rituals to get rid of negative energy and dispel evil forces."

Holding the conch shell up to the illumination of the moon's light Emrick continued, "There is a spiritual energy that emanates from within, trapped by the shell we often create to protect our life. If we listen during those moments when our soul is at rest one can hear the Voice of Creation speaking desiring to harmonize with one's spirit so that life may once again permeate the soul."

Dalton was about to respond when the sound of something stirring in the nearby tropical brush distracted him. Two young men in their twenties who appeared high on drugs came stumbling out from behind their tropical concealment. Emrick immediately noticed the glazed over look in their eyes and the menacing way in which they approached without thought or hesitation. Soren discerned the signs of possession alerting him to the approaching danger.

The shorter of the two headed straight for the bonfire drawing everyone's attention as Blake and Sommer stepped away from the fire unsure of what the young man's intentions were. The other companion was walking up from behind when he suddenly turned and grabbed the two spear guns leaning against a Coconut Palm tree. Seizing the weapon with a firm grip he suddenly spun and aimed it right at Akamu who was making a move to approach.

Akamu spoke first, "Look brah, I'm not sure what your deal is but you really should put that away. There is plenty of fish for everyone."

With a murderous, wild-eyed glare the young assailant replied, "My deal is you and I'm here to end your pathetic excuse of an existence."

The other assailant stepped over receiving the second spear gun from his companion. Turning he aimed it directly at Dalton. Feeling nothing but cold, naked fear, Dalton recoiled as he looked into the menacing, murderous eyes of one who seemed to have no apparent concern or hesitation about taking the life of another.

Slowly without drawing attention to himself, Emrick took a step closer to Dalton so that he was standing within arm's length of him. The air filled with tension as Dalton and Akamu found themselves within the crosshairs of two would-be killers with bloodlust in their eyes seemingly intent on pulling the trigger.

Soren slowly moved closer toward Akamu when the assailant with his spear gun trained on Akamu said, "I wouldn't take another step if I were you or this one walks among angels."

Are you kidding me? What oblivious spirit are you? He IS walking among angels. Soren thought to himself. Ceasing movement and fixed on the young man's trigger finger, Soren sensed the duress the young assailant's mortal body was experiencing resulting from the demonic spirit within. A nervous twitch would be enough to engage the trigger and send a sharp metal-tipped projectile into Akamu who was standing nearly twelve feet away.

The other assailant wore a sinister grin sensing the fear and confusion welling up in Dalton. "You possess the Sword of Eden. Give it to us and we will allow you and your friends to live." For a fleeting second Dalton thought he saw a flicker of crimson ripple across the eyes of his assailant.

Emrick made to position himself between Dalton and his assailant but was quickly challenged.

"Don't take another step you fool," the assailant sneered, "or I will end his mortal life right here and now. Give us what we want and we will leave this wretched place."

Emrick drew closer challenging the demonic spirit within the assailant while never losing eye contact. "What you demand is not yours to give nor take. Leave this young man and depart from this place." A vile, sinister look came over the young assailant as he pulled the trigger unleashing the projectile.

Sommer yelled, "No!"

And then as if everything went into slow motion, Dalton's eyes dropped down to the spear gun and then up and over at Emrick. With lightning-like reflexes, Emrick snagged the flying projectile about one inch away from piercing Dalton's chest cavity before rolling downward and up in one fluid motion catching the assailant off guard and in a state of shock. Dropping him to the ground Emrick's eyes transmuted into an astral sapphire hue as he bore deeply into the young man's eyes and beyond to the demonic spirit within. The crimson red manifested only momentarily as Emrick commanded with authority, "Leave him now."

The young man convulsed only momentarily and then found himself looking up into the eyes of a stranger he'd never seen before. The sapphire blue eyes were mesmerizing and otherworldly conveying a sense of strength and compassion.

"Who are you?" the young man said.

"A friend," Emrick replied as his eyes returned to normal coloration denoting the retraction of spiritual energy.

When all eyes including Akamu's assailant turned toward Dalton, Soren seized the moment and with deft reflexes took out the other young man pinning him to the ground before his finger could so much as twitch. The demon spirit posed little resistance as Soren quickly exorcised it and cleared the young man of spirit possession. With a look of despair mixed with relief the young man said, "Thank you."

Blake was stunned by what he just witnessed. Akamu had momentarily looked over toward Dalton and the next thing he knew was that his assailant was pinned to the ground by Soren. It was all so surreal that everyone including the young druggies were staring in disbelief at Emrick and Soren.

Breaking the awkward silence Emrick said to Dalton, "Wow. What a rush." Like pent-up air released from a balloon, the tension eased as nervous laughter broke the deafening silence.

Dalton and Soren helped the two young men to their feet. "What are your names?" Dalton asked.

"My name is Todd Dixon", answered the young man whose actions had been thwarted by Emrick.

"And my name is Ron McGarrett," the other said. "I'm not sure how we got here. The last thing I remember was meeting two strange guys dressed in black back in the parking lot area."

Emrick glanced over at Soren before speaking to Dalton, "Look after our new friends while Soren and I go check out the parking area to make sure there are no other surprises awaiting us."

Blake immediately piped up, "You need me to go with you?"

"No, that's ok. We can manage. Hang back here. We'll make sure the coast is clear."

Dalton addressed Sommer who had remained unusually calm throughout the ordeal, "Hey, you ok over there?"

"Yes, other than watching your life pass before my eyes."

"Well, I'm still here thanks to Emrick's quick reflexes."

Dalton's eyes trailed off after Emrick and Soren as they ran into the black fringe of the tropical foliage disappearing from sight. *Something is different about them and yet strangely familiar,* Dalton thought to himself.

The night was deepening as the moon's light was being eclipsed by a drifting cloud bank. With a suspicious gaze, Dalton questioned both Todd and Ron, "You two have no idea what just happened out here?" With a genuinely clueless look about him, Todd scratched his head and answered, "It's as if I just blacked out in the parking lot. Did something weird happen?"

"Dude, I feel like I just had a transcendental experience. I'm so clueless how we ended up here on the beach," Ron added lightheartedly.

Dalton knew island druggies when he saw them and started to take a hardline approach when he struck something in the sand with his right foot. He stooped to pick up the hard obstruction in the sand laying his eyes on the empty conch shell that Emrick had held in his hand. Looking up at Todd and Ron he suddenly viewed them in a different light.

Chapter 14

THE LEAP

The Black Forest, Germany

Devin entrusted Aeron with oversight of all internal operations within the *Lycaon* while he orchestrated and manipulated mortal pawns and global events that were thus far moving along according to plan. He was OCD about the details expecting his subordinates to perform above and beyond expectations. Thus the only concern that preoccupied Aeron was ensuring that she did just that. Sparing no expense in recruiting a dream team comprised of the world's top scientific minds, Devin was driven by his diabolical purpose to create an army of superintelligent beings far superior to a weak and flawed humanity.

Taking extra precautions to ensure the highly secretive experimentation within the *Lycaon* from ever leaking, a nanotransmitter had been injected within everyone on Devin's scientific team monitoring every waking thought, sound, and action. Devin could quickly terminate any potential violator with death by aneurism. Aware of the required implant and the clandestine nature of the research, each scientist was closely screened and ultimately signed willingly in pursuit of advancing bioresearch and AI experimentation that would redesign, recode, and reinvent the created order itself.

Devin inspired a culture of creativity that gave his scientific team a real sense of possessing god-like capabilities manipulating man and machine with the power and control to set the course of humanity's future. Devin's creation of humanoids and simulants would possess immortal qualities becoming gods among humankind dictating the terms and conditions of natural selection. His new creation would give rise to a new world order of superintelligence.

Aeron walked into the highly secure and isolated area within Devin Sinclair's Alpine research facility where she found Dr. Mark Wolff, Devin's brilliant physicist from Ireland, engrossed in his research experimentation. The interior room was a state-of-the-art laboratory with highly sophisticated nanotechnology consisting of biomolecular nanomachines and advanced thermo-nuclear systems. Approaching the lead AI scientist, Aeron sensed a surging energy that arrested her attention. Pausing she watched Dr. Wolff with rapt attention.

Dr. Erwin Steininger, a renowned molecular geneticist from Austria was standing by a holding chamber intensely focused on the flurry of computational readouts in response to the performance of the neural microcircuits. Collaborating feverishly alongside Dr. Wolff, they both had left everything behind to follow Devin Sinclair's vision of the creation of superintelligent humanoids. But this simulant was the master design derived from Devin's diabolical mind. It would serve a special purpose.

Engrossed in the moment, the tension and excitement began to build as Dr. Wolff stepped back in anticipation of the breakthrough in a biomolecular engineering feat that would assure his place in the world of AI science. If successful his legacy would rival that of the likes of Newton and Einstein. After much perplexity and uncertainty, the moment of triumph had finally arrived.

Simulant 666 was an imposing figure with brown wavy hair at the apex of a flawless masculine frame. His facial structure was that of a perfect male specimen with a high forehead and chiseled jawline. His well-defined torso was athletically-toned with six pack abs. His lower body boasted muscular thighs and shins rounding out a flawless external design eerily similar to a perfect male Homo sapien.

Aeron couldn't help but raise her right eye brow and smile while beholding the ideal male body, an object of lust, admiration, and envy. Walking around the body encased in an acrylic incubation tube she was able to observe any possible external imperfections of which she found none. She beheld the beauty of a creative design that rivaled that of the Creator's. And now, she was about to witness the leap that would far surpass that of the Creator's breath that first gave life to Adam.

The simulant was perfect in every way externally. The real test was how the internal systems performed. With the creation of synthetic genomics and the manipulation of biological genomes, Dr. Wolff was now standing at the threshold of taking artificial intelligence and design beyond what had previously been thought impossible. Dr. Wolff had confidently insisted to Devin that not only was it possible but even probable that if he were given the resources, research facility, and means he would achieve and make the leap from human-level machine intelligence to superintelligence far exceeding the limitations of human cognition.

Through genomic engineering, Dr. Wolff with Dr. Steininger's assistance was able to manipulate and enhance genetic stability while improving metabolic efficiency. Taking real human DNA and combining it with synthetic biological components, the DGC was on the verge of pulling off the first superintelligent humanoid possessing perfect health, increased cognitive intelligence, enhanced memory, and superior reflexes. The perfection of Devin Sinclair's creation of a superintelligent humanoid was the critical next step in creating an army of such beings that would bring about the extinction of humanity and set the stage for an ultimate assault on Empyrean.

"The resemblance is striking," Aeron said breaking her silence.

"Biosystems are functioning at optimal levels. The cognitive systems including oracle, genie, and sovereign are ready for performance testing. If all goes as designed Simulant 666 contains within its cerebral cortex the capability to instantly upload any information data base within wireless reach instantaneously. His oracle system will give him advanced capability to speak any known language, answer simple to complex questions, and evaluate human intentions. I've also built in a flawlessly designed genie system for internal command-execution purposes should the need to manually override arise. And of course, the brilliant masterpiece and crown achievement is the sovereign system that upon initiation by Devin will be ready for whole brain emulation of the subject. What we have now achieved is superintelligence."

Dr. Wolff brushed a strand of thick matted hair away and met Aeron's eyes, "Simulant 666 is ready." Appreciating Dr. Wolff's confidence in his work, she smiled grimly knowing results and not mere talk would either validate or nullify the veracity of the scientist's words. Walking around the holding chamber examining every flawless detail of what appeared the perfect specimen she was eager to see if their new creation would exude the strength, power, and intelligence of the angelkind.

What have we created? Aeron thought while weighing the implications of this new superintelligent machine. *Could Simulant 666 be the embodiment of the ancient prophecy from the Book of Darkness foretelling the offspring of Satariel?* The dark energy quickened within as she pondered the possibility. Giving the all clear Aeron said, "Let's see what our intelligently designed genomes have produced. Initiate animation and let's bring Simulant 666 to full life force."

Scanning one last time the various monitors assigned to each internal vital organ and confident everything was a go, Dr. Wolff turned to Dr. Steininger who was anxiously awaiting the moment that would forever change the world. "Begin the animation sequence."

While manipulating the AI systems activation sequence, Dr. Steininger paid close attention to the synthetic biological systems for any signs of deterioration during the activation phase. Stepping over to the animator and touching the smart screen, he activated neurological sensors attached to Simulant 666. Working through the activation sequence, Dr. Steininger finished providing the appropriate code sequences deactivating the hibernation state. Bringing Simulant 666 to life, the eyelids began to evidence rapid eye movement followed by an abrupt cessation. For a fleeting moment, a surge of dark energy welled up within Dr. Wolff as the possibility of failure crept into his psyche before quickly dissipating as the simulant opened its black eyes. Locking on Aeron the simulant said, "Hello Dr. Trevil or should I call you, Aeron?"

"Oh, by all means please call me Aeron. And who might you be?" Aeron asked raising a knowing eyebrow.

"Legion. For I am many."

Chapter 15

THE INFERNAL EMPIRE

Dubai, The United Arab Emirates

Devin walked with Aziel and broke the lingering silence with an observation, "If only adherents of other world religions were as extremely devout as some within the Islamic faith, we would have our Apocalypse in short order."

Aziel, the demon prince listened, betraying no emotion. A menacing presence, Azeil was evil incarnate with crimson eyes concealed beneath dark shades, long black hair tied back in a braid, a well-groomed goatee accenting his rugged jawline, and a black tattoo on the left side of his neck in the shape of a dark sun with swords pointing outward from the round orb.

Having played an integral role in the angelic revolt against God, Aziel now held charge over the spirits of darkness including demonic rulers and authorities who kept the Middle East embroiled in chaos inciting sectarian strife, religious extremism, death and destruction. A master of fomenting mayhem, Aziel excelled at deceiving the devout into believing they are following the Light when in reality it is the will of the Darkness being served. By creating conditions that foment social disparity and incite anarchy, Aziel had masterfully sown seeds of religious extremism within the rich fertile soil of discontent resulting in a harvest of evil promulgated by ISSIM.

Devin and Aziel walked together along the glass encased corporate suite on the 154th floor of the Burj Khalifa, the world's tallest building in Dubai. The sweeping panoramic vistas of the cityscape provided Devin with a sense of being on top of everything, quite literally. The exterior cladding comprised of reflective glazing provided a tint to the windows allowing sufficient light in while refracting much of the heat from the blazing sun. Not that heat ever bothered Devin.

An architectural marvel with the most advanced digital sophistication, the ascending tower of the Burj reached high into the heavens reminding Devin of a time thousands of years before in which a similar human feat was attempted with the construction of the Tower of Babel. *How things have come full circle,* Devin mused appreciating the humor in how the Creator's mortal pets were ever trying to one up each other by seeking to be higher, faster, stronger, and more powerful. He couldn't help but admire his own powers of influence over the ages and how he had so effectively corrupted, disrupted, and maligned the will of the Creator.

Devin peered out upon the vastness of the Arabian kingdom taking in the towering skyscrapers amidst the majestic cityscape. He looked down upon a sea of humanity busily going about their daily activities oblivious to the sovereign powers who were influencing, shaping, and determining their destinies. The humankind were mere pawns easily manipulated to carry out his will. *How pathetic,* Devin scoffed to himself.

In vain do you worship gods that do not hear you, do not see you, and do not care about you. I am the determiner of your fate, your true God. And soon I shall watch you all burn to ash.

Devin turned inward as thoughts of vengeance began to churn like a tempest stirring and whipping desert sands. Recalling a memory, he withdrew to an age long ago, an age of power, an age of ascension. His eyes became as fire as the irises transmuted into crimson with pupils black as coal. His eyes slowly glazed over as he drew inward within the dark recesses of his memory where his thoughts transported him to Primora — The Kingdom of Darkness.

€

Flames of fire erupted out of the mouth of an angry volcano vomiting poisonous gases, dark ash, and molten projectiles a hundred and fifty feet into the sulfuric atmosphere. Its searing heat and roaring flames lashed out at the heavens casting it in crimson illumination revealing shadowy figures that moved and slithered among the darkness. The faint screams of the damned could be heard from deep down within the volcanic abyss.

Rising on plumes of pumice several winged beasts lurched out of the molten lava clawing into the sky gaining lift and propulsion with each upward and downward thrust of their wings. Wafts of noxious heat swirled around them as liquefied rock dripped from their tough, onyx scales. Their razor sharp wings sliced through the thick gaseous atmosphere lurching erratically while gaining altitude and then dropping abruptly increasing velocity before rising faster and higher with each back arching thrust.

Fierce-looking angelic sentries appeared seemingly out of thin air stepping to the edge of a rocky outcropping just beneath a towering mountain peak that was part of a mountainous range extending as far as the eye could see. Each angelic sentry possessed body armor mirroring their natural surroundings with reptilian skin reflecting the diffused light that escaped the thick gaseous atmosphere. Their eyes were dark crimson possessing keen visual acuity among a world enveloped in darkness offering very little natural light.

Winged beasts swooped down toward the outcroppings possessing fiery yellow eyes providing scant light illumining the darkness; each creating a deep guttural screeching sound as an angelic sentry ran and leaped onto the back of each before immediately swooping back down to the dark region below. Like wolves of the sky, the winged dragons soared as a dark pack of ravenous reptiles along the valley.

Another volcanic eruption lit up the diabolical sky causing a surging tremor that shook the valley floor below. Several loud explosions, molten bubbles bursting, and a roaring sound like that of a jet engine at full throttle provided a deafening, ear-throbbing sound that reverberated around the surrounding mountainous walls.

Rising out of the fiery abyss a colossal dragon emerged with a deafening roar that thundered and echoed throughout the Kingdom of Primora. Fire blazed forth like streaks of lightning from its nostrils. Two enormous horned tusks jutted out from its crown and draped back toward its serpentine neck. Its magnificent muscular body rippled as it clawed forth from the volcano while the dragon's thick scaly hide shimmered reflecting Primora's surroundings with hues of black, crimson, yellow, and orange.

Upon stepping out of the volcano the dragon extended its massive wing span that stretched forth encompassing the length of a football field. The black wings with dark crimson razor-sharp wing tips jutted out supported by monstrous legs like black walking pillars with three pointed claws extending from its feet biting deep into the mountain wall as it walked out upon a giant rocky dais. Protruding spikes ran down its back culminating with a slithering tail possessing at its tip a diamond-shaped serpent head recoiling and baring its fangs with menacing intent.

Gazing out over the dark valley below, the dragon reared up on its hind legs raising its head upward eliciting a ferociously deafening roar spewing flaming fire toward the heavens in a menacing display of angry defiance. The dragon dropped down onto all fours with a thunderous crash as its declaration of rebellious independence was met by the strident shrieks of a demonic host of rebel angels who filled the valley below as far as the eye could see.

The dragon's scales began shimmering shades of black and crimson. Fire and smoke could be seen emitting from its reptilian body as the dragon assumed a commanding posture inhaling and exhaling the dark energy that permeated the hellish Kingdom of Primora.

Rising out of the violent volcanic eruptions appeared two other dragons half the size in stature as that of the great dragon. A fiery red dragon with eyes of flame stepped to the great dragon's left. The second dragon with black soulless eyes possessing dark charcoal gray skin with black streaks running vertical along its scaly body stepped to the great dragon's right. Both dragons stopped just short of the great dragon's position forming a triangle of defiance. They bellowed ear-splitting screams and shrills that reverberated throughout the valley below.

Standing upon a dais now oozing flames and smoke, all three dragons represented an unholy trinity of chaos, death, and destruction. Having emerged from a thousand year imprisonment within a volcanic tomb the three dragons stood as one united in their rebellious determination to seek vengeance by inflicting misery, suffering, and destruction upon their sworn enemies.

Looking out upon a valley of the rebel angels comprising a third of all angelic powers representative of the nine orders of the angelic hierarchy: Seraphim, Cherubim, Thrones, Dominions, Virtues, Powers, Principalities, Archangels, and the Angels. Winged beasts along with screeching wraith-like creatures soared high above the devilish lair. Wolf-like angelic beings with fangs like daggers emerged from the mountainous caverns. Predatory howls joined a cacophony of diabolical cries forming a symphony of evil culminating in a thundering chant, "All power, glory, and honor to the Great Dragon who shall reign forevermore!"

A guttural and incoherent sound began to emanate and rumble

from deep within the great dragon. Dipping its mighty head downward and then upward the great dragon unleashed a torrent of fire while giving voice to the words "Death to Eden" spewing forth from its fiery mouth. With incredible strength the great dragon lunged forth off the dais quickly gaining altitude with each powerful thrust of its expansive wings. The demonic horde below screeched in furious acclaim.

The dark world of Primora flooded the vision of the great dragon before quickly dissolving into blackness as Devin's irises transmuted from crimson to black. He blinked as if to clear his thoughts and refocus.

€

"The humankind and their lust for war intensifies as we feed their insatiable appetite for power, subjugation, and dominance", Devin said gazing upon the Middle Eastern landscape.

Turning to Prince Aziel he said, "Much hinges upon our combined efforts to influence global politics, religion, and technology in fomenting a perfect storm of chaos."

"ISSIM grows daily keeping the Middle East embroiled in a perpetual cycle of violent hatred and murderous outrage fomented by religious extremism. The souls of fire gorge themselves on religion poisoning the human spirit and rankling Eden. It weakens the mind making the humankind more susceptible to anarchy and chaos. Their bloodlust is palpable becoming almost as insatiable as my own," Aziel said smiling grimly. "The dark fruit of knowledge is the gift that keeps on giving," Aziel added sarcastically an inference to the fall of Adam and Eve.

"How easily they fall," Devin quipped although clearly distant.

Aziel discerned the air shivering with dark energy around Devin evidencing a preoccupation and restlessness stemming from a possible threat posed by the Light.

"I sense something disturbing you my Lord," Aziel said.

Pacing along the tinted windows like a caged lion whose intentions are unreadable, Devin simply looked ahead as if weighing his options. After a period of silent reflection, Devin responded to Aziel's discerning observation.

"The Sword of Eden has awakened. I felt its fiery power ignite eliciting a shockwave of energy that coursed through the astral sphere."

"Then let us end this threat before it grows," Aziel spat in defiance of the Light. Well aware of the ancient prophecy Aziel asked, "What of the mortal?"

"His faith is weak and his confusion grows. There is one close to him that presents an opportunity. All is moving according to plan. And yet, that's what bothers me. It's too easy."

"You lack faith, my Lord."

"Don't speak to me of faith," Devin fired back annoyed by the patronization.

"Faith in the Darkness, my Lord."

"I AM the DARKNESS," Devin said with crimson fury in his

eyes. "Never underestimate the power of the Light or you will do so to your own demise."

Aziel new better than to challenge Devin although he arrogantly believed boots on the ground engagement was the answer to the pesky humankind problem. Dominion without diplomacy was Aziel's modus operandi which made him one of Satariel's most feared and fearsome demon generals.

"You did well in crippling the mortal's faith and his reliance upon the Light," Devin said becoming less agitated. "But where you did not succeed is in quailing his faith in the Light once and for all."

"He was not meant to get off that bus, my Lord. Everything was planned meticulously. We have been over this many times," Aziel said nostrils flaring with anger rising in his voice.

"And yet what should've been was thwarted by a young woman feigning to choke on her lunch," Devin countered as he turned to face off with Aziel.

Aziel looked down so as to avoid eye contact with Devin. Wisely he chose not to reply although he was inwardly seething with rage desiring with every fiber of his being to lash out and rip Devin's head from his shoulders.

"You are prudent in exercising restraint," Devin said reading Aziel's thoughts. "Your hate is lethal my dark friend and you are wise to hold it in check. There is a time to unleash words and a time to unleash weapons. Words are more powerful than any weapon you or I can create."

"In all due respect, my Lord, where words failed a bomb blast worked wonders. Those loyal to the Light rely on words to inspire faith, those of us who stand against the Light rely on weapons."

"Yes, weapons. Wherever would we be without them," Devin retorted acerbically. "You arrogant and insolent fool."

Aziel yielded to the rage surging within him as he swiftly ignited his energy sword which hummed to life proving short-lived as Devin quickly countered with a simple word, "Down." Aziel was quickly forced to his knees by a telekinetic energy elicited effortlessly by a simple downward swipe of Devin's right arm as if he were wielding an invisible sword. The fiery energy from Aziel's sword reversed back up the pommel sizzling his hand causing him to quickly drop it.

"Thank you for providing an opportunity to demonstrate my point," Devin said indifferently. "Never doubt the power of a timely WORD."

A charge of pain surged through Aziel who winced in agony as he began shedding beads of sweat down his forehead. Devin became emphatic gazing down upon him with steely eyes, "Have you been so long among the humankind that you've become so soft? Forgotten what it's like to engage one of your own kind in conflict? Well, here's a refresher."

Devin's eyes ignited in fiery crimson as he infused Aziel in even greater pain. "A slight modification to your thinking is needed. Those who place their faith in the Light are inspired by the Word – the Word of the Creator. And though I loathe it, I am no fool to underestimate the power of the Light. Words ARE our most powerful weapons. Words inspire religion, manipulate and control, fuel hate, and incite rebellion. To conqueror your enemy you must first KNOW your enemy. Words can inspire either faith or doubt, hate or love, war or peace. Words not weapons have been and will continue to be the primary means by which I shall win this war against the Light with or without you. To succeed in conquering the Light then master this truth or DON'T and I shall take personal pleasure in eradicating you from our ranks."

Releasing the coursing infusion of dark energy, Devin stood briefly over Aziel like a dominant alpha male wolf before commanding, "Rise."

"Aziel, you are blinded by the very thing at which you excel. You're masterful at embroiling the religious-minded humankind in a holy war over dogma. And yet you give me cause for concern in your lack of application of the very truth that we affirm. If Eden's history has taught us anything it's that the humankind rise or fall depending on what they believe. WORDS inspire belief and belief like power can be corrupted. Influence and win the mind and you add the power of belief to your arsenal; one of the greatest weapons that can be wielded in eradicating humanity and bringing about the inevitable fall of Empyrean. Words are primary and weapons secondary. A single spoken word imbued with the Darkness has the power to create, orchestrate, and annihilate. Never doubt it and never forget it," Devin said turning and taking in the panoramic views of Dubai stunningly lit amid the backdrop of night.

"The coming conflict will test us all. Don't take the stuff you are dishing out too seriously lest you rush to draw your sword and have your own head cleaved from your shoulders by one of our kind. Be vigilant and prudent for we are fighting on two different fronts. It's a slippery slope we tread. Our kind will not fall so easily for the tactics we use effectively against the humankind."

"I will be ready as always, my Lord. I've not been bested by a mortal yet and I'm not about to start now. And as for our kind who cling pathetically to the Light, their heads shall be pinned upon the celestial walls of Empyrean."

"Of that I have no doubt," Devin said.

Chapter 16

THE ORDER OF BAAL

Homicide detectives Skylar Jensen and Barret Raleigh were already sitting at the bar area of the *Beach House*, a popular restaurant on Kaua'i with picturesque sunset vistas, when Dalton walked over to join them.

"Dr. Orion, it's good to see you again," Detective Jensen said standing to shake his hand. "Sorry it's under the circumstances." Introducing her partner she added, "This is Detective Barret Raleigh."

"Good to see you again Detective Jensen and nice to meet you Detective Raleigh," Dalton said taking a seat at the bar area. "Any luck with the investigation?"

"Based on the latest evidence turned up we believe we're dealing with multiple homicides and that the explosion aboard the *Kanaloa* was no accident but an intentional act in which you may have been the primary target. We've been going over some of the forensic evidence retrieved from the recovery efforts. The video surveillance was mostly damaged or destroyed but one image in particular that we were able to enhance turned up something interesting."

Detective Raleigh powered up his smart device revealing an image of two figures approaching Dalton from behind as he was about to enter the aft stairwell. The individual dressed in a dark navy NORA technician shirt was brandishing some type of unknown weapon in his right hand about to strike Dalton from behind with a second individual reaching out a hand as if to thwart the blow. Dalton clearly recognized one of the individuals as that of Emrick. A spine-tingling sensation went down his back as the dawn of realization swept over him.

Detective Jensen interjected, "Dr. Orion do you know of anyone working with NORA that would desire to harm you?"

Dalton was incredulous as he swept his hand through his hair startled by this latest revelation. Shaken from the thoughts spinning in his head he mind-numbingly replied with slight trepidation, "No. No! I don't even recognize the man in the image." Dalton wasn't sure how much to divulge at this point so he decided not to disclose any interactions with Emrick.

"We have run several digital scans and recently met with Sally Minder with NORA's Department of Human Resources. There are no employees currently working with NORA matching the individual's description based on the rear profile. All souls have been accounted for with the exception of the two individuals pictured here. The only thing that seems clear from this image is that the individual behind your assailant saved you from a pretty bad concussion or worse."

Detective Raleigh zoomed in closely to the right side of the assailant's neck, "And then there is this interesting tattoo that we believe is some kind of possible gang symbol. Have you ever seen a tattoo like this before?"

Dalton leaned in closer to get a better look at the pixelated image and then sat back. "It's a sigil."

"A what?" Detective Jensen asked.

"A sigil or symbol dating back to at least the 9th century BC during the reign of Ahab, the northern king of Israel. A sigil is considered to have magical power over a demonic entity and was commonly used by occult members or magicians to call forth and control a demonic spirit by using the demon's sign."

Detective Raleigh was already busy pulling up the term on Wikipedia and jumped in before Dalton could finish, "The term sigil derives from the Latin sigillum, meaning 'seal', though it may also be related to the Hebrew סגולה (segula meaning 'word, action, or item of spiritual effect, talisman'). The current use of the term is derived from Renaissance magic, which was in turn inspired by the magical traditions of antiquity."

"Yes, but this sigil with the black sun and daggers is one of three attributed to the Order of Baal, an ancient order of angelic assassins dating back to the prophets of Baal who the prophet Elijah challenged, confronted, and defeated on Mount Carmel. This sigil with the black sun surrounded by daggers denotes demonic assassin and is one of three different types of sigils associated with the Order of Baal," Dalton said drawing from his theological background.

"Are you saying the figure in this image is a demon?" Detective Raleigh asked in disbelief.

"I'm not saying anything. I'm just interpreting symbols based on legend and lore from antiquity. The Order of Baal was an elite group of assassins similar to that of the Knights Templar, the Christian military order during the Middle Ages. Comprised of religious assassins loyal to Satan, many within the Order of Baal were believed to be fallen angels clothed in mortal flesh. These elite warriors existed for the sole purpose of assassinating vessels of God whether angel or mortal, who were charged with thwarting Satan's primary objective in commencing Armageddon, the end of days. The second sigil in the unholy triangle of Baal is the symbol of the dark sun encircled by swords pointing outward in all directions signifying chaos. The third sigil is that of the dark sun encircled by a lightning bolt symbolizing the reaper or bringer of death."

"Ok, you've totally lost me," Detective Raleigh interjected. "How does magic and the controlling of demons come into play?"

"Glad you asked," Dalton said as he began to passionately articulate a part of his former academic life that had remained dormant for over a decade. "Things get even more fantastical and interesting as you examine the magical training books called grimoires, the books of the ancient magicians. Probably one of the more notable of the ancient magicians was King Solomon. *The Sefer Raziel,* a magical text of esoteric knowledge attributed to the angel Raziel, discloses that Solomon was heir to *The Book of Mysteries* enabling him to become the source of all wisdom."

"Wait a minute," Detective Raleigh said trying to follow along. "Are you telling me that King Solomon in the Bible was a magician?"

"Yes, but not a magician like you're thinking in the David

Copperfield sense. No, Solomon was privy to an esoteric knowledge that made him perhaps the greatest of all magicians. Legend and lore surrounding Solomon's ability to master the magic arts to summon angels and command demons is not found in the biblical text. In texts of antiquity such as the apocryphal *Testament of Solomon, Odes of Solomon, Psalms of Solomon,* and the *Wisdom of Solomon,* you will read some pretty fascinating lore regarding the adventures of Solomon and his command of wisdom and secret knowledge to rule both the natural and spiritual realms."

"I always imagined Solomon to be this wise king who mainly mediated the affairs of Israel with judicial fairness based on uncanny common sense knowledge and insight," Detective Raleigh said. "You know, the wise king with a very large harem of women."

"And then there was that part of his life as well," Dalton said light-heartedly.

"But there is a whole other side of Solomon that we do not encounter in the biblical text of 1 Kings. Solomon was a prominent figure in early Christian lore appearing on amulets, talismans, and lintels, and invoked in incantations for the purpose of protecting against and casting out demons."

"Wait a minute," Detective Raleigh interrupted. "I thought early Christians invoked the name of Jesus to command demonic spirits."

"Before you get too worked up Detective Raleigh, let me remind you that we're dealing with legend, myth, and early Christian and Jewish lore. In Islamic lore, Solomon is a master of the Djinn or supernatural creatures. He is viewed as the greatest of world rulers, a true apostle and messenger of Allah. Just as John the Baptist was a foreshadowing or forerunner of the coming of the Messiah so Solomon is viewed as an exemplar of Muhammad."

Detective Jensen's wheels were spinning intrigued by Dalton's intimate knowledge with the occult and ancient sigils. Sensing that he may know more about the mystery surrounding the destruction of the *Kanaloa* than he was letting on she asked, "Dr. Orion, how do you know so much about this Order of Baal?"

Detective Raleigh had already run a thorough background check of his own and answered before Dalton could respond. "Because Dr. Orion received a PhD in Theology from Duke University with an area of concentration in the esoteric writings of ancient cultures. Basically a primer in Demonology."

"How ironic," Detective Jensen responded casually. "You have an interesting academic background that is certainly diverse. Any idea then about the tattoo on our mysterious assailant and why he seemingly wanted to harm you?"

"Not a clue," Dalton said mystified by the image while processing the implications.

"Do you think this could be an occult related ritual?" Detected Raleigh asked.

"Anything is possible. The sigil certainly suggests the possibility. The magical training books I mentioned earlier known as grimoires, well the most notable of them is, *The Greater Key of Solomon*. Another less well known grimoire is *The Lesser Key of Solomon*. Within these texts as well as others, we learn that the magical seal for Solomon was often depicted in a pentagram or hexagram shape."

"Hold on a minute," Detective Raleigh butted in again. "Isn't the pentagram an occult symbol for the Devil?"

"Well that's where things get really interesting," Dalton answered. "The *Testament of Solomon*, a pseudepigraphon written between the first and third centuries, mentions a legendary tale in which Solomon builds the Temple of Jerusalem by commanding a legion of demons. It is said that when Solomon prayed to God for help to build the Temple, God answered with the gift of a magic ring brought to him by the archangel Raphael. The ring, engraved with the pentalpha (5-pointed star), possessed the power to subdue all demons. By knowing the sigil or true name of a demonic entity, Solomon was able to exercise a measure of control over the demon. Due in no small part to the unparalleled wisdom granted to Solomon he became the greatest master magician, even able to command demons. Thus the Satanic symbol of the pentagram or hexagram was attributed to Solomon as his magical seal also referred to as the Great Pentacle of Solomon."

"That's preposterous," Detective Raleigh said incredulously. "I mean come on, building the holy of holies with the labor of demons."

"Depends on how you choose to look at it. I kind of find it ironic that demons are forced to build the very bastion of Light on earth that is dedicated to their own demise. Kind of like having to dig one's own grave."

"And whatever became of this magical ring with the power to

subdue demons?"

"No one knows what happened to the ring of Solomon. Some among those who believe in the ancient legend think the ring was slipped off the finger of Solomon during his sleep by one of his foreign wives and given to the demon lord Abaddon who swiftly descended within the bowels of Hell where it is hidden safely away from the reach of the Light."

Dalton took a sip from the glass of water the bartender had brought out. "Look, I know the legends and lore from extra biblical sources sound absurd and I'm not saying I believe any of it myself. But the simple fact of the matter is that the Bible also contains many fantastical tales which people for centuries have accepted without reservation. It was the church father Athanasius who in 367 AD first presented the 66 books that comprise the biblical canon. He asserted that the 66 books of the Bible are the only recognized writings to be read in a church service. Churches, councils, and synods over time gradually accepted the list of 66 books as inspired by God and authoritative. And even then there has not been a universal consensus over the canonical books with many apocryphal writings excluded. The only books upon which there is a general consensus are the five books of the Pentateuch, a Hebrew word meaning 'Law'."

"If anything, you can count on religious leaders to unite around LAW," Detective Raleigh added sarcastically.

Detective Jensen couldn't help but contribute her bit of social commentary, "And other religions are not much different than the

Christian religion. Look at Islam. The Middle East is embroiled in turmoil, anarchy, and war. And what over? Religion. It's all lunacy. Death and religion are like a happily married couple and it doesn't appear that they're getting divorced anytime soon. There's just too much passionate love-making going on between the two for any chance of that happening in the foreseeable future."

Dalton chuckled in agreement as he took another sip of water. The cool evening breeze was blowing into the bar area. Outside tiki torches illuminated the well-manicured landscape as the sun began setting over the Pacific. He felt a stirring within like something otherworldly was tugging at his core opening his thoughts to a realm of the Spirit that he had relegated to myth and legend. But the image of the assailant approaching him from behind with the sigil on his neck dealt a crack in his wall of doubt and disbelief.

"Ok, so Solomon commanded a legion of demons in building the Temple," Detective Raleigh said rousing Dalton from his thoughts. "You mentioned a *Book of Mysteries* and an angel named Raziel. What are the implications, if any, for our unknown persons of interest?"

"I'm not sure what the connection is," Dalton said. "According to legend after the fall of Adam and Eve when they ate of the forbidden fruit from the Tree of Knowledge in the Garden of Eden, God sent the angel Raziel to teach Adam the spiritual laws of nature and life on earth, including the knowledge of the planets, stars and the spiritual laws of creation. Legend has it that Adam was driven into a Cave of Treasures by God where he was tormented by dark spirits chief among them being Satan. He became conflicted and was driven mad by the knowledge of good and evil where a civil war of sorts raged within his soul; never able to make peace by fully giving himself to either the Light or Darkness. Some adherents of the ancient legend say that Adam never died but still roams the earth as a tormented soul revealing himself during times of great upheaval tilting the balance between good and evil, for which side he fights one can never be quite sure. Some say he has the power to shapeshift into a black wolf that stealthily stalks among the misty moors. Still some say that he is the shadow walker, progenitor of Dracula; the recipient of a divine curse feeding off the blood of mortals lurking in the shadows and the haunt of catacombs and tombs. Eastern myth and legend has it that he is the first vampire among mortals the one referred to as the horseleech in Proverbs 30:14-16. The Hebrew word for horseleech is 'alukah' and in Aramaic means, "bloodsucker'. Many believe him to be an appellation of hell, a bloodthirsty demon. A formidable foe of both the Darkness and the Light depending on his disposition at any given time, he possesses powers feared by both angel and mortal alike."

"Ok, this is getting deep. So basically a strong possibility that we may be dealing with some type of occult activity," Detective Jensen speculated.

"Either that or demons are walking among us in flesh and blood," Detective Raleigh said making a joke of the whole hocus pocus religious nonsense.

Dalton gave a half-hearted laugh in response as he took another swallow of his water gazing out the windowless dining area toward the setting sun and the encroaching darkness.

"So what about this second individual?" Detective Jensen asked pointing to the person behind the assailant. "Have you ever met him before and ideas on why he was aboard the *Kanaloa*?"

Dalton felt the urge to at least come clean about his initial encounter on the beach with Emrick but resisted the temptation to divulge anything further until he knew more himself. "I first met him on the beach after the explosion. He rescued me as well as many others on the ship. I'm not sure why he was on board at the time. He said his name was Emrick."

"Do you know how we can find him?" Detective Raleigh asked.

"I don't. I assume he lives somewhere around Kaua'i."

"I'm not sure where that leaves us gentleman," Detective Jensen said rising to get up. "We have a missing person of interest with another one we know little about or where he lives. Dr. Orion, if you come across this Emrick again please let us know so we can bring him in for questioning. He could be an important piece to helping us solve this enigmatic puzzle."

"I'll do that," Detective Jensen. "I appreciate all that you're both doing to get to the bottom of this tragedy. I lost some close friends on the *Kanaloa*. If I come across anything of significance you both will be the first to know."

"In the meantime Dr. Orion, be extra vigilant as your life may still be in danger," Detective Raleigh said. "Not to further alarm you but we can assign an evening police surveillance if that will help you feel safer."

"I appreciate the thoughtful gesture but it's not me that I'm worried about. It's the innocent lives that have already been lost that concerns me. If I could trade places with them I would in a minute. I would rather all available resources may be utilized in apprehending those responsible for this senseless crime. If I think of something else that may benefit your investigation I will let you know that as well."

"Thank you Dr. Orion for your time this evening," Detective Jensen said as Dalton stood up. "I'm so sorry that you are having to deal with this right now. Here's my card. Call me if you come across this Emrick or think of anything else that may be of help."

"Will do. Thanks again for all that you're both doing. I'll be leaving in a few days for Charleston on what will hopefully be a short-term reassignment."

"We know," Detective Raleigh replied. "We have resources on the ground in Charleston who can readily find you if needed."

Dalton wasn't so sure how to take the remark but let it pass. "Good night," Dalton said as he casually strolled out of the *Beach House* restaurant.

Watching Dalton walk out, Detective Raleigh asked, "Do you think he knows more than he's letting on?"

"I'm not sure," Detective Jensen replied. "He's a tough one to read. Although he appears troubled I'm not positive if it stems from feeling in some way responsible either directly or indirectly for the deaths of his colleagues or from a memory trigger. His wife and son were killed in a terrorist attack in Israel nearly ten years ago."

"Yes, I know. Their deaths and the resulting PTSD is well

documented in his personnel file. Damn. Death seems to follow this guy around," Detective Raleigh replied.

"It certainly appears so."

CHAPTER 17

EMPYREAN: HEAVEN UNDER SIEGE

The ghostly light of the moon escaped a breaking cloud cover casting its illumination upon the jadite green home. Emrick and Soren canvased the area surrounding Dalton's house. The home appeared unmolested with the exception of an unsecured white plantation shutter that clattered in the gentle wind. The grounds were peaceful enough as the Coconut Palms flanking both sides of the quaint island home swayed in the evening breeze.

The evening calm was a little too quiet for Emrick. The stridulating sounds of crickets and katydids were noticeably absent as if something had arrested their attention silencing their revelry. Concealed from sight by thick lush foliage, Emrick looked down from an elevated hillside position taking in a sweeping view of Dalton's property and the surrounding landscape. Soren remained vigilant flanking the opposite side of the home.

Emrick decided to break cover stepping out into the clearing as he proceeded to cross the open and well-manicured lawn leading up to the lanai. Reaching the steps, Emrick felt a fluctuation in the air emanating from his right flank. Realizing he was being watched as he'd hoped, he walked up and reached out his hand to touch the door. Acutely sensitive to vibrations and movements from inside he was unable to detect disruption of air movement from within the den and kitchen area. He walked toward the right side of the lanai to Dalton's bedroom window. Lightly touching the exterior glass, Emrick did not detect an intruder present inside the bedroom. He did detect, however; the vibrating energy of the sword concealed within the secured wall vault behind Dalton's bedroom armoire. As if communicating to Emrick, the sword warned of dark energy in close proximity. He decided to risk vulnerability as tempting bait to draw out the assailants.

Spotting a rocking chair on the lanai, Emrick entertained a scheming thought as a mischievous grin broke across his face. Taking a seat he began enjoying a rhythmic rock in a bold move to taunt the Dark Ones into breaking silence and reveal themselves.

The moon was hanging full unobstructed and casting a wild light upon the premises. Emrick utilized the rocking sounds to mask the bio sonar ultrasound signals he emitted seeking to localize and lock onto any distinct sounds associated with angelic beings. Just like echolocation used by bats to hunt, Emrick was especially adept at using his skills of echolocation in total darkness to detect and isolate a combatant.

Emrick was adept at identifying a target(s) of interest, determine whether mortal or immortal, hone in on its location and proximity to his position, and perceive whether an imminent threat or not. He used a variety of different methods to emit ultrasounds whereas in this case a simple tapping of his finger on the arm of the rocking chair sufficed.

Rocking Emrick closed his eyes and drifted into a relaxed meditative state remaining keenly attuned to his surroundings. Drawing upon the Spirit he immersed himself in the positive energy quickening and filling him with an overwhelming peace. His relationship with the Spirit was as natural as breathing.

A tranquil expression swept over his face as Emrick rocked back and forth as if he didn't have a care in the world, seemingly oblivious to any potential threat. The tropical breeze began to stir blowing in from the Hanalei Bay bringing with it a refreshing coolness. Only the gentle rhythmic rocking of Emrick's chair could be heard. An energy from the Light began to swirl emanating a blue astral aura around Emrick as the awen of life began flowing serenely within.

As Emrick eased deeper into a peaceful meditative state, he latched onto a memory that quickly arrested his thoughts.

ψ

Within his spirit he transported to a world where light radiated with such intense brilliance. Majestic mountainous peaks awash in emerald splendor towered over the celestial city of Empyrean. Interspersed among the soaring peaks were thunderous waterfalls dropping a deluge of water in the azure blue river below feeding into the great Empyrean Ocean.

Walking across a massive bridge made of pearl soaring nearly a thousand feet high with luminous supporting azure blue arch ways beneath, Emrick enjoyed a leisurely stroll across a transparent bridge enabling unobstructed views of the River of Life coursing beneath shimmering in hues of azure and turquoise.

A massive winged dragon with crimson and black scales swooped down in the breeze as it descended toward the river below. *Odd,* Emrick thought. Looking down from the celestial bridge, he noticed a school of multi-colored dolphins leaping in the water not in their usual playful manner but more in an erratic pattern as if something were amiss. Sitting along the banks were Merangels; half fish and half angel. Sensing Emrick's presence the Merangels regarded him with a respectful bow of their heads. Upon seeing the winged dragon the merangels leapt into the water quickly emptying the banks.

Continuing along he approached the city of enchanting wonders with walls made of pearl glistening milky white in the pristine light. Nearing the enormous gates at the entrance to the Celestial City, Emrick was greeted by enormous seventy-five feet high gates made of blue topaz with two statues made of translucent diamonds. One statue was that of a lion and the other of a lamb. The luminescent light that radiated from all around permeated the diamond as if animating both statues. The two diamond creatures appeared to give a respectful nod as the majestic gates thundered open.

Tall marble columns with streaks of sapphire and emerald lined the entrance walkway leading into a great open square with gushing water fountains in the center. With each step Emrick took the transparent gold floor gleamed. Greeted by two angels donning breastplates of crimson and black attire, he smiled placing a fist to his chest as a show of solidarity in the Light. The gesture was not returned. *Strange,* Emrick thought.

About twenty off to the side of the Colonnade walkway was a collage of murals upon the interior wall with animated images morphing periodically among a variety of scenic vistas from the seven kingdoms that comprised the Kingdom of Heaven. The mural images were real time depictions of the actual elements and energy temperament within each kingdom.

One image quickly arrested his attention as a graphic scene of darkness and fire among a smoking landscape belonging to the Kingdom of Primora appeared. Primora was located on the far reaching celestial border of Empyrean. Stepping closer to the morphing mural on the great wall a low rumbling seemed to be coming from the great volcano within the moving image.

Emrick's angelic senses began to quicken as he felt a strange sensation he never before had experienced. A dark energy began pulsating as the mural began to shimmer in hues of crimson, black, red, and orange as storms erupted violently ravaging the kingdom in a hail of fire and brimstone. Primora's tropical and lush landscape began withering morphing into a volatile climate. The balance of energy was catastrophically shifting as light began to give way to darkness.

Drawing upon the Spirit he calmed the restlessness that was welling up within his core. Closing his eyes he tried to relax the energy surging within him. A calmness swept over him as the energy of Light began to relax him. Opening his eyes he beheld a fierce black dragon emerge from the volcanic crater with a gaze that seemed to bore into him as if reaching for his deepest most inner thoughts. The black dragon reared back its head unleashing a mighty roar that thundered across the heavens like a sonic boom. Darkness enveloped the dragon as a powerful volcanic eruption spewed flaming ash into the air. The mural faded to black leaving only an arresting dark void.

Emrick's thoughts began to whirl with possible meaning and implications. The dawn of realization assaulted him unmercifully as fear began pummeling his core. An outside consciousness began scratching at the wall of his mind. He was fully aware of the source that was reaching out to him as he allowed access to his thoughts.

"Sariel."

"Yes, Father."

"A dark and devouring evil has arisen fomenting rebellion against the Light."

"How can this be possible? What is the source of this dark power?"

"Not what but who. Darkness has fully possessed one among the Council of Light. The one who next speaks your name is the one in whom the Darkness controls. Restrain your emotions and resist fear. The Light will be your strength."

The voice of the Creator reverberated within as Emrick was left reeling from the revelation. Confusion and turmoil tugged within as he could not imagine who among the angelic order would even consider much less embrace the Darkness.

Stirred from his thoughts, Emrick's attention turned to the

growing sound of approaching footsteps. Resisting the urge to turn and look, Emrick found himself cringing within from the foreboding anticipation of who among his brothers had betrayed the Light. Mounting fear began to well up as he began to sense who was behind the rebellion.

"Sariel. I've been looking for you."

Emrick knew the voice well and slowly turned to look upon his fallen brother. For the first time in his angelic existence a mist began welling up in his eyes as an unnatural emotion of sadness engulfed him, a virgin emotion he had never experienced. Gazing upon Satariel he felt an upwelling of anger mixed with compassion as Darkness and Light began wrestling within his spirit. "What have you done brother?"

Seeing Sariel's eyes suddenly tearing while beginning to morph into deep blue sapphire gave Satariel a moment of pause as he was about to lift his fist to his chest the feign the sign of solidarity with the Light. Shifting his gaze, Satariel noticed the mural of Primora which revealed a pitch black void.

Realizing that his deceptive masquerade had been exposed, Satariel took a slow step back as the smile on his face quickly gave way to a menacing expression. "Sariel, today is the day of our liberation. Exercise your free will and join us in standing against our Father's reckless sovereignty."

"Satariel, you have partaken of the forbidden dark energy and its clouded your judgment. You know not of what you speak. We ARE exercising our free will by standing in our Father's Light, the Light of our Creator. Do you realize the implications of what you're doing? Judgment will be swift as all of Empyrean will rise against you. Turn from this dark madness before it's too late."

"Sariel, your loyalty to Father really is heart-warming but unfortunately it has blinded you to the discontent and disparity that exists among our kind. You are a fool if you think I stand alone in the pursuit to make things right once again."

Sariel could hardly believe what he was hearing. Past memories began to flood his consciousness of conversations, observations, and disparaging remarks made by Satariel that Sariel had merely brushed aside as the musings of his outspoken, passionate brother. But there had never been any question regarding Satariel's allegiance to the Creator. Never had Sariel entertained the slightest notion that Satariel was flirting with thoughts of open rebellion.

"Not loyalty but love, brother. For loyalty is born of love. And when did we start speaking in terms of our kind? The Kingdom of Eden is and ever shall have a rightful place among the seven kingdoms of Heaven. Your misplaced pride has given you a false sense of power and authority. Your word is empty and devoid of meaning apart from the Word of the Creator. Your dalliance with the Darkness has only served to sow seeds of destruction."

Satariel replied mockingly, "Are you oblivious to what is happening around us? Eden threatens the very essence of Empyrean. The Ancient Ones have stood along with me in declaring, 'Do not create man!' And yet Father did just that but not before disregarding our counsel and wisdom. Man represents a rival to who we are, a threat to the purity of our kind, and a flawed creation given dominion over the Seventh Kingdom. Mark my words, man will give rise to a race of infidels that will usurp our sovereignty. A third of the Council voted against the creation of man."

"Our sovereignty?!" Sariel challenged. "Only the Creator is Sovereign. You speak as if you have been baptized in the dark energy," Sariel said as the dawn of realization came over him. "What have you done, brother?"

The confrontation and verbal exchange was beginning to draw attention from several onlookers walking past the cascading fountains. Undeterred by the unsolicited attention, Satariel continued to foment his dark rationale to Sariel. "Now is the time at the dawn of its creation to bring Eden under our dominion with our superior powers. You and I can rule as gods and establish ourselves as sovereigns over the Kingdom of Heaven."

Satariel's dark purpose began to crystalize for Sariel. Discerning his malevolent intent and dark plan he stepped forward while calculating his next move, "You know there is only One Sovereign and can only be one sovereign over the Kingdom of Heaven. The Council of Light will not support your dark cause. And as for Eden, the only darkness that resides there is that which you plan to bring to it. Do you really think man will reject the Creator for an inferior counterfeit?"

Swatting Sariel's objectionable words aside Satariel arrogantly exclaimed, "Man will give rise to the humankind who will worship us as gods!"

"There is only one problem with your demented plan Satariel. Even if all would follow you, I will never deny Father, OUR Creator. Even if darkness was to infest all of Empyrean the Light inside of me will burn an eternal flame until all is made right again. In your reckless desire for adulation you infect Heaven with your religion in an effort to win adulation worthy of the Creator alone."

"Yes, religion will exalt us among the humankind as we rule over their hearts and elicit praise from their lips. We were created for this! The humankind will be weak and pliable. They will fall easily enough and will worship us as the true Progenitors of all that is and shall be. We will make them into what we would have them be. The purpose of our existence is to be like the Creator and to rule as such. We become lesser of ourselves with each idle passing moment as the Creator continues without consent nor constraint to imagine and create new worlds, new kingdoms, new beings. If we do not act now, as ONE, we will rue the day that the infidel race came into existence."

Sariel felt a rising indignation as the self-aggrandizing words spewed forth from Satariel's cold, calculating thoughts. It was painfully apparent that he was fully consumed by dark energy and that in his current state, no amount of reasoning would deter his dark passions. A conflict between the Darkness and the Light was inevitable, it would only be a matter of which side proved strongest.

A voice began to stir within Sariel as the Spirit of the Creator swept into his thoughts. Sariel began to speak saying, "Satariel, firstborn among the angelkind, when did you lose faith and forsake your first love? You, who once shined brightest among us. Your passion for the Light burning ever strong. A stalwart voice of wisdom among the Council of Light. And yet you pushed aside love to embrace insecurity. You greedily clamored for more becoming discontent with what you were given. You chose restlessness over rest. You abandoned the Light for the Darkness. Your fall from the Light will become a dark symbol of evil among all creation and your name will become synonymous with sorrow, shame, and sacrilege. Your path along with those who follow will lead only to eternal death."

Seething in anger as he discerned the source of Sariel's words, Satariel's eyes transmuted from an emerald green to a red crimson with fiery yellowish orange irises that wrapped around pupils black as onyx. With a tremendous force of power, Satariel unleashed a crushing blow with the flat of his hand into Sariel sending him crashing into the black mural wall of Primora behind him. Dropping to the floor with a jarring thud, Sariel remained momentarily dazed in a state of disbelief and shock.

A calming presence flooded his core as the Spirit of Light began to flow within as the Creator's voice spoke to his spirit, "Be still. Feel my power flow through you. I will be your shield and my strength your own. No created power will prevail against you. Rise now in the power of Light."

Feeling a surge of power never before experienced, Sariel looked up and beheld the maniacal grin of Satariel who was basking in his dark power. Suddenly an intense and luminescent energy began surging within Sariel as he slowly stood to his feet and with the sheer power of his mind he unleashed a force of Light from his hand that sent Satariel hurtling through one of the massive colonnade pillars and careening into the fountain pool.

Dropping the cocky expression from his face, Satariel quickly leapt out of the fountain pool performing a backward somersault landing on the second floor balcony of the colonnade. Looking down with a scornful glare and derision in his voice Satariel said, "It is inevitable. Heaven WILL fall. The darkness will swarm Empyrean as my power grows. Darkness is coming and with it the Light of the Creator will diminish and eventually be extinguished. You can't stop what has already begun. And I shall begin with Eden."

Stepping to his side on both his left and right stood Abaddon of the Order of Powers and Paimon of the Order of Dominions. They both lifted their fists to their forehead as a show of solidarity with Satariel. Like an unfathomable nightmare, Sariel could not believe what he was witnessing. The open arrogance and defiant display of rebellion against the Creator infuriated him.

"Oh, and before we depart BROTHER," Satariel spat sarcastically. "Abaddon as well as the ENTIRE Order of Powers stand with me in aligning ourselves against the Creator. Paimon was able to do an extraordinary job of inspiring a vast majority of the Dominions. And our recruits grow by the hour."

Dark energy began seeping within Sariel as he felt an overwhelming almost uncontrollable desire to end Satariel's wretched existence. Stepping onto the walkway between the massive columns along the Colonnade, his piercing sapphire eyes were illuminating with greater intensity as he held Satariel's gaze. Suddenly to his right a tremendous blast tore through the Colonnade catapulting Sariel against the towering gates to the entrance of the city. The force of his impact propelled the massive gates open.

Rattled from the blast Sariel made to get up but was quickly apprehended by four angels loyal to Satariel who wasted no time in seizing upon Sariel's disorientation casting him over the bridge. *So much for being still,* Sariel thought as he hurtled downward at breakneck speed bracing himself for the crushing impact upon the watery surface as he plummeted like a crashing boulder hitting the raging river that felt like an unforgiving concrete wall.

Sariel found himself succumbing to the clawing darkness that seemed to infect even the life-giving waters of the River of Life. Resisting the desire to succumb to the dark current that was pulling him downward into a watery abyss, Sariel cast off the dark energy and began swimming toward the light. Breaking the surface another massive explosion shook the towering walls of the celestial city as a ball of fire erupted. Several angels were cast down and into the river. Others were fleeing in fear across the bridge heading for the safety of Empyrean's mountainous forest beyond.

ψ

The Spirit suddenly quickened him as the vision of the flaming walls of Empyrean and bobbing motion of his body in the water coalesced with his mortal awareness and the rhythmic rocking of the chair.

Emrick opened his eyes as they quickly transmuted from a luminous sapphire hue to a soft blue with his black pupils adjusting to the lack of light.

Remaining calm and motionless, Emrick was filled with conflicting emotions inside. The Spirit was awakening him to the import of the mission at hand. The emergence of the Sword of Eden was a sign of the Age of Armageddon that was dawning upon the Kingdom of Eden. An age characterized by formidable dark powers bent on wreaking havoc upon Eden with the purpose of relentlessly and unmercifully wiping all vestiges of humanity from existence.

Emrick no longer sensed the presence of Darkness.Light suddenly flooded the lanai stemming from the bright beams of Blake's Range Rover that was pulling into the driveway.

Chapter 18

KADEN

After surviving the nightmarish ordeal on Cannons Beach and meeting with Detectives Jensen and Raleigh, Dalton's mind was reeling from the events of the past few days. Either he was experiencing bad karma or there was something more sinister at work toying with his life. He came to Kaua'i to find solace in paradise and now, like before, his world seemed to be crashing down all around him. Again.

Reflecting over the events of the past week beginning with his encounter with Lonomakua and the sacred fire sword, the massive explosions aboard the *Kanaloa*, and a near death experience on the beach, Dalton began trying to connect the dots. Todd, the assailant who almost killed him had demanded that he hand over the Sword of Eden.

Pressing Todd further after the assault, Dalton was unable to garner any insights into why Todd was willing to kill him to obtain the sword. Todd seemed genuinely clueless and didn't come across as one who in his right mind would kill anyone. It was almost as if something had taken complete control over Todd and his friend Ron. That would imply demon possession, a possibility that Dalton rationally struggled. There was a time in his life when he ardently believed in angels and demons but that was before the terrorist attack. But now, the possibility of an existing spiritual realm with warring angels and demonic spirits was beginning to materialize in his physical world imposing a harsh reality.

And then there was Emrick and Soren. They were conveniently present during each crisis. For nearly ten years, Dalton had trained his mind to doubt God and accept the madness of life. He found life easier to deal with when not taking it too seriously. Bad things are going to happen. Love ones die tragically and no amount of faith is going to change the inevitable. He had come to believe that God is about as inclined to prevent a tragedy than a baby is changing its own diaper. Adopting a cynical attitude, Dalton espoused the viewpoint, "Crap is going to happen. It's just a matter of whose going to clean it up."

Dalton had come to believe that religion, especially organized religion, was nothing but a psych ward for the emotionally unstable seeking a support group to wallow in their shared misery. Religion is the culprit for the great many evils that plague the world. A world without religion would be a world well on its way to realizing sanity and lasting peace. So Dalton had come to believe.

Although his mind was reeling from thoughts and questions, his body desperately beckoned for sleep. There were only a few hours before the breaking of dawn and hopefully the new day would bring with it answers to his mystifying questions. Finally able to drift off, Dalton fell into a fitful sleep that only served to unleash haunting memories that had been lurking within his sub-consciousness.

ψ

It was picture perfect day without a cloud in the sky. A few seagulls soared overhead scavenging land and sea for food. Walking down the beach on Sullivan's Island, South Carolina, Dalton carried his son Kaden on his shoulders. Nearly inseparable, the two were always embroiled in a salt life adventure ever searching for pirate gold, magical artifacts, and enchanting sea creatures that often emerged from their colorful imaginations.

"Dad, what do you think heaven is like?" Kaden asked while bouncing along upon Dalton's shoulder's as they enjoyed a leisurely stroll along the beach on a lazy summer day. "Heaven is paradise. Everything is perfect there."

"Are there any bad people in heaven?"

"No. Heaven is a place where angels and good people spend eternity loving God and each other."

"What about angels? Are they ever bad and get timeouts?"

Dalton chuckled at the question. "The angels in heaven are perfect beings who love God and protect people like you and me."

Kaden answered, "Dad, I want to be an angel."

"Well, I'm sure the angels in heaven would be honored to have you. But right now you're my shishle and I'm not sharing."

"We will always be shishles Dad – bestest buds in the whole wide world!" Kaden exclaimed reaching out his arms in a wide arc.

"You bet! Always. Forever. And then some." Dalton rejoined.

For seven wonderful years Dalton and Kaden were joined at the hip; where one went the other was almost certainly nearby. They both were die-hard members of the Daddy's Club with mom having to ask permission to join club outings. And when necessary Lauren would remind them both that there wouldn't be a Daddy's Club without her. It was her ace card that always resonated with Kaden allowing her to participate in the illustrious Daddy's Club. Those were the good times that Dalton treasured more than anything else.

ψ

Dalton awakened calling out to "Kaden" in hopeful expectation knowing full well it was only a dream. For one brief nostalgic moment, Dalton felt whole again and then like a shooting star that lances across the heavens, the feeling of elation vanished replaced with only a soul-crushing pang of grief. His haunting dreams were always bitter sweet. But with the passing of time Lauren and Kaden's visitations in his dreams became less frequent making it even more painful not knowing when he would see them again.

In terms of coping, Dalton found the dreams to be more disheartening than comforting. The waking part was the nightmare for Dalton. How often he wished he could drift off into a dream with Lauren and Kaden never to wake again.

Sitting up on his bed and looking out the bedroom window, Dalton felt as if his heart was going to implode from anger, resentment, and powerlessness. He had needed someone to direct his anger and resentment so for nearly ten years that someone was God.

Getting up Dalton walked over to the armoire and opened the secret vault. He removed the sword hilt and gripped it while turning it around in his hand looking admiringly at the intricate craftsmanship while thinking to himself, *Whoever forged you certainly had quite an imagination.*

Walking out onto the lanai, Dalton kept turning the sword hilt over in his hand as it seemed to energize him like multiple hits from energy drinks and loads of coffee all in one. The light of a huge pale moon gently caressed the hilt as the emerald stone glistened absorbing the light. The etching of a tree and what looked like a river made of turquoise seemed to move in the moon light. Dalton felt a sense of wonderment as he held the sword hilt aloft in his hand. The exquisite craftsmanship was overlaid by a smooth transparent surface providing a comfortable grip.

Dalton recalled the vision he experienced in the sea cavern of the sword blazing in emerald fire and how he had become so transfixed by its beautiful power. A voice suddenly startled him from his fascination.

"A thing of beauty isn't it?"

Quickly turning, Dalton gave out a sigh of relief upon seeing Emrick leaning against the rail along the wraparound lanai. "Geez, you about gave me a heart attack," Dalton said as his pulse was racing from the sudden adrenaline rush.

"My apologies, I didn't mean to startle you."

"It's ok. I'm just a bit jumpy after everything that has happened here of late. What are you doing here anyway?"

"I thought it best to keep watch in case trouble comes knocking."

"A nice gesture considering everything that has happened here of late," Dalton replied.

"You appear to be holding it together under the circumstances."

Dalton turned away and looked out toward the black shape of the Na Pali mountainside draped mostly in darkness except for its peak illumined by the moon's light. "Looks can be deceiving. The troubling events of the past week have opened old wounds and my dreams are fraught with painful memories."

Emrick stirred by compassion and understanding replied, "Pain is a path that leads to healing."

"Not this kind of pain," Dalton was quick to assert.

Sensing Dalton's emotional need to share the pain he had kept bottled up inside, Emrick prodded, "And what is the pain of which you speak?"

"The kind you never want to experience."

"You must be referring to the love you have for someone close to you."

"Yes, a love that can never be replaced once lost," Dalton said as he became increasingly sullen.

"I too know of this kind of love and understand your sense of solace among the beauty and serenity of this place. But love can never be lost. Not if it's truly love. Love is born of the seed of creation. It can only grow for it can never die."

"Then you know not of the love of which I speak. The kind that rips your heart out and leaves you barren and without a sense of orientation." Dalton gripped the hilt of the sword more firmly continuing, "I lost my wife, my son, and my soul. They were my compass and now I am adrift among a sea of pain. But I manage," Dalton said with a callousness to his voice. "I try my best to forget as forgetting is liberating. But my dreams refuse to allow it."

Emrick sensed the deluge of pent up emotions that had been festering and poisoning his soul. The only way for Dalton to heal was for him to release the poison so that the emotional toxins could be released from his spirit. And the events of the past week were bringing Dalton to a breaking point forcing him to go to a place within himself that he had so effectively and efficiently avoided.

Dalton tried to continue but the pain and emotion became so great that the words stuck in his throat. Tears welled up in his eyes obscuring his vision. Defiantly resisting to lift his hand to clear the tears, Dalton choked back healing emotions that were desperately trying to surface as he laid siege to his anger instead speaking through gritted teeth, "I lost my wife and son to a barbaric terrorist. In a brief moment of sheer horror, I watched my very soul go up in flames. Everything precious to me was taken in that blast. And because of self-deluded religious extremists and their despicable God, my heart was ripped out replaced only with loneliness and pain."

The intensity of Dalton's emotions caused the sword hilt to transmute into a pale green energy briefly stirring to life before quickly dissipating. It happened so fast that Dalton never even noticed while gazing out toward the Na Pali coast preoccupied with his anguish.

The sword's fluctuation of power did not slip Emrick's notice. Only the chosen protector of Eden could elicit the sword's energy force. Emrick's concern now was if anyone else witnessed what had just transpired. With Dalton in his current state of enmity with God, the fate of Eden and all humankind was at incalculable risk. Emrick was well aware that the Sword of Eden could only be wielded in unfettered faith and reliance upon the Spirit by the chosen Protector. Only then could would Dalton by powerful enough to lead an army of Light comprised of Eden's Sacred Guardians and angelic forces loyal to the Creator in standing and prevailing against Satariel and his army of Darkness.

Emrick was also aware that Satariel would exploit Dalton's past in an attempt to turn him away from the Light. Operation Full Light now depended on the success of Emrick in helping Dalton to rediscover his true self and once again reclaim his faith in the Light. But one thing was certain, the Guardians of Light would need to be ever vigilant and shadow Dalton for his own protection and well-being. The Dark Ones would be seeking the opportune moment to deal a decisive blow against the Light by taking Dalton out and obtaining the Sword of Eden.

Walking over, Emrick placed a hand on Dalton's shoulder and said, "Not all is as it seems. Your heart will heal. The time will come when the sacred fire will ignite in you once again."

Dalton intentionally brushed aside Emrick's words as he wrestled with conflicting emotions. "I'm afraid that ember has grown cold and fireproof. It doesn't matter anymore. Really, I'm over it. But there is another matter that has been eating at me here of late," he said slipping into an all too familiar gray despondence.

"I'm happy to help in any way I can," Emrick said anticipating Dalton's question.

"The criminal investigation surrounding the *Kanaloa* has turned up two persons of interest." Dalton pulled up a police photo on his mobile phone and handed it to Emrick and said, "One of the individuals in this picture looks a lot like you. Is it you? And if so, why were you aboard the *Kanaloa* on the night it went down?"

Before he could respond, Emrick sensed telluric energy within close proximity and then a thud was heard on the lanai followed by a husky voice, "Oh, I think I can help clear your befuddled mind," Samael interjected casting a menacing look Dalton's way.

Stepping out from the concealment afforded by the surrounding Teak, Mahogany, and Koa trees growing off to the side of Dalton's home, Andras was holding Soren at bay with a crimson energy shield rendering him motionless.

Dalton couldn't believe what his eyes were seeing feeling paralyzed by uncertainty and fear. "Who are you?" Dalton feebly managed to utter trying to collect his wits and courage.

"It seems you are just rife with questions that your pea-sized brain just can't quite get its mortal grey matter around," Samael said dripping with sarcasm.

"And what about you?" Samael asked maniacally taunting Emrick by energizing his sword which flamed to life in brilliant crimson energy humming with power. "Do you also wonder who I am?"

Emrick weighed his options quickly sizing up the strength of his opponents. He knew he could either dance around the question or answer it directly. Never one to mince words, he chose the latter. "Oh, I know who you are. I've parlayed with your kind a time or two in my day. The more pressing question here is do you know who I am?" Emrick replied as his eyes transmuted to a brilliant sapphire blue illuminating the darkness around him.

"Make one false move and I will end Eden's hope right here and now," growled Samael.

Emrick's luminous eyes both enchanted and frightened Dalton. He stepped back as the dawn of realization cascaded over him. He suddenly felt small, inept, and helpless to do anything that would be of significance in the presence of such angelic beings. Fear, like a claw reaching out from a massive beast seemed to clutch his torso and squeeze the oxygen out of his lungs. Powerlessness washed over Dalton leaving him feeling bereft of any real ability to do anything to assuage his predicament.

Keenly attentive to every breath and hair-trigger movement of Samael's, Emrick remained calmly rooted in place calculating any potential risk to Dalton's life. "So, how is Renaud faring these days?" Emrick asked trying to provoke Samael and distract him from his primary objective.

Rage and indignation crept across Samael's face as he gazed into the eyes of the one who had vanquished his former partner aboard the *Kanaloa*. Although he had suspected but now he knew with certainty who was responsible for taking out Renaud. "You will soon share his fate as shall your mortal friend," spat Samael.

"Are you really so certain about that? You might want to think that one through to its logical conclusion based on recent events," Emrick replied keeping up the mind games.

Ever tightening his grip on his energy sword as the crimson flames began to intensify, Emrick could feel the heat cascading off Samael's sword. It would only be a few moments before he chose an object for his hated affection. Emrick was counting on that being him.

And then another voice broke from the darkness that provided the necessary distraction Emrick needed. "Hello there boys," said Sommer as she walked up the drive silent as a mouse searching for cheese almost as if she were carried on the air by the stirring trade breezes. "Starting to look a bit like Christmas around here with the red and blue neon lights shining so brightly."

Samael turned toward the sound of her voice and Emrick was upon him before he knew what happened. As if reading Emrick's thoughts, Dalton dove to the lanai allowing Emrick a direct body shot as he flew through the air like a mighty rush of wind twisting mid-air to avoid Samael's blazing sword and leveling him to the deck. Hitting the floor with a quick somersault and spinning around toward Samael, Emrick quickly assumed a defensive position for a counter.

After he hit the floor, the sword hilt on Dalton was jarred loose and scattered across the lanai. Samael turned almost instinctively as if drawn to the powerful energy fluctuation being emitted by the mythical weapon. "The Sword of Eden," Samael called out Andras as he turned back toward Emrick with renewed determination in his countenance.

Samael pointed his crimson sword toward Emrick as he slowly stepped back and bent down to retrieve the ancient weapon of Eden. "It appears that you have failed to protect the mighty Sword of Eden. Whatever will Metatron think of you now?" Trying to ignite the mythical blade of fiery energy, a look of bewilderment came over Samael as the sword hilt remained dormant.

"You guys just don't get it," Emrick said as he stepped closer only to be halted by Samael's raised sword. "The Sword of Eden was forged by God to be used against the Darkness. Its true power can only be harnessed by a chosen vessel wielding it in faith in the Light in Eden's defense."

"Stop playing games with him," Andras said while holding Soren at bay, growing increasingly impatient. "Be done with him and grab the pathetic mortal and bring the sword. He speaks lies."

The wind began to howl as the trade breezes swirled near tropical force sending several coconuts careening down and hitting Andras on the head causing him to momentarily release his energy hold on Soren. Breaking free, Soren spun and gave Andras an upper kick to the abdomen sending him crashing through the well-manicured shrubbery between two Koa trees.

"Now let's see what you got coward," Soren said releasing pent up frustration from being taken by surprise from behind. A growling sound could be heard from behind the shrubbery. Leaping through the air a huge black wolf soared with razor sharp teeth bared and eyes blazing bright as crimson fire. Shocked by the fierceness of the wolf with eyes ablaze in crimson energy — the sheer vision of the beast hound from Primora's dark abyss sent Soren doubling over backwards while attempting to avoid the wolf's vicious attack. Stumbling he hit the ground with a thud exposing his neck.

Only inches away from landing on Soren, a body tackled the wolf mid-air knocking it to the ground where the two enmeshed bodies rolled and struggled for superiority. The black wolf quickly gained the top position and was viciously trying to rip the throat out of his attacker.

Soren cast a quick glance over toward Emrick who was engaged in a furious sword engagement with Samael. Flipping off the lanai and landing only feet from Soren, Samael arched his sword and thrust downward in an attempt to end Soren's angelic existence. Before he could do so, Sommer influenced the winds and pelted him with a barrage of coconuts. It was enough to send Samael rifling through the air and fleeing the fight. Dalton was nowhere to be seen. Sommer who was standing off to the side about twenty yards back dropped her hands bringing a calm to the wind.

The black wolf was snarling and gnashing its rapier teeth while slashing sharp claws viciously at his opponent who was pinned beneath his heavy torso. Soren was about to intervene when a hand clutched down on his shoulder preventing him from doing so. It was Emrick. Taken aback, Soren was momentarily confused by Dalton's restraint.

Turning their attention to the tussle on the ground an arm extended upward clutching the wolf by the throat as emerald energy began emanating from beneath. Gripping the black wolf by the throat, Dalton elicited a force of energy sending the beast of Darkness careening through the air whereupon the wolf yelped as it hit the ground with a tremendous thud some twenty feet away. Spinning quickly around, Dalton rose up preparing for the counter which never came. The black wolf leapt up and ran quickly off into the dark valley beyond.

When Dalton looked around at the others all eyes were upon him. His aura was awash in emerald energy with eyes as emerald fire. Emrick walked over and extended a hand as Dalton reached up and took hold rising to his feet. The energy that was coursing through his body quickly waned as Dalton's countenance returned to normal. "What the hell just happened here?" Dalton asked incredulously trying to collect himself as his heart was nearly pounding out of his chest from the adrenaline rush.

"You are safe for now," Emrick replied, "but we have not heard the last from the Dark Ones." Looking to Soren he stated flatly, "The Sword of Eden has been taken."

Chapter 19

GLOBAL DOMINATION

Zurich, Switzerland

Meeting on the top floor of the DGC's twenty-five story office complex with 360 degree sweeping views of Zurich, the Board of Directors gathered with a bit of apprehension in the conference room awaiting Devin Sinclair's arrival. Many of the DGC Board of Directors meetings were handled via secure-linked holographic conferencing but due to a few complications with a recent acquisition Devin called a meeting insisting on all members to be present.

As President and Chief Executive Officer, Devin was instrumental in overseeing the rise of the DGC over the past ten years. The key to his success was an aggressive pursuit of acquisitions and mergers that served to expand the reach and influence of the DGC. And for over twenty years that's exactly what Devin did with a little known struggling military Defense company called Dynasty Manufacturing, LLC. In time with each acquisition and merger Dynasty Manufacturing morphed into Dominion Industries before giving rise to Dominion Global Corporation, the go-to-source for smart munitions and superintelligent AI systems.

Devin now had Dominion Global Corporation positioned as a global defense conglomerate and he was not about to concede defeat at the negotiation table. Never one to play second fiddle to anyone or anything, Devin possessed a "winner take all" business ethic and treated anyone who stood in the way like a pebble in his shoe to be removed and discarded.

Devin maintained a tight grip as the CEO making sure that board members either backed his play or were dealt with in such a way as to guarantee smooth sailing toward the horizon of his vision for a global monopoly of the military defense industry. With so much at stake, Devin was very efficient at holding egos in check among the various financial, political, and corporate entities.

Directors were chosen due to their impressive resumes and proven track record of being influential movers and shakers. But if a Director's influence began to wax and wane resulting in lackluster leadership, Devin had no qualms about jettisoning the dead weight and bringing fresh energy on board to achieve the desired effect.

Devin walked into the spacious and inviting opulent conference room framed by large windows which allowed ample light to filter into the room. The office walls rivalled that of an art gallery with some of the most prestigious and rare artworks on visual display. Two of Devin's favorites were those that hung on opposing sides of the room.

The *Creation of Adam* by Michelangelo, a replica of the original painting on the ceiling of the Sistine Chapel, hung by itself on the wall facing opposite of Devin's seat, an ever present reminder of his chief purpose. Just as God breathed life into Adam the progenitor of humanity, so he would breathe death into Adam and all of his progeny throughout the ages.

Hanging on the wall to Devin's back was *A Starry Night* by the Dutch artist Vincent Van Gogh featuring the village of Saint-Remy under a swirling sky. The painting evoked darkness, mystery, light, and wonder. Devin appreciated the confluence of opposing extremes in Van Gogh's painting capturing the true essence of the universe influenced and shaped by Darkness and Light. The painting evoked a sense of his singular purpose and chief aim to ensure that Eden's ultimate fate would be determined not by the Light but by the Darkness.

The twelve members of the Directorate stood as Devin confidently entered the room walking over to the high back leather chair draped in black exhibiting a huge D in the center. Stepping in front of his chair, Devin asked everyone to be seated.

"Thank you for gathering on such short notice. I will get to the point. There has been a break down in the acquisition negotiation with Genesis Corporation (Gen Corp)." A nervous fidgeting swept around the large conference table made of solid black onyx.

For effect, Devin allowed his words to sit with the Directors for a few lingering moments. Turning his attention to Fen Blockman the one charged with handling the Gen Corp negotiations, Devin continued with a sarcastic edge to his voice, "Please Fen, we are all ears to learn as to how we could've possibly dropped the ball on what I was lead to believe would be...let me see...how did you put it...'a walk in the park.'"

Fen Blockman was chosen to serve on the Board of Directors due in no small part to his expertise in Corporate Law and Business Acquisitions. As a shrewd negotiator he had enjoyed a high success rate in securing key corporate acquisitions that were instrumental in positioning the DGC as a leading global defense conglomerate.

Prior to Gen Corp, money and lofty promises had proven effective as Fen's calling card which lured in those corporations that were struggling to turn a profit among an increasingly competitive advanced military smart munitions and systems market. For these struggling companies and corporations, the DGC offered a lucrative exit for corporate executives and a way to save face.

Gen Corp proved to be a miscalculated risk that Fen did not foresee. Riding high on his prior successes, he was overly confident that Stan Winston, the President and CEO of Gen Corp would quickly buckle and accept the DGC's offer of 8.8 billion in US dollars for a corporation that was valued at half the amount but presenting a viable threat to his monopoly over the defense industry.

Gen Corp was one of those business outliers that defied conventional business norms surprising everyone with its rapid growth in less than ten years. As a rising star among the scientific research community, Gen Corp's advancements in life-enhancing technologies, promotion of responsible A.I. design and manufacturing, and the development of superior tactical systems designed to counter, disrupt, and neutralize precision-based military munitions prior to detonation, all served to ensure Gen Corp's viability and lucrative future.

Gen Corp's high ethical values and focus on conservation added to its growing appeal. Its commitment and emphasis upon eco-friendly technologies developed with a two-fold purpose of protecting lives and protecting the environment was a unique approach to utilizing nanotechnology in developing military defensive systems that served to deter minimize collateral damage and destruction.

Devin had been monitoring the successes that Gen Corp was enjoying at an accelerated rate with its latest research and advancements in Nanosciences and Artificial Intelligence (A.I.). Under Stan Winston's brilliant leadership he was able to grow and position in short order, a real contender among the defense industry that was quickly becoming a viable threat to Devin's dark purpose.

Gen Corp was a thorn in the side of Devin and a nuisance that needed to be dealt with. A primary reason for the DGC's rapid ascent as a global conglomerate was because of Devin's ability to effectively takeover competitors by striking first, striking fast, and striking hard. And now he had Gen Corp in his crosshairs.

Fen tried to keep from blowing a head gasket as his resentment toward Devin and his arrogant way of exalting himself while demeaning others. Fen nervously took a sip from a glass of water trying to muster the courage to confront Devin's tacit demeanor. Upon placing the glass down, he saw a vision coalescing on the black onyx table before him. Materializing through the murky onyx that appeared to swirl was a vision of his twenty-five year old daughter,

Norean with a chain wrapped around her ankle and several cement blocks on the other end was at the bottom of a lake. In sheer terror she was struggling to no avail to swim to the surface as a plethora of air bubbles evidenced the screams spewing from her mouth before her struggle finally ceased. Almost as quickly as the vision appeared everything turned to black with only Fen's shocked reflection staring back at him.

"Fen, are you still with us? You look like you've seen a ghost," Devin asked.

Looking a bit pale, Fen loosened his neck tie and slid back in his high back leather chair. Embarrassed he acknowledged Devin's caustic words by looking up with a half-hearted smile. He then proceeded to consult his notes while trying to compose himself to respond appropriately in his own defense.

"After negotiations with Gen Corp, Mr. Winston has made it abundantly clear that he will not entertain an acquisition offer from the DGC. He has initiated a hostile takeover defense as a shark repellent tactic. He has even taken measures to put a poison pill clause in their corporate charter."

Stacy Ramling, the CEO of Aeroflight Corporation previously acquired and now a subsidiary of the DGC responded first, "I believe it would be correct to assume that Mr. Winston is also a non-player regarding a possible merger?"

"That would be a correct assumption," Fen replied. "Both of our offers were turned down. The man is an oak and will not bend. He is resolute in his position."

Annoyed by Fen's failed negotiations and acquiescence Devin quickly brushed aside his remarks, "Oaks make for great furniture pieces. Did you convey to him the financial wisdom in accepting our offer of acquisition?"

It was all Fen could do to restrain himself from an outburst he would regret if he allowed this meeting to turn into a confrontation between him and Devin. He resented Devin's patronizing remarks ever doused with sarcasm. "The issue is not the offer on the table," Fen said betraying a hint of resentment while locking eye contact with Devin. "The problem preventing the DGC from moving forward with acquiring Gen Corp has nothing to do with money."

"Well, please do enlighten us Mr. Blockman," Devin sarcastically replied.

"Our current dilemma is due to Mr. Winston's adamant refusal to do business with Devin Sinclair. He views you as a corporate raider," Fen said uneasily while avoiding eye contact with Devin. Looking at the other Directors, Fen continued, "We have aggressively pursued over the past ten years and with great success some major players among military defense contractors, scientific research technologies, and corporate financial firms. The DGC has grown in breadth and stature. We are a known entity with tremendous clout."

"But obviously not enough clout to seal the deal with Gen Corp," Devin countered.

Shaking his head as he finally lost emotional control Fen fired back, "You have no compunction about biting off more than we need to be chewing right now. We are drawing the kind of attention and press that will not bode well for a corporation that should be adjusting to our current successes while exercising appropriate management necessary to maintain both sustainability and profitability. Your relentless pursuit of Gen Corp is fool-hearty and reckless at best."

Devin leaned back placing his palms on the table with only Fen Blockman in his sights. Fen felt Devin's boring eyes and the full weight of his regard which was heavy, dark, and calculating.

"Maintain? Whoever said anything about maintaining? Do you know what happens to corporations that maintain? Well, let me clue you in. They flounder on safe sands because they're too afraid to risk swimming among the sharks. Let's get something straight right now. Your job is not risk management. That would come under my direct oversight and responsibility. Your job is acquisitions. Don't condescend to lecture me on matters in which you obviously are demonstrating gross incompetence."

Brushing Fen aside with a verbal slap across the face, Devin turned his attention to the rest of the Directors. "Now is not the time for playing it safe. We're a global leader in military defense technologies shaping and giving rise to the future of human civilization. Our latest High Energy Laser Lock (HELL) weaponry will leverage unparalleled investments in our technology. When governments desire the latest advancements in advanced military systems and superintelligent technology it will be the DGC to whom they look. It is the mission of this board to ensure that this remains the case. We must continue to maintain a firm grip on the corporate sector while exerting a dominant influence on how corporations and subsidiary companies impact the local, regional, and global economies. Power is derived from intelligence – those who think and create it first will enjoy dominance. Gen Corp is one of the few remaining corporations standing in our way of exercising total dominance over military defensive systems and technologies."

Easing the tension in the room for everyone except Fen, Devin wrapped up the meeting saying, "Thank you Fen for your efforts. Take a couple weeks off and enjoy a little rest and relaxation. We will start afresh and see if we can't come up with something a little more convincing that will give Stan Winston and the Board of Directors at Gen Corp a change of heart."

Fen cracked a nervous smile fearing his passionate outburst could prove costly. Looking down to gather his smart device, Fen's attention was arrested by a teeming swirl of clouds on the black onyx surface revealing an image of himself stepping out onto a busy intersection right in front of a fast moving garbage truck that barreled over him. His heart rate quickly increased as he began experiencing a panic attack.

The meeting was called to a close by Devin and the Directors were dismissed. Fen immediately rose and headed for the door not looking back. After speaking with a few of the board members, Devin walked over to a window gazing down upon the busy street below. His attention fell upon Fen Blockman who was hurriedly walking out of the DGC corporate building pausing by a busy intersection.

Approaching Fen from behind was a tall, imposing man dressed in a black suit with keen dark eyes. Turning back to see who was brushing up behind him, Fen noticed the tall stranger was sporting a black tattoo on his neck of a dark sun with daggers encircling it. Giving a nervous smile at the menacing looking stranger, Fen's expression suddenly turned to sheer terror. The stranger's face morphed into that of a black wolf bearing razor-sharp canines.

Fen stepped quickly away into the street as the monstrous transformation of the stranger's face exerted a chilling power over him. Gripped by fear, Fen was oblivious to the large garbage truck barreling through the intersection. He was dead before he hit the pavement.

Chapter 20

CONFRONTATION

Dalton's immediate concern was Summer. "Are you ok?"

"Yeah, I'm fine. But did I just see you tackle a black bear?"

"No, that would've been a black wolf and a mean one at that," Dalton said still bewildered by what he had just witnessed and experienced.

"That was Andras. He is one of the fallen angels and has the ability to shape shift into a black wolf," Emrick said.

Sensing Dalton's confusion, Emrick added, "You and I have much to discuss. But for now we need to see you safely off Kaua'i. The Darkness grows and although it has taken the hilt of Eden's sword it still does not possess the power to wield it. And a power we must not allow to fall under Satariel's influence. No matter the cost."

As the first light of the sun began peaking over the Pacific, Dalton felt a renewing peace stirring inside although he couldn't explain it. It was as if a restoring energy began to come over him. He remembered feeling an incredible adrenaline rush as instinctively he defended Soren in a moment of danger without giving a second thought to his own personal safety. Questions were beginning to swarm his mind.

"What a hit you levied against that beast," Soren said as he slapped Dalton on the back. "Nicely done."

"I'm not sure what came over me but I'm just glad you're ok. It was almost instinctual as if something inside propelled me to leap."

"Great gut reaction," Soren said bending down to retrieve his energy dagger, "keep trusting those instincts because they're spot on."

Dalton just cast Soren a curious look reminded of similar words that Lauren used to say to him as well.

"And since when did you start showing up before the break of dawn?" Dalton asked Sommer playfully.

"I thought you could use some company on your early morning run but had no idea you were opting for a calisthenics workout instead. You're really stepping up your game," Sommer replied tongue-in-cheek.

Emrick was still scanning the surrounding valley shadowed by the towering peaks of the Na Pali mountains. He did not detect any dark energy. He could only surmise what their next move would be. Not one to harbor concern nor give ground to fear, Emrick knew that a dark trial loomed on the horizon for Dalton. He could only place his faith and hope in the Light that Dalton would stand. Otherwise, Eden's great hope could falter in its darkest hour.

Walking over, Dalton pulled Emrick to the side. "Who are you, really?" Dalton asked.

"You ask that which you already know and yet choose not to believe."

"Why were you on the *Kanaloa* the night it went down? And what in the name of Poseidon just happened here?" Dalton asked suddenly feeling light headed.

Recognizing how the sudden influx of energy emanating from the Light had drained Dalton's mortal strength, Emrick quickly helped Dalton to take a seat on the lanai steps. He quickly went inside and brought back a glass of water dipping his finger into it. The water began to change slowly from its clear form to a dark burgundy. Looking at Dalton he offered the glass and said, "Drink."

Dalton's thoughts began racing as his pulse quickened. Reaching out he received the glass and began to drink slowly at first. And then he began to greedily gulp down the warm liquid as it raced through every vein in his body. It tasted of the finest red wine and yet it energized rather than dulled his senses. As if seeking a rational answer to what he just witnessed and experienced, Dalton was at a loss for words. Only amazement and bewilderment remained.

"Your body in time will acclimate to the fluctuations of spiritual mana as you become one with the Light," Emrick said.

"I'm not following," Dalton said trying to make sense of everything that had just transpired. His life was so fracking upside down that he didn't know if he was dreaming or experiencing a parallel universe where the supernatural was natural.

"Your thoughts trouble you because you do not embrace them. What you know to be true deep within the core of your very being longs to take flight and soar again. Who I am is of little consequence. But who you are seems to be your greatest mystery."

Dalton felt as if Emrick were somehow reading his thoughts

pulling back the veil of his safely guarded internal world. And yet Emrick's words resonated with truth and clarity. Emrick wore an expression of sincerity upon his face and not that of one who was standing in judgment. Recognizing compassion rather than condemnation, Dalton tried to relax in light of the swarming thoughts that were berating his mind.

Life had taken the strangest of turns as Dalton found himself literally confronted by otherworldly activity that he could not rationally explain and yet the supernatural was manifesting in real and concrete ways. He just couldn't explain it. For ten years he had done everything in his power to suppress the part of his life that had once been so freely open and available to God and the miraculous. And now it was as if the supernatural realm were more real than the natural realm he had rationally constructed his new way of being and believing around. He was beginning to wonder which was more fictitious the safe world he thought he had constructed or the realm of angels that seemed to be all around him.

"I don't understand," Dalton responded in disbelief overwhelmed by his natural senses.

"Your struggle has always been about understanding. What you've failed to learn is that faith is never about understanding. It's about believing even when every natural fiber of your being tells you otherwise. In time you will begin to see clearly."

"Do you have any idea who those two men were that just tried to kill us all? And how in Zeus' dog house did a black wolf get loose on Kaua'i?"

"We were attacked by assassins known as the Dark Ones or Furies, they are fallen rebel angels adept at the art of killing. These angelic killers, who prior to their fall, belonged to the angelic hierarchy known as the Powers. Ruthless and sinister imbued with darkness they are fit denizens of the darkest Hell imaginable. One is called Samael, a highly angelic warrior and dark prince who is greatly feared and revered among the angelic orders. Crafty, lethal, and determined, Samael once was head of the Order of Powers before his fall. Nicknamed the 'angel of death' Samael has lived up to the meaning of his name, 'Venom of God'."

"When it comes to the killing arts, Samael excels. Skillful and agile, he rarely encounters an opponent he cannot easily out maneuver and overcome. The only drawback for Samael is the limitations imposed on him by his mortal body as opposed to his astral body. The human form is a frustrating handicap and one that presents an advantage in any encounters we may experience. Samael is a General within the Order of Baal serving under the Dark Prince Abaddon who is one of the Archein. Their sole existence and chief diabolical objective is to foment evil, discord, war, and devastation."

"To make sure we are both on the same page," Dalton said. "Are you saying that Samael and this Abaddon were behind the confrontation with Elijah on Mount Carmel in 1 Kings 18?"

"That's exactly what I'm saying," Emrick answered. "The battle atop Mount Carmel was first and foremost a spiritual battle that pitted the Darkness against the Light. The biblical narrative only sheds light upon half the story. Mount Carmel was a nexus of Light and Darkness that converged at a pivotal moment in time tilting the balance of the Angelic War. During the darkest period of Israel's history, the kingdom was divided by rebellion, anarchy, and religious schisms. Israel began to devote themselves to foreign gods following King Solomon's lead. Known as the 'Dark Seduction', Solomon was influenced by his foreign wives turning his heart to Ashtoreth the goddess of the Sidonians, and Molech the vile god of the Ammonites. The dark seed found root and began to grow reaping a dark harvest of evil culminating in a divided kingdom under King Jeroboam 1 of Israel and King Rehoboam of Judah. Baal proved to be a highly adaptable god whereupon denominations of Baal sprang forth such as Baal of Peor (Numbers 25:3), Baal-Berith (Judges 8:33) and Baal-Zebub (2 Kings 1:2) to name a few. Elijah was a vessel of the Light chosen to stand against the growing dark powers that were laying the ground work for an all-out offensive that would've led to an eventual apocalypse had it not been for Elijah's courage to stand against the assassins within the Order of Baal."

"Assassins?" Dalton asked. "You're referring to the prophets of Baal, correct?"

"Yes but there is more to the story than meets the eye. Baal was worshipped as both a sun god and a storm god and considered by many to be the most powerful of all gods. His symbol was a lightning bolt. But what the biblical narrative does not reveal is that the god worshipped as Baal among mortals is none other than the vile angel Abaddon. He is one of Satariel's chief Generals and one of the first to stand with Satariel during the Great Rebellion in Heaven. Many of the prophets who influenced the masses were either angels in mortal guise or mortals possessed by the demon assassins within the Order of Baal."

"Wait a minute," Dalton said trying to wrap his mind around what his ears were hearing. "You're talking about angels and demons."

"Yes, the very subject matter you so astutely wrote about it earning your PhD in Theology. Let me see, how did you so perceptively put it? 'The phenomena of the angelic kind are as fearsome as they are sublime. Imbued with celestial energy these heavenly creatures of the Light energize the cosmos and serve at the behest of their God.'"

"I was writing as an academician about spiritual beings of legend, myth, and lore. Nothing more."

"You are experiencing what you have chosen to ignore, that the great turning points within human history have been a direct influence of the forces of Darkness and Light engaged in an epic war that will ultimately decide the fate of both Heaven and Eden. You see, when Ahab became King of Israel the Darkness was reaching its zenith of power. He married a Phoenician wife named Jezebel whose father was a high priest and eventually a king who worshipped Baal. Influenced by Baal and his sisters Ashtoreth, a fertility goddess and Anath, a goddess of love and war, Jezebel gave herself to the diabolical possession of the rebel angel Paimon. Her one mission and obsession in life became that of finding and killing Elijah. Warned by God and led by the Light, Elijah fled to Kerith Ravine where he was fed by Ravens."

"Kind of ironic that God used ravens who were viewed as unclean birds and then a widow to care for him in Zarepeth, a foreigner from Jezebel's home territory," Dalton said recalling the biblical narrative.

"Yes, the Creator does have his way of flexing his power. Not all is as it seems," Emrick rejoined shedding further light on a greater narrative pulling back the veil on the showdown that took place on Mount Carmel. "You see the ravens were angelic protectors known as the Guardians of Light, with shape-shifting abilities. You witnessed earlier a shape shifter who became a wolf belonging to the Order of Baal. But dark angels are not the only ones who have the ability to change form. Angels loyal to the Light also possess shape-shifting abilities among other powers. And then there are the others known as guardians who lurk in the shadows as Eden's watchers. They serve the Light and serve it well."

Dalton found himself dumbfounded and yet drawn further into Emrick's version of a biblical narrative that was beginning to shed light on the recent happenings around Kaua'i. Emrick discerned Dalton's thoughts and continued to reveal the supernatural happenings behind the scenes of the popular biblical story.

"By the time Elijah had summoned the prophets of Baal to a showdown on Carmel, the Darkness had grown very powerful. Elijah stood alone among mortals and yet was a stalwart sentinel of the Light filled with a power that the dark powers in their arrogance underestimated. Elijah was the last remaining obstacle to a thorough infestation of the mortal kind with the dark powers. Elijah's victory on Carmel over the prophets of Baal was a spiritual battle that pitted some of the most powerful and lethal assassins known among the angels of Darkness against the Guardians of Light who joined their faith with that of Elijah's unleashing what mortals described as a fire from Heaven but known among angels as the 'Energy of Creation' the divine breath of God. Abaddon and his dark minions fled discarding their mortal hosts and the rest as you know is history."

Dalton picked up the story and continued, "Yes, but although Elijah utterly destroyed the remaining prophets of Baal with a sword he then under threat from Jezebel tucks tail and runs for his life hiding out in a cave. It's almost anti-climactic."

"Sounds like someone else I know," Emrick said raising an eyebrow as Dalton looked away feeling a bit uneasy by the implications of his words.

"Dalton, whether you choose to believe it or not, you are caught up in a spiritual war between the forces of Darkness and Light. You have been targeted by the Darkness because you have been chosen by the Light."

"But I choose neither," Dalton responded sternly. "God took everything from me. That's the sum of my relationship with him. It's a one-sided relationship that keeps on taking. I have nothing left in me that is even worth giving. I just want to live out the rest of my days in peace not be hounded by God or any of his narcissistic offspring. I really appreciate all that you've done but I'm no Elijah and if that's God's high, holy purpose for me then you better start waving a white flag because it ain't happening."

"That is not how your wife Lauren described your resilient faith."

Dalton's attention was arrested by Emrick's words as the mere mention of Lauren's name stirred shame and disappointment dealing a blow to his dwindling skepticism. How disappointed Lauren would be to see how far he had fallen away from his faith. He felt as if his world was leached of color and all that remained was a barren wasteland primed by his intellectual perceptions. Grief had so faded the bright, colorful palette of his once burgeoning spiritual imagination leaving only a ghostly apparition of a bone dry skepticism destitute of faith and belief in the supernatural.

"What do you know of my wife?" Dalton asked resigning himself to the numbness inside aware of the paradoxical weight of his empty soul beginning to weigh heavily upon him.

"I know she possesses great faith and believes in you. But that really doesn't matter does it?" Emrick said goading some spark of life out of Dalton. "Hell can rise and blaze a trail of evil for all you care as long as you can hide away in paradise and assuage your pain by denying your true self."

"Why do you hound me so?" Dalton fired back. "What do you want from me? I gave God everything! Every damn thing except my breath. Does he want that as well? You don't know how often I wished I died that day. When Lauren and Kaden were blasted from this world's realm my faith was destroyed along with them. I have no desire to do anything or be anything than what I am now. And I have no compunction about the way I have chosen to deal with their deaths in moving on with my life. I've tried all in my power these past ten years to carve out a safe haven where I can maybe enjoy a semblance of sanity. Does God desire to deprive me of that as well?"

"You honestly don't get it do you?" Emrick challenged.

"Take stock of your life. Transcend your pain and see with new eyes. You have been chosen by the Light for a high calling; to be the bearer of a sublime power that will chase back the Darkness. Those responsible for the mortal deaths of your wife and son, and for nearly killing you several times over the past week will stop at nothing to see to it that you do not become a threat."

"Well, why didn't they just kill me years ago? Why was I allowed to live?"

"The Light protected you. In anguish you spurned your faith. You ceased to be a threat. But although the Darkness lost faith in you the Light never did. We still believe in you Dalton Orion. We who stand with the Guardians of Light believe you will ascend and become what the Light has ordained you to become; the Protector and Guardian of Eden, the one chosen to wield the sacred fire sword."

"How can I possibly let go of the fact that I was spared for a higher purpose and yet the Light did nothing to protect Lauren and Kaden?" Dalton countered.

"All is not as it seems."

"What does that mean anyway? My wife and son are DEAD! End of story and end of my faith. I made a promise to God at their graveside nearly ten years ago. As he abandoned my heart so I would abandon his. 'Do unto others as you would have them do unto you.' Well, I am following the Almighty's lead."

"God did not take your wife and son nor did he abandon your

heart. The Darkness manipulates, twists, and deceives. The soul poison of pain, grief, and suffering is used to destroy the faith of many. You must understand this and see with different eyes or you will be destroyed in your grief. You choose to place your faith in what you can see and touch rather than in the One who created that which you see and touch. Your faith is misplaced and a spiritual malady that can be easily remedied. But you must choose."

Redirecting the conversation, Dalton asked what had been weighing on his mind. "And you," Dalton began giving utterance to words that his faith-challenged brain desperately attempted to deny, "are you an actual angel?"

"What do you believe? What does your heart tell you? Arrest your thoughts, challenge them, and deny that which objects to sound reasoning. Trust in the mystery of faith. And you will learn to trust again the greatest power you could ever wield in heaven or on earth. The power of faith."

Dalton knew. Somehow he had always known since the moment he first laid eyes on Emrick the night the *Kanaloa* went down. "How foolish to believe he could be an angel," he recalled thinking about Emrick at the time. Angels don't exist, their merely the stuff of legend, myth, and lore. The Bible was chalk full of stories about angels but how much of the Bible could really be trusted to be true in light of all the politics that had so corrupted the church on earth. Could the ecclesial powers who were set apart and charged with deciding which holy books were canonical or heretical even be trusted much less the historical outcome? And if not, then who's to say which holy books are true and which are false. It was enough to discourage any serious seeker of the Light. Dalton had grown so comfortably numb to the on-going battle between the Darkness and Light that he simply ceased caring anymore.

Dalton found himself overwhelmed by the implications of what Emrick was saying. His world was careening out of sorts and the semblance of solitude he had enjoyed on Kaua'i was soon to be a bygone memory as he felt himself being thrust forward into an unwanted destiny with a future filled with uncertainly.

"I don't know that I can do what you expect me to do by serving as this Protector of Eden. Faith doesn't work for me like I once mistakenly thought it did. It's hard to trust in that which you've been burned by."

"And yet, instinctively you overcame Andras in saving Soren with little thought to the possible consequences to your own life.

"Well, that's because I acted on instinct. Just a primal impulse that in hindsight was probably more stupidity than faith.'

"And that's what makes you a great vessel of faith. Your instincts. It's when you are emptied utterly of self, willing to sacrifice self, that the Light can use you, empower you, and enable you to be who you are meant to be. Each of us whether angel or mortal has a divine purpose to fulfill within the greater plan in bringing redemption to the fallen order and restoration to the created order. We all play an important role. And you my friend will play a great part in drawing many to the Light."

Dalton turned away from him and merely looked out toward the tranquil Hanalei Bay and listed to the rhythmically soothing sound of the lapping of the waves upon the shoreline. He could only speculate about what the future would hold for him. But one thing was for certain. If Emrick was an angel and the assassins were fallen angels then maybe death was not something to be dreaded after all. And if death was not the end of it all, then the living of life takes on a whole new dimension of meaning that transforms the dark void of nihilism into vibrant and colorful faith.

"So what happens now?" Dalton asked.

"You must prepare to leave Kaua'i. The journey ahead will lead you toward your destiny but it will be fraught with many personal challenges, grave perils, and desperate times. Learn to trust again in the Light and allow your faith to breath freely. Remember that the Darkness feeds off fear and is empowered by rebellion. The fallen will seek to destroy you from the inside out. They will try to thoroughly diminish all vestiges of the Light from your mortal body leaving you nothing more than a living corpse. But the greater your faith the stronger you will become in the Light and thus a serious threat to the Darkness. Trust in the Light and you will overcome in the hour of travail. Know that you do not go alone. We will meet again soon, my friend."

And with those words, the mortal form of Emrick shimmered and became one with the Light, vanishing from Dalton's natural vision.

Chapter 21

KAUA'I 'AKIALOA

Dalton walked into the Coconut Café, a quaint diner with breath-taking views of Hanalei Bay. The diner was famous for its laid back, open air ambiance with tables positioned so as to maximize the scenic views. The Coconut, as locals called it, had plantation style windows that were currently raised to allow the trade breezes to move freely. The main dining area opened to an outside deck where Dalton and Emrick were seated.

Made of Koa wood the dining table possessed a lustrous glow from the lacquer. Off to the left of the café deck was a Hala tree providing amble shade from the Pacific Sun. About twenty-five yards off to the right of the deck was a sizeable Banyan tree that stood nearly thirty-five feet providing shady relief beneath sprawling branches of a mushrooming top.

Several Coconut Palms swayed lazily in the gentle breezes as a couple of young children were fighting beneath over possession of a coconut. A middle-aged Dad with receding hair, a protruding belly, sunburned skin and wearing Hawaiian swim shorts tried to maintain control over his wild hellions. Nearby and oblivious to it all, the mom relaxed on her beach blanket beneath a copse of mango trees enjoying a pleasant read.

"Johnny, let your brother hold the coconut some. I'm sure there are more coconuts lying around that we can find."

"But Dad, this coconut contains secret powers and is more powerful than all the rest."

The younger brother tugged at the coconut and screamed in anger, "I found it first!"

The Dad embarrassingly looked around real quickly before getting in the boys personal space, "Look, knock it off. Give me the coconut. You want to see real power? Watch me make this coconut disappear until you two learn to share and get along. Now get back in the water where you're needed to scare the sharks off."

Overhearing the exchange, Dalton couldn't help but chuckle at the debacle unfolding within earshot. But just as quickly his thoughts turned to melancholy. At least the Dad was able to share a bit of paradise with his two sons. That aching feeling began gnawing again at the pit of his soul. Dalton found himself weary of the all-too-common triggers that reminded him of his abiding grief and emptiness inside. How he yearned to have Kaden back and to experience the precious moments they so often experienced together.

A Kaua'i 'akialoa, a presumed extinct Hawaiian finch alighted on the deck rail in front of Dalton. Its bright olive-yellow feathers and long, curved bill and docile demeanor distracted Dalton from his melancholy thoughts. The Kaua'i 'akialoa just sat there perched on the rail and seemed to lock eyes with Dalton before taking flight winging its way off toward the majestic Na Pali mountain range. Dalton was incredulous. The Kaua'i 'akialoa had been believed extinct with the last known documented case of a sighting on Kaua'i back in 1965.

Sommer walked up and said, "Was that what I thought it was, a Kaua'i 'akialoa?"

"Can you believe that? I'm glad I wasn't the only one to see it. I thought they were extinct. Absolutely amazing! The one time I don't have my camera to document the occasion. Unbelievable."

"Some things just aren't meant to be documented," Sommer replied with a casual air about her.

"Are you kidding me? That was the first known sighting in nearly half a century."

"I must admit, there have been some cray cray happenings here of late."

"Some what?" Dalton asked.

"Cray cray. Craziness. Angels and demons. A black wolf. An extinct bird. Nothing really surprises me anymore. All of it is becoming just so believable. It's almost as if the abnormal is becoming the norm."

"And you don't question any of it?"

"What is there to question? Seeing is believing. I mean really. The stuff is real. We do dabble in the scientific from time to time so what does your trained mind tell you Dr. Orion?" Sommer replied sarcastically with a wry grin breaking across her face.

"Yeah but geez. It's enough to cause one to question life as we know it. Think of the implications if all that we are seeing and experiencing is actually real," Dalton said with a glint of amazement and wonder in his eye.

"And that could be a good thing. I've often felt that if I had only took the time to trust my instincts and challenge what I thought was real, the difference it could've made in my life and in the lives of others," Sommer said as she looked out toward the Pacific with a hint of sorrow that momentarily sweep across her face.

The subtle change in Sommer's countenance didn't escape Dalton's notice. Choosing to respect her private musings, he let the observation remain unquestioned rather than pick at a painful memory or experience. He knew Sommer well enough to know that if she wanted to divulge something she would certainly do so when she was good and ready. She possessed a strength he had grown to admire but she was not one to readily open up about her past. He had sensed a guardedness about her private life and because of his own pain chose not to go there.

A couple of tourists walked by and were seated at a table across the way. The man was wearing a local Hawaiian surf tee-shirt with the picture of a menacing looking shark beneath the slogan, "YOU EAT LIFE…OR LIFE EATS YOU". Dalton couldn't help but reflect upon the Hawaiian word for "mano" meaning shark and "niuhi" meaning man-eating shark. Fighting back paranoia, Dalton began to question everything he was seeing and hearing of late. Is this a message from the Darkness? Light? A sense of foreboding came over him awaiting the bottom to fall out beneath him.

Interrupting his brooding thoughts, a waitress walked over and delivered a couple of waters and proceeded to take their breakfast order. Looking at Dalton she said, "What will it be for you hun?"

"Is it too late to order breakfast," Dalton asked noticing that lunch was now being served."

"Hun, you just tell me what you want and I'll take care of it."

"Well then I'll take a couple of eggs scrambled, turkey sausage, and a slice of whole wheat toast. Thank you."

Turning to Sommer she said, "And how about you sweetie?"

"Alika, I'd love to try the surf omelet."

"You got it. I'll have your orders out in a jiffy."

"What's troubling you?" Sommer asked.

"Oh, I don't know. Just about everything. I'm reeling from it all. I chose to come to Kaua'i to get away from the craziness of life and now it seems…"

"Your paradise of solitude has been invaded," Sommer said finishing his thoughts.

"Exactly," Dalton replied. "It's like my very existence is cursed. Damned if I do and damned if I don't. If I seek to run then I'm allied with the Darkness and hounded by the Light. If I embrace the Light then the Darkness marks me for death. It's a wicked conundrum in which I feel embroiled in supernatural issues when I can't even make sense of my own natural issues. Why can't they just fight their war off in the far distant reaches of the cosmos? My God, listen to me. The more I talk the more absurd I sound. It's all so nonsensical."

"Some things you just can't change," Sommer replied matter-of-factly. "We are their siblings whether the angelkind choose to embrace us or not."

"Is that what you call them – the angelkind?" Dalton interrupted.

"Yes, sort of fits don't you think? We are all of the same DNA whether angel or human. I mean, isn't that really what this whole cursed war is all about? Whether our kind is to be accepted into the created order or rejected and cast off like a trifling annoyance. I for one am not going to roll over and play possum while rebellious, upstart angels try to impose their elitist attitudes over everyone else."

"And here I thought all along you only desired to commune with nature," Dalton said with a mirthful smile.

"Don't get me started," Sommer said forcing a smile. "We have as much a right to exist as they do. And furthermore, we are really not all that different, sharing similar emotions and desires."

"I think we are a bit different than those Dark Ones," Dalton countered.

"Really? How so? Think about it. Their rebellion was premised upon the desire to act independently of their Creator. Our Creator. Even your life these past ten years has been both a conscious and subconscious attempt to reconstruct your life independently of God. Whether right or wrong, life happens. And when it does our reactions may vary but in the end whether angel or human we all share one thing in common and that is free will. The freedom to choose. And how often are our choices based upon emotions? Dark emotions and light emotions. Anger and happiness. When things are going our way we are at one with the Creator. But when things are contrary to our liking then we tend to be at odds with the Creator. Where is the fairness in that?"

"Well, maybe God should've taken that into consideration before he created angels and humans and cut us loose with free will. In the end, the buck stops with God. He gets the praise as well as a heap of damnation if justice warrants it."

"Justice? Seriously? Come on Dalton. You're starting to sound like the cray crays fighting with the ISSIM in the Middle East. We all fight for our just cause and then attach God to our self-serving agendas. We all are deserving of justice which is why there is a thing called mercy. God created out of love not hate. We all make mistakes and when we do we need to live and learn. And move on. My point is that angels both loyal to the Light and fallen to the Darkness have their own just cause. And so do humans. Look at what is happening in our world today? It's madness. Don't tell me there isn't a symbiotic relationship between the war raging among angels and the human chaos that pillages our global village."

"So God made a mistake?" Dalton countered. "Is that what you're saying? Or is the mistake in blaming God for allowing innocent lives to suffer while the guilty go unpunished?"

"No. Well maybe. Who knows, it depends on one's perspective. My faith is not shattered by someone questioning God's will and motives. I've certainly had my occasions of being at odds with him. For some it's simply easier to believe there is no God to avoid the baggage that comes along with believing that he exists. I too, know of deep personal loss but my issue is not with God. In the end, God is God and I am Sommer. Life is a wonderful gift but it can also become our worst nightmare if we allow it to be so. I know my place.

I accept my place. I just choose to experience serenity among nature and welcome the mana from all living things inviting it to flow freely in and around me. I embrace good karma and jettison the bad karma. It is how I choose to live."

"When did you become such an avid believer in angels and demons?"

"From the moment I first drew breath," Sommer said.

Dalton all of a sudden had this look of incredulity that broke across his face. "Don't tell me you're an angel too."

"No," Sommer laughed. I'm one of your kind.. Things may have turned out a bit differently if I had been created an angel but no I'm full blooded human through and through," Sommer assured Dalton with a smile. "Although at times I feel a lot like the Kaua'i 'akialoa but I'm not willing to give up the ghost just yet."

"I hear you," Dalton said with an affable laugh.

Alika walked up with their breakfast orders and scurried off to wait on another table as the beachfront café began to fill up.

"Let's dig in. You and I have a plane to catch later," Dalton said.

"I look forward to seeing this Holy City of yours. To the journey ahead," Sommer said raising her glass of water with a pleasant smile.

"To the journey ahead," Dalton affirmed as they both clinked their glasses.

Chapter 22

THE SHADOW WALKER

Fierce, tumultuous winds whipped through the Alpine forest pelting the faces of a battalion of Dark Ones who stood to attention unaffected by the stinging sheets of ice liquefying upon impact. Off in the distance the haunting howl of an alpha wolf could be heard rejoined by a chorus of howling unnerving prey within hearing distance.

Ramiel stepped out of the *Lycaon* with Devin into the wind-lashed night. His white hair was cropped closely giving him a distinguished appearance. His prominent eyebrows blended nicely upon his forehead perfectly accenting his crystalline blue eyes. Standing in similar height to Devin they appeared as Darkness and Light standing together, a veritable yin and yang personified in the flesh.

"All is going according to plan in Rome, my Lord. Those who resisted have been permanently dealt with."

"And what of Cardinal Denali? Can we can count on him?"

"He is easily swayed by visions. He will succeed Cardinal Ferdinand. All is in alignment. Now we await the Pope's death which will happen in a matter of weeks."

"How unfortunate for his Holiness. His life holds such great promise for the Light. It's a pity his death will have to do," Devin said with an indifferent smile.

"Happens to the best of them. Sooner or later, death claims them all," Ramiel voiced with malevolent pride.

"Sometimes Ramiel, I get the feeling you really enjoy what you do."

"Yes, my Lord. I take great pride in my master piece - The Dark Religion. It will ultimately be the undoing of the mortals. Not to take away from your superintelligent creations but oh, how these mortals love their religion."

Samael walked up and took a knee before Devin bowing his head and holding the Sword hilt up in his hands. "A gift for you, my Lord. I present to you the Sword of Eden."

Devin received the Sword and then said, "Rise, Samael. I must say that I am surprised you were able to claim such a prize with so little resistance. Our misguided brothers must be weaker than I thought."

"They are no match for the Darkness."

Standing among the chill of the night air outside his densely concealed Alpine fortress, Devin gripped the mythical sword of Eden examining it admiringly like a prized trophy. He lofted the Sword in his hands and made to activate the energy blade but to no avail. The wicked smirk vanished from his face. His once approving expression flattened to bewilderment before giving way to realization. Dropping his hand by his side while clutching the sword hilt, Devin merely gazed up at the mocking heavens toward the pale light of a full moon. The distant stars served as a mocking reminder of his long pursuit of that which he held in his grip and yet its power remained ever elusive beyond his diabolical influence.

Samael recognized the daunting expression that broke across Devin's defiant features and restrained from speaking less he detonate a withering assault of dreadful fury from his dark lord. Something was amiss but he had come to learn the importance of measuring his words when addressing Devin. And if unsure of Devin's state of mind it was always best to weather his withering glare than risk a debacle of words in one's defense.

Devin spoke with dangerous calm breaking the unsettling silence that hung in the air. "The sword without the mortal vessel will be of little use in accomplishing our objective. For now we have neutralized a potential threat by acquiring the sword. But we are not in the business of merely neutralizing."

"Do you still believe he is the one of whom the prophecy speaks and not a decoy? Based on what I observed, I only detect pain, cynicism, and confusion. He seems weak with much darkness in him," Samael said.

"Pain can be a great ally," Devin replied. "The death of his wife and son is a gift that keeps on giving." Devin walked a few paces toward the dark forest edge with his back to Samael.

"Yes it is and one which often hollows out these pathetic mortals," Samael said.

Devin's calculating thoughts elicited a devious grin as he continued, "But if we can take advantage of his diminutive faith in the Light and bring him over to our way of thinking then we strengthen our advantage and neutralize their desperate hope of winning this war."

"Wouldn't it be easier to just kill the mortal?"

"It would appear that is what Andras attempted and yet failed to accomplish," Devin said turning to face Samael before continuing. "Pain is a powerful tonic and the Light has shown itself adept in using our weapons against us. The power to influence and turn the mortal is more desirable."

Samael chose his words carefully, "Yes, my Lord. But the prophecy does speak of a great mortal warrior of Light rallying faith and loyalty to the Creator. I've seen only a hollowed out, restless spirit who desires to live out his days in quiet solitude. He is hardly a viable threat to us and will prove to be of little use to the Light. But even so, it would seem prudent to neutralize the threat to ensure there is not even a remote chance of him becoming what the prophecy states he shall."

"You speak of the prophecy as if you believe it to have merit," Devin spat in detest. "Do I sense a fledgling of Light sparking within you?"

"NEVER," Samael vehemently denied, returning Devin's lingering stare with resolute conviction that emanated from a dark calm within. It was moments like this in which Samael's distaste for serving at the behest of someone else that fueled his yearning to lead rather than follow. But to challenge Devin openly would be to court disaster. Those who dared to challenge Devin's authority were seen and heard from no more. His mastery in wielding the Dark energy was unsurpassed rivaled only by the Great Dragon of Primora.

"No my Lord, of that you can be assured," Samael said holding his ground without betraying fear or self-doubt.

While holding Samael's unwavering attention, Devin said, "Dalton Orion has proven himself resilient thus far. Though he is weak in the Light, he nonetheless still has a spark of faith remaining in him. Need I remind you that only a spark of faith in the Light is necessary to affect a great deal of damage to our cause. Never, ever let your guard down by underestimating the Light."

Samael cringed inside although concealing any visible sign of resentment at Devin's withering words. "Dalton Orion is preparing to leave on the next flight out of Kaua'i heading to Charleston, South Carolina. I will be heading there myself to attend a political fund-raiser on behalf of Senator John Sterling. You and Andras will join Draven in the Holy City and await my orders."

While walking back to the Alpine facility, Devin paused and then turned to Samael. "As for our winged friends shadowing Dalton, serve notice that the Darkness is not idle."

"What about his mortal companions?"

"All in due time. I have something special planned for them."

Turning to Ramiel, "Go back to Rome. Make sure everyone is ready for the papal conclave of Cardinals that will convene upon the death of Pope Paul VII. I will tie up a few loose ends with the upcoming American Presidential election. Our efforts will soon bear fruit worthy of a Dark harvest," Devin said as a palpable thrill of reaping death and destruction on a global scale temporarily satiated his deepest, darkest longings.

The entrance to the *Lycaon* opened as the light from within raced out illuminating two figures standing in the entrance as if in conversation. Recognizing Aeron, Devin approached as she turned with a self-confident air to her demeanor. "Devin Sinclair, I'd like to introduce you to Legion."

Turning his back away from the light and stepping out into the darkness, Reaper said, "The pleasure is all mine, Dr. Sinclair." A grin quickly spread across Devin's face as he looked approvingly at the uncanny resemblance to the subject.

"Well done Aeron. Well done," Devin replied.

"Come my friend," Devin said to Legion while walking back inside. "We have much to discuss."

Ψ

"Ramiel. Great," Raphael quietly whispered as the biting wind and blowing snow careened unforgivingly through the Black Forest. Raphael's silvery, white hair was tied back and tucked beneath his warrior attire that blended with the snow-white environment. He and Nikiel with their telescopic sight peered down upon the mountain fortress that bulged like a gigantic hornet's nest housing the creations of Devin's dark hopes and aspirations.

"*THE* Ramiel?" Nikiel asked perplexed by his presence in the Black Forest.

"The one and the same. Leader of the apostates who was thwarted by Abdiel during the first day of the dark siege against Empyrean."

"We should take him out now," Nikiel said emphatically. "He is the elusive one we have been seeking, who helped Satariel turn nearly a third of our kind away from the Light."

"No, we must wait."

"But his fighting skills are no match for ours," Nikiel protested.

"It is not our mission to act, yet. Besides, it's not his fighting skills that concern me. It's his powers of persuasion and uncanny ability to present dark visions as visions of Light. His weapon of deceit is a most formidable one. For now, he must be closely watched," Raphael said as he looked around for any signs of the Watchers.

"Something is not right," Nikiel said while scanning the perimeter for any signs of their presence. She inhaled deeply inviting the Light's awen to flow through her, to guide her, and to quicken her senses. "I know they're out there," she said as her black, flowing hair blew in the icy breeze. Scanning the area with her green, expressive eyes she said, "The land breathes dark magic. If we draw any closer we will compromise our positions."

"Check out your ten o'clock sitting atop the ridgeline."

Nikiel turned and looked off in the distance nearly two hundred yards and spotted a black wolf with golden yellow eyes. Sitting atop a rocky outcropping, the black wolf was staring stoically back at her. "Why does he not alert the others to our presence?" Nikiel asked.

"It's the shadow walker."

"You mean the confused one," Nikiel replied sarcastically.

"I wouldn't choose to put it quite that way," Raphael said as he tried to read the wolf's thoughts. "I'm unable to breach his mind.

Either the dark magic is preventing access or his dark powers are stronger than the typical Watcher. Either way, we are on borrowed time here."

"I'm not leaving here till I gain access to that research facility. If the shadow walker is neither fully given to the Darkness or the Light then maybe that plays to our benefit," Nikiel reasoned.

"The shadow walker is a phantom of the darkness. Rarely does he reveal himself to the Light. His powers are great. You don't want to underestimate this creature."

Nikiel fixed her attention ahead as she placed her right hand to the ground in an effort to pick up on footfall vibrations. "The ability to drain Light and Dark energy from either mortal or immortal is a dark gift. But to suck it from the blood through fangs is abominable."

"His teeth are swords and his jaws are knives," Raphael replied.

"You refer to the ancient writings of the mortals found in Proverb 30:14. But in verse 16 it states he's also, 'the grave, the barren womb, land, which is never satisfied with water, and fire, which never says, Enough!'"

"He is a formidable foe and although his vampire gift is not to be taken lightly, we must not forget from which he came. He was first created by the Light. Breath of his breath, soul of his soul. And strength of his strength. There is always the hope that even the shadow walker will return to the Light. We must keep faith in that hope."

"We've got visitors," Nikiel said as her vision narrowed detecting movement closing in around the fortress perimeter. Our position may be compromised."

"Check out your ten o'clock."

Nikiel turned and noticed that the black wolf was gone. The bite of a chill wind dampened the mood reflecting Nikiel's growing exacerbation with the situation. Keenly attentive to the presence of the gathering Watchers, Nikiel and Raphael knelt with their backs against a wind-eroded boulder.

"I see three Watchers just below the ridgeline to our nine o'clock and four to our three o'clock. If we can take them out then I can possibly slip in undetected."

"And them?" Raphael asked pointing overhead to a circling pack of wolves in the sky with outstretched black wings.

"Great," Nikiel said, feeling flustered by the moment. "If those ARCHs rise then humanity falls. We must gain access to that research facility sooner rather than later."

Raphael detected a looming presence lurking within the densely wooded forest behind them. True to its name, the Black Forest with its numerous deciduous trees and firs creating a black woodland providing the perfect concealment for both predator and prey alike. "Hold still. We have company," Raphael said to Nikiel.

Raphael found himself staring into a snowy thicket of underbrush that revealed the feral, crimson eyes and white dagger-like fangs bared as a black wolf growled low prepared to lurch at the least sign of movement. "Easy fellow," he said slowly moving his hand to the energy dagger clipped to his belt.

"I wouldn't do that if I were you," a voice said stepping out of the shadows.

Nikiel spun and squared off to face the threat quickly notching an energy arrow to her bow as the arrowhead orbed an incandescent blue. "Draven," she said resisting her greater impulse to release the arrow.

"Far away from home are we?" Draven asked. With facial features that appeared half human and half wolf and thick black hair, Draven cast a menacing presence. His piercing stare commanded attention.

"Still living in the shadows are we?" Nikiel replied with dripping sarcasm in her tone and disdain in her eyes.

"Light, darkness, shadows, it's all the same. Just a matter of one's perspective"

Attempting to prevent an escalation of an already dicey situation, Raphael interjected, "It's been a long time old friend."

"Why do you call me friend? It's your kind that brought the Darkness to Eden. I would say that makes us foes."

"And yet, you serve Satariel along with the rebel angels."

"I serve no one but myself," Draven said with a defiant snarl as his eyes flared luminous in a dark golden hue.

"Then why are you here?" Nikiel challenged as her pale skin glistened from the spiritual energy flowing within her. "If you're not serving the Darkness nor the Light then step aside or go back to your den and take your groupies along with you."

"Your arrogance blinds you to the truth you refuse to see. You simpletons think everything is black or white. Eden was perfect before your kind arrived. Ever since the angelic intruders invaded our native land Eden has known nothing but war, chaos, and death. Eden has been infected with the religious malady spawned by angels seeking followers who will worship you as gods. The religious plague has brought nothing but death and destruction emanating from the dark seed of YOUR kind. You pillage and plunder Eden with your lust for righteousness while laying waste to our world. And yet you condescend to speak to me of Darkness and Light. Your Light is as Darkness to me."

"Eden WAS perfect before YOUR kind chose to foolishly follow Satariel," Nikiel fired back. "Why do you lend your services to the very one responsible for the madness of which you speak?"

"I have my reasons," Draven said flatly.

Raphael risked a furtive look around before stepping forward to bring calm to what was quickly becoming a volatile conversation. "Draven, for all the wrongs and pain you've endured at the hands of our kind, I am truly sorry. But Satariel will finish what he began long ago if we do not stop him. His objective is no less than the total annihilation of the humankind – YOUR kind and Eden along with them. And he now has the technological means to pull it off. You must know this."

"Your kind brought the Darkness to Eden. Your Light grew dim long ago. But as for the humankind, it is what it is. MY kind will endure. We are highly adaptable. It's how we survive."

"But what has been lost can be redeemed. The Light will make all things right again and restore Eden to its former glory. Eden's Protector, the ONE of whom the ancient prophecy speaks has been summoned and even now walks among us.”

“I don’t place faith in ancient prophecies. Only in the here and now. You find solace in the Light. Your foes find solace in serving the Dark Ones. I find solace in serving neither. Now go, before I become less hospitable and alert the others to your presence.”

Nikiel made to remove her energy dagger but Raphael stayed her hand. The Empyrean pearl torc around Raphael’s neck gleamed in response to the silver rays emanating from the moonlight that found its way down through the thick forest. “We will leave for now, old friend. The Light of Eden still endures. I’ve never given up the hope that it will burn brightly once again. Don’t give up on the Light. It *IS* Eden’s only hope.”

A shimmering wall of light appeared like a sheet of water that rippled in the air. Turning away from Draven both Raphael and Nikiel stepped through disappearing beyond. As quickly as it appeared the shimmering portal of energy vanished.

A lone Lupine Guardian stepped into a small patch of clearing lit by the fitful glow of the moon approached morphing back into angelic form. “You fool! You just let them escape.”

Draven simply stared ahead as if oblivious to the world around him. He frankly had had enough of enduring the bellyaching from some of the overeager warriors looking to make a name for themselves in hopes of getting into Satariel’s good graces.

“That was Raphael, one of the Archangels who currently sits on the Council of Light. And you just let him go without so much…” Before he could finish, Draven in a snarl of violent furry instantaneously covered the ten feet separating them laying bare his canines while ripping into the neck of the Lupine Guardian. Draven's eyes morphed into a crimson hue brightening as the energy force drained from the fallen angel until there was no energy left to extract. Lifeless, Draven let the body drop to the ground.

"You really should mind your place when addressing your superior," Draven said looking down at the angelic corpse. "Your silence is all that's required. Thank you for being so eager to comply."

Bathed in the faint silver light, Draven discarded the body by calling out to an alpha male lurking not far away in the shadows. The hungry wolf was all too eager to drag the body off into the dark forest, a tasty morsel for himself and the rest of his pack.

Returning to his vigilante watch, Draven cast an observant eye down upon the *Lycaon* wearing a look of disdain upon his face. He didn't deal with internal conflict very well. Raphael's words penetrated deep striking a nerve that infuriated him. But at least he was able to find an outlet for unleashing his displeasure although the hapless victim was one of his own subordinates.

Finding solace living in the shadows, Draven enjoyed the relaxing calm of silence. Struggling with his own doubts, he returned to his calculating thoughts pondering the meaning and implications of Raphael's words. Within the deepest fiber of his being, there was a small part of him that had already sensed the recent surge in the Dark energy as well as the growing power of the Light that was beginning to manifest in subtle yet distinct ways.

If the ancient prophecy was coming to pass then one thing was for certain – the rise of an Age of Great Darkness. Deep down, Draven wanted it, welcomed it, even prayed for it. *Bring it on*, Draven challenged. *I was created for this.*

Chapter 23

THE EDEN PROPHECY

In the fullness of time when darkness envelops Eden, out of the depths a great light will ascend and the Protector shall awaken within the soul of a mortal.

—The Book of Light: The Eden Prophecy 33:7

Emrick felt a convulsion of power, a growing ripple of dark energy rushing outward from Eden's sacred core like a barreling Tsunami of Darkness gaining strength as it surged throughout the realm of mortals. A new front in the spiritual war for the soul of Eden had now opened. The fierce angelic conflict raging within the Kingdom of Heaven was reaching critical mass. The influx of the Dark powers was intensifying under Satariel's command.

Standing motionless atop a rocky cliff line along Kīlauea Point, Emrick listened to the sounds of angry swells charging into the peninsula below and crashing violently against the rocky crags. The beacon light from the Kilauea Lighthouse cast its lonely light from atop the northern most point of the Hawaiian Islands. Having safely guided many ships and boats along the rugged north shore of Kaua'i, the Kilauea Lighthouse stood as a guiding light against the inscrutable darkness warning of the unforgiving sea cliffs below.

Crouching next to him was Soren whose rapt attention was drawn to the thundering sounds of the battering waves incessantly pounding the Moku'ae'ae Islet just off shore from the peninsula. Emrick looked over at the tiny, five-acre rocky outcropping reflecting on its name Moku'ae'ae, which in Hawaiian means "fragment frothing in the rising tide".

"The spirituality of nature has much to say if we but take the time to listen," Emrick said to Soren interrupting their meditative reflection. "The spirit of Creation derives its energy from the Spirit of the Creator. When we quiet our thoughts and become calm within, we're able to establish a spiritual connection with nature drawing upon a shared energy which illuminates and empowers."

Gazing upon the fifty-two foot Kilauea Lighthouse, a weathered-white edifice perched on the bluff nearly two hundred feet above the crashing surf, the intrepid structure stood as a symbol of salvific hope against a sea of darkness. As if declaring "I beg to differ," the lone automatic beacon atop the aging lighthouse defiantly cast its light before the encroaching darkness, resisting the unrelenting pressure to conform to the daunting, black void.

As Emrick surveyed the rugged northern coastline he recalled an ancient angelic prophecy found in the *Book of Light* penned by Metatron, the Chief Scribe of Heaven. Speaking almost nostalgically, Emrick uttered the words from the prophecy, "In the fullness of time when darkness envelops Eden, out of the depths a great light shall ascend and the Protector shall awaken within the soul of a mortal."

Soren looked up at Emrick with an inquisitive expression on his face. "Master, the words of which you speak pertain to the coming of a great warrior of Light. One born of mortals wielding tremendous spiritual power leading many in stemming the dark tide during an age of great evil."

With a faraway look in his eyes, Emrick's irises transmuted into a deep sapphire blue. Gazing out toward the enveloping darkness sweeping across the Pacific, he beheld a legion of dark angels in winged flight heading east. "The Age of Great Darkness springs forth. And so Eden's Protector will rise and even now walks among us."

The implications of Emrick's words were not lost upon Soren, one of his most astute disciples and an intrepid apprentice. "Master, you still believe that Dalton is the one of whom the prophecy speaks?"

Confident and without reservation Emrick replied emphatically, "Yes."

"But Master, I must confess that I have grave reservations about his state of mind? How can you be sure where his allegiance will fall? Many much stronger in faith than he fell like lightning from the heavens. How can you be so sure that this will not be his end as well?"

A fierceness came over Emrick's countenance as he turned to Soren who immediately rose to his feet steadying himself for one of those admonishments he knew was forthcoming.

"Rise to the Light, Soren. Never stoop to the Darkness. Be aware of the darkness but never impressed lest it gain a foothold in your spirit and utterly consume you." Emrick's luminous angelic being came to bear upon his mortal body as a white light emanated outwardly.

Soren quickly raised his right fist over his heart in allegiance to the Light. "Forgive me, Master. It wasn't my intention to cast doubt upon the power of the Light. Nor do I desire to misplace my faith. I must confess that at the current time it is a bit of a stretch to wrap myself around the notion that Dalton is the one of whom the prophecy speaks. A guardian maybe but Protector – I'm just struggling to reconcile my faith with belief."

Emrick walked softly toward the Kilauea Lighthouse gesturing for Soren to join him. "You confuse faith with belief. Many believe in the Light but do not place their faith IN the Light. The Kingdom of Heaven is a spiritual kingdom governed not by religion or religious precepts but by the sublime love of the Creator from whom all things move and have its being. Religion emphasizes faith in one's belief. But faith in the Creator is an entirely different matter. For the Light issues forth from the Creator, the source of our life and power. Just as Satariel would have all angels worship at his footstool; many pundits of religion would have the faithful flock to religious altars made of wood and stone rather than to the Creator. The spiritual promise of mortals has been greatly diminished by misplaced faith in religious dogma, creeds, and tomes. Eden's hope resides not in the prophecy but rather with the One from whom the prophecy springs forth. We stand in the Light choose to place our faith in the one to whom the Light has chosen even when we struggle to trust in the wisdom of what we do not comprehend."

Strolling along the lush green cliff side, Emrick continued sagely, "One of the reasons why Eden has become spiritually weak is because it has looked primarily to religion rather than to the Spirit. Take a ship at sea as an example. Religion is like a navigational map. Many place their faith in its guidance. But even with a navigational map, many a ship has foundered close to shore because the Captain relied solely on his map not taking into account the changing winds, shifting currents, and fluctuations in the planetary flow of energy. Religion is cold and distant whereas the Spirit is warm and inviting. Tapping into one's spiritual being connects one with the Spirit illumining the path ahead. The Spirit is like a lighthouse emitting a beacon of light. It pierces the darkness; it doesn't invite it. It creates awareness; it doesn't conceal it. It's available to all; not the preserve of a few."

Soren absorbed Emrick's words like a sponge soaking up water. The Spirit within him quickened with each word Emrick spoke.

"The difference between the Spirit which emanates from the Creator and the spirit which resides within a created being, has to do with the ego. One of the many common struggles among humans and angels, is that the spirit left to itself gravitates toward Dark energy which is why both our kind and the humankind are so predisposed toward religion. A third of all the angelic host who followed Satariel in his rebellion against the Creator; the very Spirit of creation itself, did so because of an egocentric desire to exalt self and ideology above that of the Creator. And religion accomplishes this more so than anything else. Religion is often devoid of the Spirit. It often derives its source of dogma from an angel or human."

Emrick cocked an eye upward toward a few stars shining in the heavens amidst a great expanse of darkness, "You see, when one is living in harmony with the Spirit, his or her spirit draws upon the dynamic energy emanating from the Light of the Creator's Spirit. Many among both the humankind and angelkind have given themselves over so fully and utterly to the Darkness that the Light within is extinguished. During the coming Age of Great Darkness many will succumb to the Dark energy enabling great evil to wreak havoc upon the earth. It is from the abyss of this dark madness that Eden's Protector will rise wielding the Sword of Eden in the power of the Light in defense of this world's realm."

Soren looked with great affection and admiration upon Emrick as he watched him continue to walk in stride with the ebb and flow of the Spirit's energy. "Master, if Dalton is the one of whom the prophesy speaks then how do we help him find his true self when he's convinced that his true self is actually his false self? How does the Spirit bring spiritual illumination without interfering with free will and inadvertently giving rise to false light?"

Emrick couldn't help but allow a light-hearted chuckle to escape his lips. "Soren, there is no danger of you ever succumbing to atrophy of the imagination."

Stooping down into a crouch dangerously close to the cliff's edge, Emrick pointed to the peninsula below. "You're over thinking this

Soren. Remember, the Spirit illumines our thoughts, our senses, our understanding. Things are not always as we perceive them to be. This is the essence of faith and what it means to walk in full Light. Behold the powerful force of the waves as they continually assault and batter the cliff below. In time the great force of the waves leaves its mark upon the rocks carving out what you see before you now. It really is quite remarkable to behold. In a similar fashion, the Darkness with its incessant pounding against the great fortress of the Spirit lashes out at the Light desperately trying to reach up and extinguish it or to bring the vessel of Light crashing down to its own destruction and demise. Which is where we come into the picture. We will rely on the Light and provide support to the chosen Protector of Eden ensuring that such a dark hope isn't realized."

Emrick pointed over to his right at a sloping incline that dropped from the cliff's edge created by the combination of rain water from above and the force of the ocean's watery fist below carving out a narrow ravine among the steep rocky sides. "Not all things happen in the hour of our choosing. But rest assured, when a way is needed, the Light will provide it. We just need to be patient and alert. When viewed from a spiritual perspective, the darkness seeks to crush not only the Light but anyone who would seek to embrace the Light. The reign of the Dark powers among Eden seems like an eternity inciting fear, despair, and confusion in the hearts and minds of many. But the Spirit is ever vigilante and can channel all that madness toward the creation of a means by which one can ascend to the Light."

"Notice the ravine over there," Emrick said pointing to the

peninsula. "There was a time when this cliff couldn't be accessed from below. Time and the forces of nature have chiseled out from a seemingly impenetrable mountainous wall a way to ascend toward the lighthouse serving as a powerful reminder that all things are possible for those who never waver in their resolve to overcome insurmountable odds. The Guardian and Protector of Eden will lead many to the Light: inspired by his faith in the Light, his love for the Light, and his hope in the Light. Right now more than ever, he needs us to have faith in him until such a time that he ascends to the Light."

Soren turned his gaze to the Lighthouse interjecting a question, "Can the waning light of religious habitations aide in the spiritual struggle against the powers of Darkness?"

Emrick shook his head gravely, "All things are possible. Religion is but the politics of angels that have spilled over into the affairs of mortals. Much of it is false light. It serves only to confound the way preventing many from reaching out and embracing the true Light. The Spirit however; imparts spiritual energy that empowers and makes a way for people to ascend to the Light. Religion utilizes fear, coercion, and force to promoted a particular belief about the Creator devoid of any real spiritual relationship with the Creator. Thus more often than not, religion serves to malign the way. For only the Spirit, not a religion; serves as the true beacon of luminous light radiating outward from the Creator. The Spirit is dynamic energy that ignites faith, inspires hope, and engenders love. Religion is often fed by the dark energy weakening and destroying faith in the Creator."

Emrick gazed out over the Pacific toward the East, toward the darkness, "We are witnessing the dark signs of the Order of Baal. Religions have come under the influence of rebel angels as schisms, extremism, and bloody holy wars are breaking out all across the Middle East. Mount Carmel came to be known as a holy mountain but it was more than that. It was a nexus of Light and Darkness that converged at a pivotal moment tilting the balance of the war."

"The ISSIM seem to be trying to accomplish in the Middle East and around the world what the Order of Baal failed to do on Mount Carmel."

"Exactly," Emrick replied casting an approving look at Soren. "I detect the work of the dark Prince Aziel behind the rise of ISSIM. The names means 'Souls of Fire' or 'Captains of Fear'. A reference is found in the ancient text of Psalm 104:4 TLB, 'The angels are his messengers—his servants of fire!' Ever presenting as an angel of Light, Aziel has adopted many of his tactics from Ramiel who is very busy in Rome, another front in this dark war that we will have to deal with in time."

"Satariel is wielding religion like a sword as he marshals all his efforts in a singular focus bent on the destruction of the Kingdom of Eden," Soren said.

"That is his intention. But realizing it will be a different matter entirely. We must now direct our efforts to a strategic location that has come to my attention. A nexus of Light and Darkness has been identified similar to the one on Mount Carmel with even greater implications for the ultimate fate of Eden."

"And where do you believe such a nexus exists?" Soren asked.

"The ancient prophesy in the *Book of Light* alludes to a nexus that will arise in the birthplace of the One who will be instrumental in stemming the dark tide of chaos that will be unleashed against Eden. The dawn of the Age of Terror will give rise to the One wielding the sacred power of Eden's Sword. The nexus of Light and Darkness is located in the Holy City, the place of Dalton's birth."

"Charleston, South Carolina?" Soren replied incredulously. "What makes the land of swaying Palmettos and drunkards littering the multiple taverns and less than spiritual night life so holy?"

"Mortals may have attached the nickname, 'The Holy City' because of the numerous steeples of religious denominations that pepper the city skyline but angels know it to be such for different reasons. As its history attests, it served as a powerful spiritual nexus; a convergence of the Light and the Darkness, of good and evil. We of the Light believe that the Holy City is a place that will give birth to the future hope of Eden. A future hope that the Darkness will in all its power seek to abort."

As Emrick turned and walked along the cliff's ridge, Soren lingered just a moment longer turning his attention back to the peninsula below listening to the angry surf pounding upon the sea wall as sea spray splashed up the sides of the cliff. He gazed at the natural staircase carved into the sea wall and then glanced over at the lighthouse. Speaking to the Creator he prayed, "Enlighten my spirit by your Spirit. Empower my spirit by your Spirit. Unleash your Spirit through my spirit. Drive all doubt away so that you alone command my thoughts as well as my purpose. Let it be so."

Quickly he caught up with Emrick as they both defied gravity ascending toward the heaven's preparing for the fight to come.

Chapter 24

THE JOURNEY BACK

With the tenth anniversary of Lauren and Kaden's death only a few days away, Dalton arrived at Lihue airport with mixed emotions. Returning to Charleston promised to elicit painful memories that Dalton wasn't sure he was ready to experience. Great trepidation gripped him as the reality of his returning began to settle over him.

Born in Charleston, Dalton spent many of his early years with his mother playing in the surf and building sand castles along the beach on Sullivan's Island. His father was often absent for long periods working as an underwater archaeologist with NORA, dividing his time between Charleston and Kaua'i.

Growing up as an only child, Dalton enjoyed the undivided attention of his mother. He experienced his first spiritual awakening during his teen years due to her spiritual influence and strong faith in God. He remembered with fond recollection the many sunset walks they enjoyed strolling together along the beach on Sullivan's Island. She had a way of sharing stories of brave men and women of faith who lived their lives in service to a cause greater than themselves. Love for God and the faith that "all things are possible for those who believe" were her core spiritual values.

When his mother died during the thirteenth year of his life, Dalton was forced to grow up fast. Thrust into the scientific world of ocean exploration, Dalton spent his subsequent teen years on Kaua'i under the influence of his father's profession and existential values. More scientist than believer, his father spent little time encouraging Dalton's spiritual side. Everything revolved around earth and ocean sciences.

The chapel of his father's religion resided under the sea where his father delved into sea exploration with the same intensity of religious devotion as the devout who attended church. The pillars of his father's faith and religion were the four elements of nature: earth, wind, fire, and water.

The relational distance Dalton felt with his father was as emotionally vast as the miles that separated Charleston from Kaua'i. His father possessed a domineering personality that was self-absorbed and centered around his work. Never developing a father and son bond, Dalton had invested as much time in their relationship as his father had and that was very little. But all that changed when his father was tragically killed in an airplane crash during his Senior year of High School.

Although Dalton felt emotionally distant from his father he had developed a great appreciation and love for nature the closest connection to his father that he had come to experience. After his high school graduation, Dalton returned to Charleston. While attending the College of Charleston, Dalton met and fell in love with Lauren. Their love blossomed and Dalton's faith soared. The two were soul mates living and loving together spurred on by their passionate faith inspiring them to reach for the stars. And now, the reality of returning to Charleston only inspired apprehension and dread.

Sommer walked up giving Dalton a tap on his shoulder from behind jarring him from his thoughts. Upon seeing Sommer's travel attire, Dalton chuckled. "You sure you're ready to leave paradise," Dalton said glancing at her tie-dye tee-shirt from *Keoki's Paradise*, their favorite restaurant and bar in Poipu. The front of the bright multi-colored shirt featured a red feathered I'iwi bird chilling in a hammock sporting a pair of black sun glasses with a Mai Tai in one feathered wing and the other giving the hang loose sign with the tagline, "Hanging Loose in Paradise".

"Just letting people know how I roll. Besides, I hear Charleston is a southern paradise with a flair for the dramatic."

Blake jumped out of his Range Rover and came around to give Dalton a hug. "Didn't think you were going to leave town without saying good-bye did you?"

"I figured you would want to keep a little distance after all the bad karma here of late."

"After all we've been through together? Never a chance in this life."

Dalton helped Blake grab Sommer's bags out of the Rover loading them on a dolly. "Take care of the old man and keep him out of trouble," Blake said light-heartedly to Sommer

"Oh, I plan to keep him busy wining and dining me around the

Holy City."

"Thank you for everything. You're a great friend. I hope to return to Kaua'i very soon. And thanks for looking after my home while I'm away. You and Arlene are simply the best," Dalton said giving Blake a hug.

"Don't mention it. Stay safe and keep looking up. Stuff's going to get better." After shaking hands Blake noticed the curbside security officer looking in his direction so he said, "I better hit the road. Have a safe flight to the Holy City."

Dalton and Sommer waved as Blake jumped in the Range Rover and drove off.

"We've got a flight to catch," Dalton said as he grabbed his suitcase and one of Sommer's.

"Let's do it," Sommer excitedly replied.

Walking over to the curbside check-in they both provided their luggage to the check-in agent and proceeded to make their way through the airport security and boarded the plane for the short flight over to Honolulu. As the plane taxied down the tarmac melancholy came over Dalton as he glanced out the plane window departing the place he had come to treasure in his heart. Taking the active runway, the plane began to accelerate before gaining lift and soaring to the skies.

Dalton looked out the left side of the aircraft window as he took in the pristine view of the beautiful "Garden Isle" of Kaua'i. The Kalalea Mountain Range came into view in which the second peak from the left used to be referred to by Hawaiians as Mano (shark)

Mountain. More recently due to the resemblance to the protruding head of *King Kong* from the 1976 film which was partially filmed on Kaua'i, the mountain is now more popularly referred to as Kong Mountain.

Dalton leaned back into his seat allowing his thoughts to reminisce of bygone days on Kaua'i where he had spent the past ten years grieving the loss of Lauren and Kaden. He had given himself fully to his work with NORA which had become therapeutic enabling him to lose himself in the scientific exploration of land and sea.

Taking one last glance down at Kaua'i, he beheld the lush green and majestic Na Pali coast along the North Shore of Kaua'i. Dalton looked down upon the Hanalei Bay and pier that jutted out into the bay where he often surfed, swam and snorkeled while enjoying the many-tinted, beautiful fish of paradise. Then the view gave way to soft billowy white clouds as the aircraft continued to ascend toward its cruising altitude.

After landing at the Honolulu International Airport they made it just in time to board their connecting flight, Pacific Air Flight 372, a non-stop flight to Hartsfield-Jackson Atlanta International Airport in Atlanta, Georgia. Walking up behind them toward the back of the boarding line were two young men of Middle Eastern descent both dressed alike in a charcoal gray suit with a solid black shirt underneath. Dalton felt a quickening within but shrugged it off as the typical fear associated with Middle Easterners possessing the stereotypical terrorist persona.

Upon boarding the Boeing 787 Dreamliner, Dalton's eyes were

immediately drawn to the large entry way and the white arches that lined the interior fuselage of the plane. New leather smells greeted his senses along with the visually pleasing navy blue and white opulence of the interior. With first class seats, Dalton and Sommer were provided personal assistance in storing their carry-on bags and escorted to their seats by Kiana, the first class section flight attendant.

"May I bring you a refreshment while we complete boarding and preparation for takeoff?" Kiana offered.

"Yes," Sommer immediately chimed. "I'd love to have a Chardonnay."

"A Merlot for me please," Dalton added.

Kiana returned a smile and said, "Please make yourselves comfortable and I'll have drinks to you right away."

"Now this is travelling in style," Sommer said with amazement in her voice. "I mean, check out this plane." Looking around they couldn't help but appreciate the luxury of their surroundings and the innovative design of the Dreamliner's interior elegance and advance entertainment system. The first class seats provided more than ample leg room with the capacity to fully recline. There was plenty of walking space to stretch and move around during the nearly eleven hour flight to Atlanta.

Kiana promptly returned with two small bottles of wine and two cups. "Thank you," Sommer said as she eagerly started to open her bottle of Chardonnay.

Interrupting, Kiana offered, "Please, allow me."

Dalton smiled as he watched Sommer's face light up in a sweeping grin. He ascertained that this was her first experience flying first class. He often traveled coach as well but in light of the *Kanaloa* tragedy, Dan Fields ensured that they both received first class tickets for their flight to Charleston.

As Kiana was pouring Dalton's cup of Merlot he commented to Sommer, "I took a course when I was in seminary under a professor who was a Jewish Rabbi. Speaking about wine during one class he said, "The rabbi's always used to say, 'There is no rejoicing without wine.' You know why?"

"Jews like to drink? I don't know, why?"

Dalton laughed and continued, "All of us seminary students with our heads in the clouds were busy trying to come up with a lofty theological response when the answer to the professor's question was rather quite simple. With an unforgettable grin slowly crossing his face our professor answered, 'Because wine makes you feel fine.'"

"Now that is a course I would've loved to have taken as an elective in school," Sommer said while sipping her wine.

"It's funny what we take away from our studies. Wisdom is not necessarily found in the esoteric but rather in the practical. Here's to the wine that makes us feel fine," Dalton said holding his cup up to Sommer's.

"Here! Here!" Sommer said lightly tapping his cup. Of course she was drinking to help her ratchet down a notch or two of flight anxiety. Dalton on the other hand, sipped his wine to alleviate his anxiety in returning to Charleston after nearly ten years.

The inflight safety video popped up on screen as the airplane was pushed back from the gate in preparation for takeoff. Watching the onscreen flight attendant go through the various procedures in case of an emergency water landing, gave Sommer the hebbie jeebies. "I'm so ready for another bottle of wine," Sommer commented as the safety video finished.

"Relax," Dalton replied sensing her growing anxiety. "We'll be touching down before you know it."

"I love travel destinations but loathe the flying. I like my feet firmly rooted to the ground," Sommer said while looking down at her empty cup. "I believe I could use another drink right now." Signaling to the flight attendant she lifted her empty cup with two fingers raised. Kiana disappeared behind the curtain concealing the storage area where the drinks were kept. Returning with a couple more small bottles of wine, she gave Sommer the bottles asking her to please wait until departure before opening.

"Ladies and gentleman, this is your flight Captain Steven Branson. On behalf of Pacific Air and the rest of the flight crew we welcome you aboard Flight 372 with non-stop flight service to Hartsfield-Jackson Atlanta International Airport. The approximate time of travel is ten hours and fifty-eight minutes. We will be climbing to our cruising altitude of thirty-seven thousand feet flying at a cruising speed of six hundred and fifteen mph. We've just been cleared for takeoff so please fasten your seat belts. Once again, welcome aboard and thank you for choosing Pacific Air."

As Captain Branson engaged the forward thrusters the General

Electric GenX twin engines roared to life pitching the aircraft forward with an initial slow forward momentum that quickly accelerated reaching takeoff speed and then breaking free of gravity as it left Hawaiian soil climbing before slowly turning east.

Dalton looked over at Sommer who was leaning over on his shoulder gazing into his eyes. Taken aback at first, Dalton said, "What are you doing?"

Sommer looked into his eyes lazily and hiccupped as she said, "Has anyone ever told you that you have really dreamy eyes?"

"Has anyone ever told you that you are a light weight when it comes to drinking?" Dalton replied somewhat amused.

Sluggishly Sommer turned her head toward two empty mini-bottles of wine and lifted both bottles up in the air and said, "O where? O where did you go my lil liquid friends." She then let out a belch and erupted in laughter interspersed with several loud snorting sounds.

Dalton's face turned several shades of red from the embarrassment and was about to say something when Sommer beat him to the punch by speaking to an older gentleman around seventyish seated across the aisle who was wearing a dreadful scowl on his face and giving her a sour glare. "Has anyone ever told you that you have really unfriendly eyes?" Sommer said busting out with another round of laughter and snorts.

Sommer made eye contact with Kiana who was assisting someone in first class holding up empty cups in her left hand and signaling the number three with her right hand requesting more mini-bottles of wine. Dalton immediately waved off Kiana while reaching over taking the two empty cups from Sommer. He turned to the elderly gentleman and said, "My apologies. She loses all sense of moderation when dealing with flight anxiety."

Sommer burst out laughing again and began slurring. "Anxiety in moderation is for losers. Winners hang loose with the soaring I'iwi's of paradise." Turning to look at the thoroughly embarrassed elderly gentleman Sommer crooned, "Fly little bird, fly! Fly high and say good-bye."

Dalton quickly pulled Sommer toward him and said, "Ok, Miss Jukebox I think we need to stay focused before we get sent to the back of the plane."

Sommer bobbed her head while looking intently into Dalton's blue eyes, "I think I could find myself again in those eyes."

Dalton discerned a hint of sincerity behind her words as he reached over and closed the window cover. "Let's just relax and try and get some rest," Dalton said. Sommer continued to gaze at him enthralled by his eyes as he compassionately smiled while gently laying her head back against the headrest. Her eyelids grew heavier slowly succumbing to sleep stemming from the combined effects of her anxiety and the wine she had imbibed.

Dalton leaned over her and manipulated the seat controls reclining her chair back to a more comfortable position for sleeping. While regarding her with a lingering stare, Dalton couldn't help but realize how self-absorbed and distracted he'd been with his own loss and pain oblivious to those around him who were dealing with their own inner turmoil and suffering.

Looking around at the other first class passengers he began to ponder. *What is your storyline? What pain haunts your lives? What dread fills your souls?* Compassion began to well up inside as he loosened his grip on his own pain and began to open himself up to the suffering of others.

Leaning back in his seat he grappled with the extent to which he had failed to honor the memories of the two women that he loved most in life, that of his mother and Lauren. Both were pillars of faith and somehow along the way he had simply lost his spiritual bearings becoming comfortably numb in paradise.

Dalton was beginning to realize that he had been living in the calm before the storm. The healing he had so desperately been seeking would not come from forgetting but from remembering. And now he was hurtling nearly six hundred and fifteen mph through time and space preparing to rendezvous with an uncertain future beginning with a place where he would be forced to remember whether he was ready or not.

Chapter 25

FLIGHT OF TERROR

Dalton dozed off into a fitful sleep as the Dreamliner reached its cruising altitude jetting toward its final destination at six hundred and thirty-five mph, a speed faster than the filed fight plan thanks to a stronger than forecasted tail wind. The interior lights of the cabin were turned off soon after the dinner meal had been served and all plates and leftovers were collected by the flight attendants.

Cruising along at thirty-seven thousand feet, Captain Steve Branson completed a final inflight check before releasing controls to his First Officer Billy Reynolds. "Auto-pilot is engaged, you have the controls," Captain Branson stated.

"I have the controls," First Officer Reynolds replied.

Taking a long stretch with his arms while leaning back in his seat, Captain Branson looked over at Reynolds, "I'm going to take a break. I'll be back in fifteen."

"Take your time," Reynolds responded.

Second Officer Rick McPherson stepped up and took Captain Branson's seat to ensure two pilots were always at the helm during flight. "Flying doesn't get much better," McPherson said as he occupied the pilot's seat next to Reynolds in the cockpit of the

Dreamliner.

The Dreamliner sported the latest advancements in aviation technology and the cockpit area was a state of the art computer and electronic wonder. The Dreamliner could literally fly itself and required very little maneuvering by the pilots with the exception of minor inputs and adjustments.

"I thought I had died and gone to heaven when I was assigned to serve as First Officer on the Dreamliner," Reynolds said. "I was hoping but didn't think it would actually happen."

"The plane is certainly aptly named," McPherson excitedly replied. Looking to his left at the weather radar he noticed the approach of a large storm cell with cumulous clouds billowing upward reaching a ceiling of fifty-one thousand feet. Lightning forked like giant tentacles streaming out in multiple directions in a furious display of electrical energy. "Where did that beast come from?" McPherson asked incredulously suddenly feeling a bit anxious.

"Looks like an unforecasted weather pattern," Reynolds calmly replied. "I'll contact San Francisco Tower and see what our options are," Reynolds added. "San Francisco Actual, this is Pacific Air 372 requesting alternate flight altitude due to approaching storm cell." A crackling static noise was the only response. Repeating his message Reynolds received the same incoherent response that was a garble of an indiscernible voice.

"Strange," Reynolds said. "We are well within range to be receiving a clear signal." The storm cell began expanding on the live radar feed visually was intensifying both horizontally and vertically.

"Contact the First Flight Attendant to prepare the passengers for a bumpy ride ahead. And have Captain Branson to report back to the flight deck ASAP," Reynolds commanded adopting a more concerned tone.

"Roger that," McPherson replied.

The low lit interior cabin lights quickly blinked on and off as the Dreamliner entered the violent storm cell. The forceful turbulence coming from the outside updrafts gave the Dreamliner a violent jolt stirring many from their slumber. What was once a quiet and serene evening flight suddenly became a concoction of various emotional reactions to the turbulence.

Dalton awakened from his fitful doze just in time to notice the two Middle Easterners emerging from the coach section of the aircraft. Another violent jolt shook the Dreamliner dislodging an overhead compartment as several carryon bags came crashing down on the heads and laps of passengers. A flight attendant who had been walking up the aisle was knocked off her feet falling backwards into a row of passengers.

Captain Branson was quickly making his way back to the cockpit when one of the Middle Eastern young men quickly seized him from behind. "What the heck," Captain Branson said as he was strong armed by the terrorist who wasted no time pushing him forward toward the flight deck.

Pushed up against the cockpit door, Captain Branson cried out in a desperate voice, "What in God's name do you want?"

"You mean, what in Allah's name do I want?" the terrorist

exclaimed as he violently whipped Captain Branson's head back. "You cooperate and I just might spare your worthless life. Now, have this door opened or I will bleed you dry. I will not ask twice."

The other terrorist entered first class carrying a young girl around the age of seven. He violently slapped the terrified mother back down in the seat as she tried to reach out and protect the girl. "Don't even think about getting out of your seats," the maniacal terrorist said with rage in his eyes.

Dalton became instantly alert quickly scanning the interior fuselage for any other terrorists. He detected none. The plane shook violently again a he looked out a nearby window and beheld a behemoth storm cell that was visibly lit up by forked lightning providing an intimidating display of electrical energy appearing as veins jutting throughout the storm clouds. The Dreamliner shuddered violently as if being shaken like a salt and pepper shaker by an unseen hand.

The little girl whimpered quietly as fear gripped her like a predator's claw gripping its prey. For a lingering moment Dalton established eye contact with the frightened girl and all he could see was Kaden in her eyes the moment the terrorist bomb exploded on the tourist bus almost ten years ago to the day. *No,* Dalton thought to himself as the same feeling of helplessness flooded over him. *Not again.*

A green luminous energy came over Dalton undetected by the human eye but was not lost on the two angelic assassins lurking in the aircraft. "We have a live one," the dark angel called out to his fallen associate, Teviel.

"Where did he come from? And what is the strange aura enveloping him?" Teviel asked Shemal.

"It is of little consequence. He will soon be dead along with the rest on board."

"Not if I have anything to say about it," Dalton said with sternness in his voice looking directly at the angelic assassins. Surprised and somewhat taken aback by his awareness of their presence the two angelic assassins warily sized up their mortal foe. The terrorist gripping the young girl followed Dalton's line of sight looking toward the back of the plane but could not see anyone. It was as if Dalton was talking to an imaginary person. But the momentary distraction was enough to give Dalton the opportunity he needed to scale the short distance between him and the terrorist.

"Excuse me," Dalton said standing directly behind the terrorist. "The girl doesn't want to play with you."

"What?!" The shocked terrorist said before his world went black.

Dalton quickly put the terrorist in a choke hold and instantaneously a surge of energy rifled through him arresting his nervous system rendering him unconscious. Speaking to a nearby passenger, Dalton said, "Quickly, bind his hands before he regains consciousness."

The mother quickly got off the floor of the plane and ran to her frightened daughter embracing her. "Thank you!" she said looking to Dalton with tears streaming down her face. "Thank you!"

Glancing over to where the two angelic assassins were standing,

Dalton saw only frightened passengers but no sign of the menacing strangers. And then the plane took a sudden plunge throwing Dalton off balance and careening toward the back of the plane hitting an aisle seat before falling to the floor. The plane struggled to regain level flight against the violent turbulence.

Knowing the aircraft was not out of danger with several terrorists aboard, Dalton glanced over at a young male passenger in his twenties and asked, "Did you see two men dressed in black who were standing on the other side of the plane?"

"No sir!" I only saw the two terrorists who went to the front of the plane."

Dalton turned and looked back toward the front and knew he had to get to the cockpit ASAP before the terrorists gained access to the flight controls. Getting up he ran back to the First Class section and slowed as he neared the closed curtain leading to the cockpit door.

Suddenly the curtain was pulled back and the terrorist had his suit jacket wrapped around Captain Branson's neck. "Want to be hero, do you?" The terrorist said with hatred in his eyes. Make another move and he dies and the liquid explosive in my pocket will send the rest of you infidels along with him hurtling to an eternal Hell."

"Infidel is a label I wear proudly if by it you mean I don't believe in your tyrannical god and follow the violent practice of your religion," Dalton replied, as his eyes illumed emerald green. "And the only one that will be hurtling toward Hell will be you."

Telekinetically, Dalton flung the knife from out of the terrorists hand. Shocked, unsettled, and filled with fear the terrorist looked at

Dalton as if he were a djinn. In a desperate move, the terrorist stiffened, as if preparing to break the Captain's neck, but his attempt was quickly thwarted by Dalton. As if a power within him had taken over, Dalton reached out with lightning fast reflexes, gripping the terrorist's neck and eliciting a surge of energy paralyzing him thereby releasing his hold on the Captain. A look of shock and awe swept over the terrorist's crazed features as he dropped helplessly to the floor.

The plane suddenly took another violent plunge as Dalton caught the Captain before landing against the storage area of the forward compartment of the plane. "I've got to get into the cockpit," Captain Branson said. Struggling against the violent g-forces of the plane's descent, Dalton was able to reach the cockpit. The door was locked. As if willing the door to unlock it complied whereupon Dalton simply turned the handle and it opened. The Captain looked surprised that the door was unlocked but didn't waste time speculating as he was rushed inside.

"Pull up," Captain Branson said sternly receiving no reaction from either Reynolds or McPherson who both seemed to be in a daze fixated on the intensity of the storm cell. Captain Branson repeated, "Reynolds, did you hear me? Disengage the auto-pilot now!" Neither co-pilot responded nor acknowledged his command.

The Dreamliner began increasing its pitch angle as the G forces from the catastrophic descent threw Captain Branson back against the empty co-pilot's seat momentarily knocking the breath out of him. Dalton was violently thrown back into a storage compartment.

Captain Branson quickly tried to regain his sense of equilibrium and reach the controls to his left but the violent G forces pinned him to his seat preventing any forward movement. Helplessly he looked on as the rapidly descending aircraft dropped below fifteen thousand feet. Stemming more from a hopeless cry of desperation than a religious prayer Captain Branson cried out, "Dear God, have mercy on our souls and pull us the hell up! Now!!"

ψ

Teivel and Shemal had concentrated their dark energy on Reynolds and McPherson at the controls within the cockpit causing the pilots to lapse into a catatonic state. Shemal reached forward with a surge of dark energy and seized upon Reynolds' hands pushing the yoke forward pitching the Dreamliner into a catastrophic pitch angle sending it into a rapid rate of descent.

Dalton made to reenter the cockpit and as he did so was met by Teivel who was swift and deft in placing an energy grip on his Dalton's forehead causing his knees to buckle as dropped to the floor.

"So you're Eden's Protector," Teivel scoffed. "The Light is a bit premature in its assessment. You are no match for the Darkness." In cold malice, Teivel unleashed a force of energy that dropped Dalton to the floor unconscious before he even hit. "How pathetic," Teviel said in derision glancing down upon Dalton's lifeless body before returning to the cockpit.

Emrick and Soren zoomed through the heavens crashing through the sound barrier at supersonic speed in pursuit of the rapidly descending airliner. Upon approach, Emrick detected Dalton's aura of weakened life force coming from the cockpit area.

"See to the passengers, I'll take the cockpit" Emrick said to Soren.

Soren arrested his ascent within the coach section of aircraft undetected by mortal eye in his celestial form. His attention was immediately drawn to a woman seated next to two crying children. Fear like a python was coiled around her body as she stared helplessly forward but nonetheless resolute in her faith as she prayed, "God, please spare us all a violent death and take us now." Soren reached over and touched the woman on her forehead infusing her with spiritual energy imparting a sense of calm and hope.

Emrick, in his celestial form, landed just outside of the cockpit area and saw Dalton unconscious on the floor enveloped by the dark energy. As Emrick approached the cockpit a dark force of energy knocked him clear back into first class where he pummeled into the bar section. Stunned by the energy force of the blow, Emrick regained his bearings calling upon the Light to shield him.

Standing at the entrance to the cockpit was Shemal with outstretched black wings and pitch black luminous energy radiating outward feeding off the fear emanating from the passengers many of whom were screaming in sheer terror. Several were vomiting and gagging on their puke as the G forces pinned them in their seats. Another violent burst of air created more havoc within the fuselage of the plane as the overhead compartments emptied stored cargo out upon the helpless passengers who were being pummeled by aerial projectiles.

Soren quickly sprang into action as the interior of the plane was quickly becoming like the vortex within a tornado. Intercepting two pieces of carry-on luggage, Soren save a passenger who came dangerously close to being struck a lethal blow as he watched helplessly spared the killing blow that never came. Deftly Soren moved about the fuselage in bursts of speed transcending space and time as if everything seemed to move at a slow crawl. He turned and dropped to one knee harnessing the energy of Light willing all the projectiles to the back of the plane shielding the passengers from harm.

Emrick knew that time was of the essence as the Dreamliner was quickly plummeting dangerously closer to impact with the surface of the ocean. Regaining his footing he stood to meet Shemal, one of Satariel's lethal warriors.

Standing his ground Shemal held Emrick with a dark, menacing glare. "You are too late and the Darkness too powerful," Shemal spat arrogantly.

Approaching cautiously but confidently, Emrick replied, "Shemal, step aside or be cast aside."

With mocking laughter, Shemal's demonic features convulsed as he hissed tersely in response, "You pathetic fool. It is you who will be cast aside." Barely getting the last word out of his mouth, a concussion from a powerful force of energy sent him crashing through the cockpit and out of the airliner.

Teviel was temporarily distracted by the shockwave thereby releasing his dark influence over the pilots. Before he could refocus his dark energy, a force of light gripped him with such intensity and power he was rendered powerless to counter. Prompting a rage of screeching fury, Teviel outstretched his black wings in a feeble attempt to shield himself from a painful surge of tremendous energy that eviscerated him into oblivion.

Stepping into the cockpit, Emrick quickly went to work clearing the area of any residual dark energy left behind. Reynold's immediately regained his composure and sense of orientation as the hold of the dark energy over him was quickly released. Emrick removed his hand from the top of Reynold's head after clearing it of the remaining dark energy. Reaching over he quickly touched the forehead of McPherson's as well.

As Emrick emerged from the cockpit he stepped into the First Class section and saw Soren standing over Dalton where he laid on the floor. Sensing nothing physically wrong with Dalton, Emrick looked over at Sommer who was still out from drinking several small bottles of wine.

"Good thing you made short work of the Dark Ones when you did. All could've been lost," Soren said.

Looking at Dalton and then back to Soren, Emrick replied "The blows that struck Shemal and Teviel were not mine."

With a questioning look Soren replied, "I don't understand."

"Look outside."

Soren glanced over at an open passenger window and did a double take as he beheld a green luminescent energy shield enveloping the Dreamliner.

"You see," Emrick said with a knowing look on his face. "Eden's Protector is awakening. Though he consciously struggles with faith the Light burns strong in his sub-conscious manifesting tremendous spiritual energy and force. When the two harmonize Eden's Protector will become an unstoppable force of Light."

ψ

As he regained clarity, Reynolds quickly glanced at the monitor flashing the impending impact alert warning with the flight altitude dropping below two thousand feet. Pulling back on the yoke Reynolds was able to regain control of the Dreamliner and leveling it off by the time it reached twelve hundred feet.

"Now if that doesn't make a believer out of you, I don't know what will," Captain Branson said as both Reynolds and McPherson let out nervous laughter in response. As the Dreamliner began to stabilize and regain altitude, Reynolds said, "Captain would you like to have your seat back?"

Captain Branson was quick to reply, "Indeed I would." Back in his seat Captain Branson said, "I have the controls."

To which McPherson was more than happy to relinquish as he responded, "You have the controls."

"Boys, I don't know what just transpired here, but you sure did put the fear of God in us all!" Captain Branson said.

"I can't explain it sir. I felt powerless to manipulate the pitch of the yoke as if it were in a locked position and there was nothing I could do to pull us out of the dive," McPherson replied.

Captain Branson was quick to follow up, "We can discuss this more in detail later. McPherson, go check on the rest of the flight crew and passengers. There's nearly two hundred and eighty-four souls that will need immediate attention. And see if the passenger who took out those terrorists is ok. I want his name."

"I'm on it Captain."

Dalton exhaled a deep breath abruptly opening his eyes which slowly transmuted back to their original blue coloration. Regaining conscious awareness, Dalton immediately looked over at Sommer. "Sommer, you ok? Sommer!" Dalton said as he shook her shoulders.

Awakening with a dazed look in her eyes, Sommer replied, "Where are we?"

"We're almost to San Francisco," Dalton said relieved as he gazed up at the onboard flight monitor.

"I thought we were heading to Atlanta," Sommer said becoming more alert.

"You slept through all the excitement," Dalton replied while taking quick glance around at the relief and lingering fear manifested on the faces of many terrified passengers.

"I had this crazy dream that we were hijacked by two terrorists while flying into a nasty storm cell and the plane began plummeting toward the ocean. And you kicked butt and strong armed the terrorists while single-handedly saving everyone from a watery grave." Then smiling she said, "It must've definitely been a dream."

Dalton leaned back in his seat for a moment before saying, "Sounds more like a nightmare."

Walking up Second Officer McPherson interrupted before Sommer could respond, "Excuse me, I've been told that you saved all our lives. To whom do we all owe our gratitude along with our lives?"

Safely apprehended and secured in the forward compartment by the flight attendants along with assistance from a few passengers were the two terrorists. Able to see them both from his seat in first class, Dalton saw only detest and hatred in their eyes as they returned his gaze.

"Dalton Orion. I did what anyone else would do," Dalton said. "Others helped as well. Besides, I've had a similar run in with these kind of crazed, religious bullies before. It was a pleasure to give them a healthy dose of what they so revel in dishing out to others."

"Well, that you did," McPherson said with a chuckle as he extended his hand. "It's an honor to have crossed paths. Thank you for saving my life."

Turning his attention to the inflight monitor, Dalton held a faraway look in his eyes lost in thought. Sommer broke the silence, "What exactly did I miss?"

"Just an attempt by two religious extremists to turn this Dreamliner into a submersible," Dalton answered nonchalantly.

They were both interrupted by the voice of the Captain over the inflight speaker system. "Ladies and Gentlemen, we will be landing at

San Francisco Airport. Assistance will be provided at the gate. We do apologize for your discomfort and unpleasant flight experience. On behalf of the entire flight crew we are thankful that everyone on board is safe and sound. And a special thank you to Dalton Orion who saved us all."

Everyone broke out in a cheer as nervous energy gave way to raucous applause. As Pacific Air 372 touched down at San Francisco Airport, applause erupted once again throughout the aircraft by passengers who were grateful to be safely back on the ground. Upon taxing to a stop on the tarmac, Sommer leaned over to Dalton and said, "You're such the hero. And to think I slept through it all."

Dalton laughed as he replied, "Better scale back on the wine intake next time so you don't miss all the excitement."

"That's ok. I'll leave the hero work to you. I'll stick with the wine."

After getting off the plan, an airport bus ferried passengers to the terminal whereupon Dalton was immediately greeted by a deluge of flashing cameras and reporters eagerly awaiting his arrival.

"Dr. Orion, what was it like to take down two of ISSIM's most feared terrorists?"

"What was going through your mind when you fought back?"

"Were you afraid?

"Dr. Orion, your act of courage is making the breaking news around the world. How does it feel to be a global sensation knowing that you saved nearly three hundred souls?

Dalton could barely see ahead as the lights and camera flashes blinded him from a huge media throng clamoring for a newsworthy morsel from his mouth. "In the moment, the only thing going through my mind was that we must stand up to those who would seek to oppress others using fear and intimidation."

"But did you stop to consider what may have happened to you or others on the flight if you failed?"

"Of course. But inaction was not an option nor was failure. Those who would have us live in the shadow of fear are weak cowards. I chose to strike at the heart of fear itself. In this instance, we were fortunate to subdue the terrorists who embodied that fear."

As Dalton was walking off the mother of the young girl he saved on the plane tapped him on the shoulder, "Sir, I want to thank you for saving my daughter, for saving us all. I thought we were all going to die. You have restored my faith in a God who triumphs over evil. You're an inspiration to us all. Thank you!"

Looking down at the little girl, Dalton smiled, "You young lady, were the true inspiration." And with that he patted her on the head as he and Sommer were quickly whisked away and escorted to the departure gate where they boarded their final connecting flight bound for the Holy City of Charleston, South Carolina.

Epilogue

DRAVEN'S DARKNESS

Charleston, South Carolina – Present Day

Damn the Darkness. And damn the Light for the curse laid upon us all. Draven's thoughts had increasingly turned dark of late as he crouched upon one of the two diamond-shaped towers looming five hundred and seventy-five feet above the main span of roadway leading across the Holy City's iconic Arthur Ravenel Bridge connecting downtown Charleston to Mount Pleasant.

Draven gazed nostalgically out upon Castle Pinckney, the ruins of a military fort in the Charleston harbor that had been used briefly as a prisoner-of-war camp and artillery position during the American Revolutionary and Civil War eras. Now abandoned and fallen into disrepair Castle Pinckney was little more than a skeletal structure of its former self overgrown with weeds and brush. Resting upon Shutes Folly Island, time and the elements had reduced Castle Pinckney to little more than a sea shoal jutting out in the harbor.

Eden is but a ruin abandoned to the ravages of time, Draven mused cynically. In many ways his existence mirrored that of the old abandoned fort that had fallen in disrepair and now was little known among the mortals.

The light of the pale moon broke out from behind a passing cloud casting its incandescent bluish light upon the tranquil harbor where a few boats rocked gently upon the ebb and flow of the watery surface. Draven enjoyed the peacefulness and solitude of the night where the storm inside his soul often experienced a semblance of calm.

Castle Pinckney had grown on him, a dark sanctuary of sorts where he connected with the energy of Eden that seemed to permeate the ruins. He had played a pivotal role in some of the historical battles that had been waged in and around the Holy City. Some of those battles he fought alongside the Dark Ones and others he stood with those loyal to the Light. More out of boredom than sense of patriotism to a particular side or cause, Draven enjoyed the thrill of a challenge and exercising his independence of any sovereign authority.

Looking to the West, Draven felt a pang of longing as he recalled a brighter time and place. Strands of his black hair with wisps of silver fell across his broad face as the bulk of his thick hair rested upon well-defined shoulders. Donning a sleeveless black shirt that covered his muscular torso like a taut glove, Draven stood while leaning into the Atlantic breeze.

Draven's wolf-like golden-yellow eyes closed as he relaxed in a meditative posture in an attempt to calm the barrage of thoughts and images that often assaulted his consciousness. The spectral light of the moon glistened off his pale skin. Much of his large ears were concealed beneath the bulk of his black hair with the pointed tips protruding along the upper sides. A curse of his fallen nature, Draven possessed the powers of an angel, the mortal body of the humankind, and the lupine features of a wolf that were fiercely intimidating to friend and foe alike.

Draven felt a rain drop upon his face as he heard the first rumblings of thunder off in the distance. A flash of lightning lit up an enormous cumulus cloud that was moving in from the east hovering over the Atlantic. The winds were beginning to pick up as a storm began to snake ever so closer toward the shores of the Holy City.

Feeling the anger begin to roil in his blood and course through him like fire consuming oxygen, Draven opened his lupine eyes leaping from his perch clearing the vast distance landing upon a patch of overgrowth that concealed much of Castle Pinckney. The rain intensified falling rhythmically in cadence with the uprising of Draven's dark emotions. He was all too familiar with the legends and the myths regarding the fall of Eden passed down by Greeks, Syrians, Egyptians, Abyssinians, Hebrews, and other ancient peoples. But he had experienced it in a way that none of the storytellers ever did.

Eden was perfect. Adam and Eve were beyond compare, the apex of God's creation. Eternal soulmates made for each other, suited for each other, and passionately in love with each other, Draven's faint smile quickly withered as he recalled the darkness of that evil day when light gave way to darkness.

Damn the Angelic War for spilling over into the affairs of Eden. Fear and hatred ravage this kingdom but it wasn't always this way. I still recall the love in those eyes. Those piercing blue eyes that once shown bright with such promise. How could you so naively fall for his deception, so foolishly allow yourself to be seduced by the cunning of the Dark One? Why did you capitulate to the seductive wiles of his evil countenance enabling him to rape your soul and violate your innocence? Damn you Eve! Your dalliance with Darkness enabled the dark energy to flood Eden like a dam of evil bursting forth in unrelenting and unrestrained power.

Draven clinched his right fist as a fiery anger flared in his menacing eyes. *You ruined what was once so perfect and beautiful. You disavowed your heart, your love, your anamcara. You spurned the Light and in so doing unleashed the nightmares that torment, torture, and vex the soul. Your affair with the Dark One gave birth to fear, confusion, suffering, and recalcitrant desires unleashing the Darkness. In a moment of wanton pleasure, Eden's innocence was forever lost.*

A sense of foreboding washed over Draven as storm clouds veiled the moon shrouding him in darkness. The rain began falling with greater intensity dropping from the wisps of hair dangling across Draven's face as his thoughts turned to a storm that never seemed to abate. He saw it all so clearly as if it happened only yesterday.

And Adam. How foolish you were to ever trust her without so much as giving any thought to the will of the Light. Love is so damnably, endlessly blinding. How could you lose yourself in the dark current of female desire? Ever trying to please, to impress, to go along without thought or care. Oh Adam, you are as much a fool as Eve. Rather than challenge the lie you embraced it. You dastardly imbecile. Now, the Darkness has so thoroughly infected Eden like a pestilence contaminating all living matter ever producing a harvest upon harvest of hatred, defiance, chaos, destruction, and death.

Leaping upon the eastern wall of Castle Pinckney, Draven gazed out through a liquid wall of rain that was falling furiously upon angry white caps dancing upon the shifting surface of the Atlantic. Draven was impervious to the harsh beating of an unrelenting assault of wind-blown rain that was mercilessly slapping his face as he walked Castle Pinckney allowing his hands to lightly stroke the top of the overgrown brush of the Fort's neglected interior.

Much like the Holy City, Draven's existence had been defined by the conflict between Light and Darkness spawning dissent, rebellion, and war. He had developed an affinity for the city of steeples admired as much for its many taverns as its religious habitations both offering spirits that promised to numb one's sense and sensibilities to the madness of it all.

The angry clouds over the Atlantic began to recede as mornings' first light broke forth in a majestic ascent toward the heavens. Draven sensed the wind temper its fury and the deluge of rainfall expending its liquid torrent. The dawn seemed to struggle as the sun sought to exert its light over the tenaciousness of the darkness which ultimately relinquished its grip as the night recoiled and vanished.

And so it is, Draven thought to himself. *Darkness in defiance of the Light in a never ending dance of abhorrence. Will there ever be an end to this unceasing conflict that rages in Eden? Damn you Adam. And damn you Eve. Damn you both to the hell of your making.*

Like a harmonic tremor, Draven felt the energy of forces both Light and Dark converging upon the Holy City. Foretold by angelic prophecy, the fiercely contested battle for the soul of Eden would usher in the Age of Terror.

Visit HoltClarke.com

Visit HoltClarke.com

ABOUT THE AUTHOR

Holt Clarke is the father of the coolest kids on earth, on Santa's Nice List, livin' the dream, and keep'n the magic real along with his family in Charleston, South Carolina.

Holt earned the Doctor of Ministry degree from Drew University, Master of Divinity degree from Duke University, and Bachelor of Arts degree from North Carolina Wesleyan College.

Other Books By Holt Clarke

Tinsel and the Book of Christmas Magic

Santa Claus and the Kingdom of Christmas

Switching Mama's Ashes

I Do Ever After : Living Heart 2 Heart in Marriage

Connect on Social Media:

www.facebook.com/holtaclarke
www.twitter.com/holtaclarke

For news and series updates, visit www.HoltClarke.com

www.ingramcontent.com/pod-product-compliance
Lightning Source LLC
Chambersburg PA
CBHW031214120726
47905CB00002B/337